PROLOGUE

DAMON

THE FIRST TIME I see her, my cold heart stops.

And it's not hard to see why.

Every single aspect of the girl appears to have been meticulously crafted to perfection: from her stunning, flowing platinum blonde hair, a striking contrast against her flawlessly fair complexion, to her form – slender, and yet bewitchingly endowed with alluring, delectable, impossible curves that speak of an underlying athleticism.

But it is her eyes that really get to me. One eye sky blue and the other eye grass green. An out-of-the-ordinary combination that is so damn striking - and so damn enticing - to a man like me.

A man who likes his women *unique.*

And that's what makes my cold heart stop.

She must be in her early twenties at most. Clearly an adult, but still so very young. College age, I bet. But she has a fiery look about her that hints at a maturity beyond her years; a hidden resilience behind her mixed-color eyes.

Oh, yes. A resilience very, very unique in a girl this young and beautiful.

And I am a man who really, *really* likes that.

She has clearly been eagerly waiting for me to emerge from the elevator doors: sitting on one of the plush leather chairs in front of my personal secretary's desk that face the elevator. It is exactly the right place for her to catch me when I arrive at my office.

I think it is fair to say it seems like the perfect girl *wants* to find me.

Damn. That certainly does titillating things to me.

At the very moment I walk out of the elevator doors and my cold heart stops, she rises stylishly from her seat, and the very first word that graces my ears from her pretty mouth is none other than my own name.

"*Damon Penmayne!*"

I respond to her proclamation with a derisive curl of my lip. It's an instinctive retort to a tone as cutting as the one she has employed against me - using my name with that noticeable venom in her voice. Nobody addresses me in such a manner and escapes my wrath.

Suppressing the icy grip that seizes me at the sight of the stunning girl, I feign nonchalance and stride purposefully into my office through the reception area. I glimpse my bodyguard rushing forward to deal with the pretty intruder as I pass, just as he is paid handsomely to do.

And I desperately try to put the girl out of my mind.

Keep moving, Damon. You don't have time for this. Restart that cold heart of yours.

Getting all shook over a woman is typically not something I strive to do. A total *stranger*, I might add. And I certainly do not believe I am one to partake in choking up in front of a cute face and pretty lips. It might be crude to say, but women, to me, tend to be mere *playthings* to have a good

THE CRIMINAL'S CUSTODY

CRYSTAL RIVER BILLIONAIRE BROTHERS

REBECCA CASTLE

ISBN: 9780645587746

"Love me, cherish me; make me your slave; my life and fortune I place in your hands."

DRACULA

time with. Pawns to be used by rich and powerful men similar to myself, in just the same manner in how I use my bodyguard to deal with angry intruders who try to confront me in my office's reception.

Nothing to spend a moment's thought on.

Sure, sometimes I indulge in casual, no-strings-attached fun with someone I know I will never encounter again, but that is the *only* emotional investment I dare make in the opposite gender.

But that girl waiting for me in the other room really did something to me when I saw her. Something I have never experienced before...

Why did my entire body freeze when I saw her?

Why am I still thinking about her?

This is so unlike me. It truly is.

For fuck's sake, I've got to snap the hell out of this insanity before I lose myself.

With my office door safely shut behind me, I stand in front of my ceiling-to-floor window overlooking the New York City skyline and take in a long, meditative breath.

Remember who you are, Damon. Don't be weak. Forget that strange girl outside the door...

It's early afternoon. The sun is up. New York is in full swing.

Despite its sunny cheerfulness today, the view over the Big Apple can't help but take me back to my self-described *dark years*. My painful past. The months of foraging for scraps in an uncaring metropolis while I learned to survive on my lonesome. The months of sleeping rough in the city's pitch-black alleyways and suffering the sharp winter chill that ate at my very bones.

The dark years that made me the man I am today.

The years that gave me my aforementioned cold heart.

But I now no longer have to beg for a pittance on the

mean streets of New York City. I now technically live in my hometown of Crystal River: a small town mercifully far, far away from this mega metropolis and the lingering pain of my dark years. I only fly back to this damned city - on my luxurious private jet - from time to time to conduct necessary business, and then I get the hell out.

Truth be told, I don't like this city. I prefer the small town life of a quiet place like Crystal River: a place pleasantly distant from other people. For all my hard reputation as a man of swift and violent action, I prefer my solitary moments and the leisurely time to think. To *strategize*.

Running an organization as large, powerful, and as complex as mine takes a hell of a lot of mental energy.

Stating the obvious, my office in this skyscraper is substantially bigger than a lot of the apartments below. I gaze upon my reflection in the window glass. I admire the well-fitted tailored suit I'm currently wearing. An all-black ensemble, as I usually prefer. My cropped short hair is tousled in its customary manner. My eyes, a hue as dark as midnight, peer dispassionately back at me from within the glass mirror's depths. I have long become accustomed to a habit of never showing my emotion.

Even to strange girls who wait for me in my office...

The most noticeable thing about my face, however, is the long, thin scar that runs down my left cheek. It is a permanent reminder of my violent years. Something I can never escape from.

It's something that I know people notice the moment they set their eyes on me.

Something that can't help but make them truly afraid.

Just the way I like it.

I turn around from the view. I can feel someone's eyes on my back. My trusted lieutenant, Jim, is standing by the door, watching me. He's waiting patiently for my next command.

"What the hell was that?" I ask him, my voice naturally filling the room with a low, resonant baritone.

"The girl?" Jim asks me, dispassionate. His own voice is gravelly. It's like he downs a gallon of nails every morning. "The one waiting outside?"

"Yes. *Her.* The pretty little blonde devil-woman we practically had to fight off on the other side of that door."

"She's been trying to get hold of you for some time," Jim replies. "Like her life depends on it."

I raise an inquisitive eyebrow. "Elaborate, Jim. Why would she be trying to get a hold of me?"

I tend to find people are typically trying to run *away* from me, not seek me out.

This is alluringly curious.

"She's here because her father owes money to you," Jim explains. I trust the man with my life, and that allows us to talk frankly with each other without fear of retribution from me or my famous fiery temper.

"And this is the first time I've heard of this girl?" I ask. "When she ambushes me outside of my private office? An office that's supposed to have some of the tightest security in this city?"

Jim shrugs. He has short red hair and strong green eyes. He is a man that has been weathered by plenty of hardship in his time. "She was, apparently, really rather *insistent* on seeing you in person," he replies.

"Hm. Was she now?"

"Yes. She has been making rather a big... *disturbance* about it with the office staff. They've been complaining non-stop about it."

"And she wasn't removed?" I ask. "No one has simply tried picking her up and escorting her out?"

"Security have tried exactly that," Jim replies. "On multiple occasions, in fact. But she refused to follow through with their demands."

"Jesus," I mutter. "What is the point of being an actual fucking *gangster* if I can't get women thrown out of my private reception space?"

Jim merely shrugs. "The laws around eviction from commercial properties have been strengthened in recent years. And, like I've said, the girl is rather insistent on seeing you no matter what."

"And how long has she been waiting for me?" I ask him, moving behind my long desk. The office is sparse and minimalist in design, and deliberately so. I've found that both the incredible million-dollar view and the spartan nature of this place can be quite... intimidating to guests, and that is *precisely* the impression I wish to evoke as they cross the threshold to meet me in here.

Jim clears his throat and takes a moment to think. Aside from my other five brothers, he is the smartest man I know. He's been with me for years now, ever since I first took over this New York outfit. Ever since I dragged myself out of the New York dirt to become one of the most powerful crime bosses in the country. Jim has loyally followed me all the way since that first day he joined my side, and he has been rewarded comprehensively for it. And not just financially, mind you, but with my loyalty and respect - two things that are a hell of a lot harder to acquire than money. He's even got brains: right now, he manages my sprawling businesses and is also studying criminal law on the side.

"She's come by here for the last three days," Jim replies. "She hasn't moved from her seat, according to the staff. I do apologize that she's out there and that she was able to create a disturbance with you. I have made it very clear to your secretary and the building security that she really was to be removed before you even arrived in the city. But that's clearly failed. To be honest, I thought she would have given up seeing you by now."

"She's waited *three* whole days?" I ask, incredulous. "Out there? Has she eaten? Has she even slept?"

"Not that I know of."

Interesting. I was right about that fiery look and hidden resilience. She is persistent. I like that in a woman. That and her mixed-color eyes.

"Well obviously she hasn't been removed from my office reception despite your orders," I snarl. I am really trying to refuse to acknowledge what that girl did to me when I first laid my eyes upon her. "And clearly, she hasn't given up on seeing me. That was quite a surprising welcome out there, I must say."

"Again, Mr. Penmayne, I apologize for the disturbance."

"What is her name?" I ask.

"Ava Matson," Jim replies softly.

I do not recognize that name. To be honest, there are a hell of a *lot* of people all around this country that owe me money. My operations have far-reaching tentacles that have wormed their way into the entirety of our nation. There are simply too many people that my various businesses deal with who I cannot reasonably keep track of, despite my characteristic attention to detail.

"Bring her in here, then," I say to Jim. "If she wants to wait three fucking days to talk about her father's debts, then let her talk about her father's debts. Let her get what she so desperately came here for. Let her meet me. Right now."

Jim's eyes narrow. "Are you sure, Mr. Penmayne?"

"Yes. I want to speak to her," I reply darkly. And then I add one more, vitally important, command, "*alone.*"

1

AVA

"GET YOUR HANDS OFF ME!" I bark angrily at the brute. And trust me, I've got every right to be pissed. The man's attempting to shove me back into the elevator, but that ain't happening, and certainly not if I have anything to say about it.

Not on my watch, sir.

I am going to resist with all my willpower and determination and all my natural *fuck-this-bullshit* attitude. See, being a top-tier ex-cheerleader ain't all just about pompoms and skirts and looking pretty, it's got me some serious muscle too, and that muscle's getting put to work as I hold my own against this massive security dude and his insistence on forcing me inside the closing doors of the plush skyscraper elevator.

The burly bald man clearly thought it was going to be easy, pushing some girl around. I am hell-bent on proving him dead wrong.

"You need to leave," he grunts at me, breathless, as his

hands continue to try to drive my shoulders backward into the elevator.

Ha. Nope.

I find my opening and slip out from his grasp, duck under his massive steroid biceps, and take my seat again by the reception desk of Damon Penmayne's impressive penthouse office.

I cross my arms and look up sternly at the perplexed bodyguard and his sweaty bald head.

Yeah, I'm slippery when I want to be, meathead.

"I am not going anywhere," I say to him, triumphant.

The big man simply sighs, dropping his huge shoulders, and shakes his head at me. It's only his first attempt, and yet he's clearly already tired of my *fuck-this-bullshit* attitude.

Well. *Good.*

"I've waited a long time to see Damon Penmayne in the flesh," I continue. "So I'm not going to stop now. You can try all you like, dude, but you ain't making me budge. Plenty of other dudes like you have tried these last few days, and I have resisted all of them. You're not the first."

The bodyguard raises an eyebrow. "Yeah. I can see that."

I smile. This time I'm even more triumphant.

Even though I despise the guy, I really gotta say that Damon's reception room is pretty damn impressive. It's a vast space of shiny marble flooring and a soft ambiance provided by some cool embedded LED lighting dotted all around. There is even a discrete filter water refreshment station set up in the corner with classy crystal carafes ready for pouring and everything. The vibe in here is proof enough that the guy is exorbitantly rich. I've never been in somewhere so effortlessly... *cool.* The walls are all a dark gray, decorated only by black and white photographs. I've been able to study those artworks as I've been stuck here waiting over the last few days, and they're way more intense than I initially thought.

They are photos of Damon Penmayne with various famous people, shaking hands and smiling.

Presidents.

Celebrities.

Dictators.

And also, just for laughs, the freaking *King* of freaking *England*.

So totally normal.

It would appear that Damon Penmayne moves with the very highest of high society.

Yeah, this office is pretty damn mind-blowing, to say the least.

It has been a hell of an effort to get my ass into this very room. I mean, I shouldn't even *be* in New York City in the first place. I've never come here before in my life: I'm just a small town girl from Crystal River who's never really been anywhere. And, besides, I should really be in class right now back home at Crystal River University and not holed up in an office for some billionaire and his big, dumb, 'roided-up security.

But I've skipped home and classes for the last week to do this.

Whatever the hell it is I'm actually doing...

To be honest, I never truly expected to really meet Damon Penmayne when I set off from home a few days ago. I simply just had to *do something*. You see, my dad is in debt. *Big* debt, in fact, to none other than Damon Penmayne.

The infamous vicious criminal with the famous last name.

The very last man I should ever, ever, ever get involved with.

But despite my misgivings, my dad's heavily in debt to the man, and I am here to fix it.

Everyone in my hometown knows who the Penmaynes are. Well, so do most of America, to be honest. Six brothers, all of whom lucked out in the looks department. And as if they needed handsome looks as well: their dad's a billionaire media tycoon who's one of the most powerful men in the world with his far-reaching TV and internet and newspaper empire. But despite their family wealth, each of the brothers has found success in his own right. One's some super smart professor, another's a famous Hollywood actor, one is some well-regarded doctor, one is a beloved firefighter back in Crystal River, another one is some former air force pilot...

The family holds every job under the sun, apparently.

And Damon Penmayne? Well, he's got the worst reputation of all of the brothers - a bad boy with a black heart. He may pretend to be the suave businessman, but he is the rumored head of one of the most powerful gang operations on the East Coast. Well, it's the worst rumor in the whole freaking world because it seems like everyone and their dog knows who he truly is.

And I personally don't know why he isn't rotting in a jail cell by now.

It's honestly damn terrifying to even *contemplate* ambushing the man himself at his own fancy skyscraper office, and yet somehow, I have found the balls to do so. I seriously don't even get why I spontaneously yelled out his name when those elevator doors popped open and I caught sight of him for the very first time. I guess I was just swept up in the moment, you know? Being a former cheerleader does also give me - as well as muscles that come in handy in a fight with grumpy security guards - a sense of the dramatic flair that comes in handy in times like these.

But I was angry. And I *wanted* to be dramatic when I saw Damon. His name did escape my lips with plenty of built-up spite within me. All I could visualize when I saw Damon Penmayne as those elevator doors opened was Dad's face when he told me he was in debt to the same man standing just yards away from me.

He is the man I want to see. The most terrible man I've heard of.

I'm not gonna let this known criminal get away with dragging my dad through hell. The research, planning, and fluttering of my eyelashes to get me up here, in this room, was crazy and demeaning and hard and vile, but I would do anything for Dad. Yeah, he's not perfect; he's got a gambling addiction - the thing that got us into this mess in the first place - and I am making sure he gets help with it, but I love him with all my heart, and I would walk to the damn ends of the earth for him.

And I am going to make this right, no matter if that means confronting a man who could probably have my body thrown into a river with just a word from his pretty lips.

And so, I end up here. Damon Penmayne is now in his swanky office, shielded by an imposing shut and locked door, and I am engaged in a stare-off with his burly bald brute of a bodyguard.

And I have zero clue as to what the hell happens next.

And I am freaking *starving*.

And I am holding in the most desperate pee in the history of the world.

"Have fun working for a man who's a psycho?" I ask the suited security as we both pant after our little altercation.

He grunts back at me.

Ugh.

"What a riveting and witty conversationalist," I reply to his incoherent grumble.

I lean back in my chair and keep my eyes peeled on Damon's office door. I cross my legs to show how serious I am.

I can wait here all day if that's what it takes...

"Nothing is going to happen," the pretty brunette secretary smugly coos to me from behind her desk next to the penthouse office door. "That was your one and only chance to see Mr. Penmayne, and you blew it."

The secretary and I have been engaged in a tense Cold War these last few days, ever since I first managed to smuggle my way through security downstairs to plonk myself down in this reception seat. It has been a Mexican stand-off of epic proportions between her and me as I've waited and waited and waited and waited and she's done nothing but glare at me from across the room, completely damn powerless to do anything about the annoying small-town blonde girl in her reception, no matter how many security guards she calls up.

"Mind your own business," I retort back to the preppy receptionist. "Protest always works. Power to the people, and all that. I *am* going to meet Damon Penmayne, mark my words."

She simply rolls her eyes at that. "Sure. You have fun with your delusions."

I stick out my tongue at her.

I'm not going to be negative. I am going to see Damon properly. This insane not-moving-until-I-meet-him protest in his office will be worth it, I am sure of it.

I hope.

As if responding to my thoughts, the door to the office suddenly swings open, and a man who isn't Damon Penmayne steps out. I must've not noticed this guy when he came in with Damon from the elevator. I'm guessing he must be good at blending into the background. He's got short red hair and striking green eyes.

And he looks directly at me with those striking green eyes. He is cold. I get that vibe from him. I see a man that I know has seen some real shit. You probably would have to witness some crazy things if you work for a man like Damon Penmayne.

And I'm suddenly very terrified.

What have I let myself in for here?

"Mr. Penmayne will see you now," the man says in a dark, slow voice, looking toward me.

I gulp.

"Me?"

The man nods.

"Yes, *you*. Mr. Penmayne will like to talk to you right now."

I am actually going to meet this guy? Right now?

I look at the secretary. She's looking fearful.

And I realize she's fearful for *me*.

Oh, God. This is all starting to feel very, very real.

And very, *very* dangerous.

2

DAMON

AND, just like that, the girl who had somehow stopped my heart mere moments ago strolls proudly into my office: her blonde hair trailing behind her, and her mismatched eyes locked firmly onto me, and her head held high.

And I freeze up all over again.

But the voice in my head is screaming at me at the highest possible volume.

What the fuck do you think you're doing, Damon? Letting this girl have this weird hold over you?

I need to remind myself of who I am. Fuck this girl and the bizarre spell she has seemingly conjured on me - I need to remember the reputation I've worked hard to forge for myself and the walls I've constructed through all these years of struggle to get to where I am today.

I need to remind myself that I am a man who doesn't ever, *ever* get weak at the knees for a girl.

I am Damon fucking Penmayne.

Yet, look at me right now, going fucking *weak* over a female.

Time to shake this shit off.

She storms in, readying for a fight even before Jim has a chance to squeeze past her out of the office. The girl's shoulders are up. Her chest is heaving with quick sharp breaths, allowing me to notice her perky breasts under her shirt...

She's clearly been anticipating this very moment for days.

Well, I'm going to give it to her, just not the way she expects.

"Why are you here?" I ask before she has a chance to open that pretty little mouth of hers. "Who are you, girl?"

I am merely playing: I know *precisely* who she is. Jim has given me the low-down on her, after all, but I do want to see the expression on the girl's face when my question hits her ears.

And, *oh*, the expression does not disappoint.

It. Is. Delicious.

Ava Matson stops dead in her tracks in the middle of the large office facing me and huffs like a child being denied a cookie as I growl at her. It's very adorable.

"It's pretty damn insulting that I have been waiting days to see you, Damon Penmayne" she starts, "And yet you don't know a single freaking thing about me."

Her entire sentence rambles on in one long, breathless word. She's either terrified or she's angry at me, I can't tell for sure. But I'm going to take the assumption it's a bit of both.

An uncharacteristic smile begins to form on my lips.

I am very much enjoying this.

"Oh, but I know *exactly* who you are, Ava Matson," I reply.

She crosses her arms, her face subtly dropping with the mention of her full name. "Hm? You do?"

She's being sarcastic. And I can be equally passive-aggressive back.

"You were born and raised in Crystal River," I explain from the corners of my smirk. "You're the only daughter of your father, who is a gambler and borderline alcoholic. You attended the only high school in town, where you held the position of head cheerleader and were the most popular girl in your grade. You've only had one serious relationship in your life, and that was with Luke Abbott, the star quarterback and captain of your high school football team. You enjoy listening to music; in fact, you already have tickets for the next tour of the band called Ravaged. Your dorm roommate goes by the name Olivia Weldon, and she's from out of town. And you've just spent three days annoyingly squatting in my reception and being a general pain in the ass for my staff."

She merely shakes her head at my cold summation of her entire life.

"You're a pain in the ass," she mutters.

"Is that everything, or shall I continue?" I ask, easily recalling the information that Jim has just passed on to me. "I could mention, for instance, that your first kiss with said Luke Abbott was on the football field immediately after the high school quarterback threw a game-winning touchdown. Or I could mention how you spent your entire weekend not three weeks ago consuming nothing but ice cream and coffee and reading online fanfiction smut in the darkness of your dorm room."

"That's enough," she whispers in disbelief. "How the hell do you know those things about me?"

"I have my sources," I reply.

"It's *stalking*," she retorts, her confident defenses already slipping away.

"I am always prepared for anyone I might potentially have the pleasure for meeting," I reply. "Even for sarcastic little girls who occupy my office."

"I am not some little girl. Give me some respect."

"But you have been occupying my office, haven't you? Why should I respect you?"

"You've really just brought me in to insult me," Ava sighs. "What is this?"

Oh, I am *really* enjoying this now.

"Now let's turn to the subject of your father," I say. "He's the reason you are here, is he not? He's the man whose... *predicament* has brought you into my office today, correct?"

"Don't talk crap about Dad," Ava says through clenched teeth,

Hm. Seems like I've hit a nerve. Let's exploit this...

"Your father owes me a lot of gambling money. You know that, right, Ava Matson? I think it's fair to say I can talk whatever crap I like about the man, don't you? Especially when he has done such a grave disservice to me."

"Don't you dare insult him."

"*Yes*. I like that fight in you, Ava Matson. Do you consider yourself a fighting girl?"

"Only when I have to be," she replies quietly.

I'm really pressing that nerve now.

"Are you going to fight me?" I ask. "Is that what you've came here for?"

She sighs, not taking my bait. "Are we going to actually get down to hard tax and discuss how to get rid of my dad's debts or are we just going to continue to do nothing but feed your enormous, ugly ego?"

"Watch it," I growl. "You've got a venomous tongue,

Ava, but this is my space, and I've invited you in here. I could have just ignored you and left you sitting out there twiddling your thumbs."

"Don't act like you're doing me some big service," Ava shoots back. "You ain't Mother Teresa. Are you just going to mock me all day, or are you actually ready to talk business, Damon?"

"Call me Mr. Penmayne," I reply. "And, yes, I would prefer to mock you all day. Seeing your face like this is *very* satisfying."

I'm loving this little bickering we've got going. It makes a fine change from my usual business transactions.

I'm actually having fun for once.

Ava rolls her eyes. She's clearly *not* having fun. "Okay, that's it," she says. "This is a total waste of my time and I ain't gonna waste a second more. Goodbye, Damon Penmayne. I'll find some way to get you your stupid money, even if I have to beg for it from some stupid bank. To be honest, I would rather do anything but hear you jerk yourself off for another hour at my expense. I truly, *truly* hope I never see you again for the rest of my life."

And she stands up. She turns her back to me. She's going to the door that leads out of my office.

I nod slowly in respect. People don't tend to bite back like that.

Damn. She's good.

And she's totally irresistible.

Even with her little speech, she must know she needs my help if she's ever going to get rid of the money her father owes me. Despite the confrontational flame that burns so bright in her, she has no bargaining position to play around here. She can't just leave this room and expect all her problems to have evaporated simply because she had the guts to tell the mean criminal billionaire a piece of her mind. I have all the power here, not her.

Look, I could easily let her go and deal with her father in the same way that men who owe me money have usually been dealt with in the past. A way I seriously doubt she would like.

But where's the fun in that?

And it's only now that I realize what I earnestly want from this spicy little interaction with the pretty girl.

I want *her*. Completely. Wholly. Utterly. I want her mine with a ferocity that I can barely control. I've wanted her since she made my heart stop in the other room.

And I am a man who gets what he wants.

I like the idea of corrupting a woman as pure as Ava, if she's into that. And Ava is positively *sinful*. She's very bad for me. She's a darling little temptation, like a perfectly ripe cherry on top of a freshly baked pie – too damn delectable to ignore.

And that's probably why I say the next few words out of my mouth before she can reach the door. The words that make the girl immediately halt in her tracks.

The words that I know are gonna change a hell of a lot of things.

"Ava Matson, I want you to stick around. I've got an offer for you."

3

THREE DAYS EARLIER

AVA

THE FIRST SOUND I hear when I wake up is my dad crying in the kitchen downstairs. With my muscles aching and my head pounding, I get out of bed and immediately go to him. I'm not going to let him suffer in silence.

Oh, God. What time is it?

It must be early morning. Very freaking early.

It feels like I haven't slept at all.

It's not with surprise that I hear him crying, it's with a familiar weariness. I have heard him crying far too many times now in the last couple of days. A few weeks ago, it would've been so shocking to hear my own dad tear up. Now it's so, so painfully common.

I really can't leave him on his own. Not when he is like this.

When Dad first confided in me about his secret debt a

few weeks ago, my whole life completely changed practically overnight. It's like I've done one of my old high school cheerleader routines and did a total backflip, becoming an entirely different person to the carefree girl I was at the beginning of this year. Back then, I had a reputation as the fun, extrovert socialite who liked to party and had a boyfriend who was the most popular guy both in high school and on the university campus and everyone knew my name and wanted to hang with me and I was, most of all, *happy*. But now that girl is utterly gone.

And it makes me so sad.

I'm not meant to be the sad girl. I never had that planned.

Since the big reveal of the debts, I've temporarily left the dorm room I've shared with my friend Olivia and have moved back in with Dad on the other side of town, even though I'm still attending classes at Crystal River University. While my friends have been having a great time with new boyfriends and new once-in-a-lifetime college experiences, I've had to go back home and look after the man who raised me.

It really was *not* supposed to be like this. I hate to complain or to whine, but it's the honest truth.

Everyone I know except for Olivia has shunned me because of my dad's debts. Word gets around fast in a town like Crystal River, and people in small towns don't like families with bad reputations – even if the bad reputations in question have sprung up overnight.

I stand by the kitchen door, observing the crying man. Dad hasn't noticed my presence yet. He sits at the table, his shoulders slouched, and his head lowered in complete surrender. He appears shattered. I've been deeply affected by all of this, too. Ever since Dad confided in me about the situation, about the mounting debts and his struggles, I've been on the brink of tears as much as he has. I've cried, in the darkness and solitude of my childhood bedroom, more times than I can count. I can honestly say, with my hand on my heart, that I had no clue about any of these problems or Dad's addictions until that one fateful day when he opened up to me out of the blue.

Even my boyfriend dumped me when the word got out around town. That was hard. *Apparently*, he can't be seen around with a girl whose family now has this kind of reputation. *Apparently*, it all comes down to image with Luke. Ha, that image he cherishes. *La di da* – the quarterback for Crystal River High and his cheerleader girlfriend. The power duo of high school. He loved the attention that position gave him. He loved being a self-described *alpha male*. He loves being that image of the all-American hero.

We were together for years. I truly loved him. I trusted him with everything. We were totally inseparable. He would even drop in mentions occasionally of how he was meant to marry me someday. My whole future was getting built brick-by-brick, and it was swimming along perfectly.

Maybe I was foolish and naïve. A dumb girl in love. Maybe it's my fault I never saw any of this coming...

It's like the whole deck is stacked against me. But I still keep fighting. I'm trying to keep my head above water. For Dad's sake.

I try not to complain. I try to not bring negative energy into Dad's space.

He needs someone to be there for him otherwise he would be long gone.

I silently hand Dad a box of tissues, gently tapping on his shoulder to pass them to him in the dark kitchen. No words need to be spoken between us, not anymore. We've exhausted all the words we can say to each other in these past few weeks. All that remains is the debt and the pain and the worry. There is no need to discuss anything else. We're drowning, and there's no way up to the surface.

I make Dad a cup of coffee without a word. I offer it to him. He takes it without a *thanks*. He takes a sip as I sit down opposite him.

I watch him for a while.

The lines on his face...

He has aged a decade in a week.

"What's the worst thing that can happen?" I ask him softly, breaking the silence.

My dad finally glances up from the table and looks me in the eye for the first time in days. He gives me a look that means one thing.

They will kill him. *That's* the worst thing that can happen.

It's all so very real...

Okay, that's it. I'm done with this.

He doesn't say a word as I stare back at him and finally decide what I am going to do.

"I'm going to New York to see Damon Penmayne," I say bluntly.

Dad blinks.

"No. Don't."

Like how he's just looked at me, it's the first time Dad's spoken in days. And it's with a fearful urgency.

But I'm not listening to him. There is a fire within me now. I know I have to be strong. For him.

"I'm going to go, and I'm going to hunt the man down, and I'm going to stop this craziness, Dad," I say quietly. "I am sick and tired of not being able to sleep or eat or do anything other than stress out. I simply just want to go back to my normal life and forget about all this. Seeing Damon will be the only solution."

"Please don't go, Ava," Dad mutters, a little more

forceful now. "Please don't see that man. You don't know who he is or what he's capable of."

He's practically begging. I can see the fear in his eyes. He's terrified of Damon Penmayne.

And I know I should be too.

"I'm going to do what it takes," I reply. "I don't care who this guy is or what he's done or what he can do to me. I don't care if he is the devil incarnate. I am going to see Damon Penmayne and I am going to make things right."

I will do anything for my dad.

He stares at me. He knows me well enough to see when I've got my mind on something and when I will not budge. It's just like my cheerleading; once my focus is set, then it is impossible to shift me even an inch.

I am going to do this. I am going to New York. I am going to see Damon Penmayne and I am going to hash out a solution to all of this.

And I am not going to leave that city until I get it sorted.

And so, I get up from the table and head straight upstairs to pack my bag.

4

AVA

I BLINK in total confusion at the gangster.

What. The. Hell.

"What did you just say?" I ask.

Standing in the middle of his fancy office, glaring at me, Damon Penmayne seems completely at ease.

A predator relaxed in the full knowledge of his coiled power.

"You heard me, Ava," he replies coolly. "You've heard what I have to offer you."

His voice is so dark. So low.

So... *unsafe.*

I blink again. I did hear him. I did hear his offer. I am just so totally blindsided by what he actually *is* proposing, and I don't know what the hell to say.

This is nuts...

"Explain again," I mutter. "Just one more time. Just so I can process that insanity."

The office we're in is even more impressive than the reception next door. There is both the air of dark intimidation and minimalist grandeur here in a way that I've come to closely associate with Damon. The floor is a dark polished marble. Everything in the office is all sharp angles and clean edges, including the slab of a desk with a solitary computer monitor sitting on top. There is a black, leather-backed chair behind the desk. There are panoramic city views all around, showing off the whole of New York: his domain. It's all so very Damon. So very rich. So very scarily gangster.

He's acting like the king of New York City.

At me asking him to clarify his offer, the man lets out a sigh and thoughtfully strokes his impeccably chiseled chin. The thin scar on his left cheek is a reminder of his always-present violence. His dark eyes lock onto me, gleaming. I can't read his mind, but I have a strong feeling whatever's going on in there isn't all sunshine and rainbows.

Especially not considering the insane offer he just laid out on the table.

"You are to be my mistress for two months," he says, reiterating his offer.

"Okay, two months? Mistress? Are you being serious?"

"I am being deadly serious, Ava. Two months is long enough to pay back the thousands your father owes me," Damon says, "don't you think?"

"But... hang on. You've forgotten the craziest part of your statement: your *mistress*?"

I am stuttering, unable to process what he actually just freaking said.

"Yes," the gangster replies. "You are to be my mistress for two months, Ava Matson. Am I not being clear enough? I'm not going to repeat myself."

"Hold your horses, cowboy," I say. "Let's not rush through this. Let me get this straight. As in a *relationship*? With you? A *mistress* mistress?"

"Yes."

"As in *sleep* with you?"

I am really stuttering and spluttering now in incredulity.

"Yes," Damon calmly replies, as if we were talking about something as simple and ordinary as negotiating over a used car and not a discussion over the use of my freaking body. "Fine, I *will* repeat myself. I am offering you to be my mistress for two months. Eight weeks precisely."

"Sounds like some kind of... *captivity*."

"This is not some flimsy backroom deal," Damon replies. "We will draw up a contract and get your signature. We will make it formal and legal in the eyes of the law."

I'm rolling my eyes.

"As if the law has ever stopped you before..."

"It is going to be the only way I'm willing to let go of your father's debt," Damon continues, ignoring my snide comments. "Unless he pays me, of course. But I seriously doubt that would be any time forthcoming, considering you've made the incredibly difficult journey to be with me here today."

So. He *is* being serious.

The smug bastard.

Now that I'm up close and personal with the infamous man, I can see him for what he truly is: a devil. *A gorgeous, handsome, sexual devil.* Square jaw. The hint of a dark stubble. Sharp high cheekbones. Under his cuff, I notice the black ink of tattoos on veiny arms. He must have the markings covering a good percentage of his body like a true bad boy with a wild nature. I can't avoid his midnight-black eyes that conceal a whole inner world.

And the most prominent feature about this particular devil in a tailored suit is that slender scar tracing down his left cheek. I really bet there's a story behind that. It certainly doesn't look like it came from just some accident.

I bet it's come from a fight. A scar from some kind of scuffle that he clearly survived.

Yeah, and I wonder what happened to the other guy...

Looking at him, I instantly get the vibe that this is a man who knows how to move and how to strike, in both a physical and strategic mental way. This is a man who possesses a deep intelligence and an unending ability to inflict pain on others.

And he is *so* terrifying. So much so that I have to say it kinda turns me on to be so close to such danger. Kind of like that feeling you get when you stand too close to a cliff edge and think "I could just jump right here and now", but... *sexier*.

No. This is insane, Ava. You can't be attracted to Damon Penmayne, and not even a tiny, tiny bit. It is so wrong on so, so many levels.

Gangsters should not be sexy, especially not ones who hold your own family members in debt.

But something about Damon *thrills* me in such an innate, primal way...

And so do his batshit crazy proposals that make me question his sanity.

"So, what's your response?" the man inquires, scrutinizing me with that deep intensity he's got going on. "What do you say to my offer?"

"Hell no to this," I say to him, shaking my head vehemently.

"You're rejecting me?" There's a hint of a smile on Damon's beautiful face. He's really savoring this. He knows there's little I can fight back on.

He knows – because of my love for Dad – that I have to seriously consider his batshit crazy proposal.

But I'm stronger than that.

Well, I think I am...

"Yes, I am rejecting you," I reply. "You want to threaten me to get me to sleep with you? That's definitely a *hell no* in my books. Blackmail, you'd be surprised to know, is not the way to woo a woman."

"You're a pretty girl recently single, Ava, I know that," he says. "You are not tied down to anyone else, and I am a hungry man. What more does there need to be said?"

"You're disgusting."

"I am a man with hot blood running through my veins," he replies. "I like what I see, and I want it. And I usually get what I want. And I want you, Ava Matson."

Is he... *flirting* with me?

"I am rejecting you, Damon Penmayne," I retort. "And that's final. Come up with a better offer that I might actually consider, and not one where I become your prisoner."

"I would advise you against rejecting me, Ava," he says darkly. "People don't usually reject the only offer on the table. You should think over this very, very carefully. It really is the only offer I'm willing to allow. It might be the only way to save your father."

"If you seriously lay one hand on him, then..."

"What?" Damon laughs darkly. "What will you do? You'll kill me? Have you ever killed a man before, Ava? Have you ever held someone's life in between your hands and *squeezed*?"

"No, but..."

"I promise you that I wouldn't even think about touching your father if you become my mistress. He will come under my personal protection. No harm will visit him."

"Now *that* is definitely blackmail."

Damon shrugs. "It seems, Ava, that right now you have a choice to make. Reject me and reject all hope for your father or embrace my deal and live happily forever after."

He takes a step toward me, shortening the gap between us so very dangerously. I can smell his sweet expensive aftershave. I could drink him in if I wanted to. But I steadfastly refuse.

I won't dare allow his dark charms work on my sorry ass.

He's a man unlike any other I've seen. A *real* man. A man who oozes power and confidence that I am positively sure bowls over other women left, right, and center.

And I do have to say that there is a small, *minuscule* part of me – right in the very back of my mind – that secretly fantasizes what it may be like to be the mistress of a man like Damon Penmayne. There is a tiny part of me that thinks it will be a hell of a lot of fun to be under his control.

And I haven't had fun for a very long time...

Damon reaches into his suit pocket and produces a shiny gray card.

"My personal phone number," he explains as he hands the card to me. "Call me when you change your mind."

"I *won't* be changing my mind," I snap back. "You can count on that."

There's a knowing glint in the man's dark expression. "We'll see, won't we," he utters.

I shake my head at his comment, but I feel my cheeks blushing. I can no longer look the man in the eyes; his gaze is just so... *consuming*.

"And how are you going to get back home to Crystal River?" Damon asks in a near-whisper. "It's a hell of a journey back. You are a girl in a city so very far away from home."

He is so damn close. So very close.

"I... haven't planned that far ahead," I stammer. "I just came to see you. I guess I'll get a train, and then a bus, and somehow find my way to Crystal River."

"And you're hungry," he replies. "And you're tired. You have just spent days squatting in my office, unmoving."

"I am so very tired," I sigh.

Damon nods deliberately. "You could take the train and then the bus to get back home, but I do have a quicker route I am willing to propose to you, Ava. If you *are* willing to let me handle this one thing for you..."

5

AVA

TURNS out the so-called *quicker route* home that Damon was suggesting back in his office wasn't some kind of high-speed train or even a chauffeur-driven car, but instead the man's private jet.

Yeah, as if.

I really did not believe it when he told me he'll get the jet on standby to fly me back to Crystal River.

Wait, I'm actually getting flown back in a freaking private plane?

I still don't believe it as I sit in the back of his limousine through New York City traffic on the way to the airport. I simply refuse to believe *anything* the man has uttered until I actually see the private plane with my own eyes.

That secretive man with the red hair and the hard eyes - who turns out to be Damon's second-in-command - is along for the ride with me to the airport. I've since learned his name is Jim, but that was like getting blood from a stone with a man of such few words. He sits opposite me in the long limo, staring emotionlessly out of the window probably trying to avoid any interaction with me.

He's certainly not the talkative type.

I was practically ushered into this vehicle the moment I left Damon's office – with a quick, and very much needed, pitstop in the restroom on the way down. I didn't really get the chance to say yes or no to his offer to fly me back home, let alone spend a moment to think about it, before I was whirled downstairs of Damon's office building and into the limo. That's probably why my heart is pounding as I sit here and look at all the rising skyscrapers of this big city and think about what the hell has happened today.

Damon. Waiting days for him. Confronting him in his office. His crazy offer of being his mistress. Riding in his limousine. Going on his freaking private jet.

A girl in a city so very far away from home...

It's all a bit too much for a simple small town cheerleader like me.

Yep. I think I'm suffering from whiplash.

"You're on babysitting duties, then?" I ask Jim, grasping at straws to break the tension that exists inside this limo and to also get my mind off all the craziness that's going on.

The man regards me coldly. "I've got business back in Crystal River. It is convenient to fly on the plane."

"Ah. Right. Cool."

His response is short, sharp, and to the point. No fucking around.

What is even going on?

I'm getting a bad feeling from all of this, but it's too late to back out now. Why did I allow myself to get tangled up in this mess? I can't exactly jump out of a moving vehicle, so I'm pretty much stuck in this weird gangster movie I've somehow ended up in.

"I've kind of ruined your solo trip, haven't I?" I mutter to the man.

I tend to babble on when I'm nervous and losing my freaking mind. It's the downfall of being such a people pleaser.

"I do everything that Damon says," Jim replies, just as cold as his last answer.

Yeah. Definitely not a talker, this guy.

Jim is just like the meathead security brute at the office. Does Damon only hire men who can't string a sentence together?

"You do everything Damon Penmayne says?" I ask. "Like *everything* everything? What's that like, I wonder? He must be a pretty powerful guy."

That gets a tiny chuckle from the man. "You have no idea," Jim answers.

And we fall back into uncomfortable silence all the way to the airport.

I don't like silences. And I don't like weird men who would do anything for a man who might be a cousin of Satan.

Damon told me, back in his office, that this trip back home on his plane is *just* a gift. Nothing more. He said it in such a way that he made it seem like flying on a private jet across the country was like getting two candy bars for the price of one. *Free of charge*, that's how he put it. Well, I don't want to be in debt to such a dangerous man, even if my dad is, but Damon insisted this isn't like that at all.

But I still don't know.

Why would he do this if I've said no to his mistress proposal? Does he think I'll suddenly flip my mind and go all gooey-eyed at his offer now that he's flashing his wealth and material power toward me?

Well, that ain't how I do things, mister. I'm not that kind of girl.

We soon arrive at the airport, and now I can truly believe that what Damon was saying was real. There is his private jet waiting for us, all fired up and ready to go.

It's probably been the only truthful thing he ever said to me in his office.

This is next-level crazy.

We're taken up into the plane. Jim walks casually across the tarmac and through the doors inside the jet as if he rides private all the damn time. I, however, feel like a kid on Christmas morning, although I am doing my best to hide it. I am still on a gangster's plane, after all.

A gangster whose offer I just rejected...

I can't help thinking of all those mafia movies I've seen. Am I gonna get whacked on here?

The inside certainly doesn't *look* like a plane that a gangster would own in one of those movies. It's all plush leather seats and indulgence and soft lights. Coffee tables and TV screens.

It's all so very nice.

As I take a seat, the hostess onboard offers me a glass of champagne and a plate of lobster tail in a creamy garlic sauce. It's like they just knew I would be starving after three days holed up in Damon's reception.

Maybe he even let them know to do exactly this.

"Oh, no. Thank you, but I won't," I mutter to the hostess, embarrassed, as she raises the champagne glass toward me.

"Take it," Jim tells me from across the aisle in his own seat. He still doesn't seem fazed by all the surrounding opulence. "It's free."

"Okay," I say, uncertain. "As long as you promise me this isn't poison."

"Trust me," Jim replies. "If Damon wanted you dead, you'd be dead by now."

"Ah. Very reassuring, thank you."

And so, I do take the glass of champagne, and I do hungrily stare at the lavish dinner presented in front of me. I'm not going to lie, there is still a part of my brain that reckons the golden liquid in the glass has been tampered with, but my paranoia goes away the moment I taste the bubbly and realize that Damon probably has better ways of getting rid of troublesome girls like me than inviting them onto his private plane and drugging them with expensive sparkling wine and lobster tails.

"You're lucky to have got the chance to see Damon," Jim quietly tells me as we take off and I start to devour the food. "He rarely lets strangers into his office, especially crazy, baffling girls."

"Who are you calling crazy? Or baffling?"

The man raises an eyebrow at me. I can kinda see his point.

I am a little crazy – waiting for three days to see an infamous gangster and then rejecting his offer.

"I am not lucky, though," I continue. "The man is insane. A monster. He should be locked away behind bars and the key should be thrown away into the deepest, darkest ocean."

Jim chuckles again. It's like I'm really opening him up with my charm and wit. "Damon Penmayne is very different once you get to know him," he says.

I dab away at a drop of creamy garlic sauce that has somehow ended up on my cheek.

"Okay," I retort. "So, he's less of a cold-hearted killer and more like a warm-hearted one?"

"The man has never killed anyone innocent or in cold blood," Jim replies. "That's not who he is."

"I seriously doubt that. I think that's *exactly* who he is."

"Do you have any proof?" Jim asks.

I scoff. "No, I don't. But I just know, right? I mean, simply take a look at him. The man doesn't exactly look like an angel, does he?"

This makes Jim actually laugh. "No, he certainly does not. I can admit that. But he really isn't the terrible monster you make him out to be."

"How so?" I ask, curious now that I seem to be finally squeezing complete sentences out of the man.

Jim shuffles in his seat. He's plainly uncomfortable with disclosing too much. "Damon is the only family I've ever known," he mumbles. All chuckles have drained from his face: he's deadly serious now. "That man has done some *impossible* things for me, things I can't even say out loud. I owe my life to that man. He's dragged me through hell. Without any expectation from me to pay him back in any way. He's a true friend, and the most loyal person I've ever known."

"Nice speech," I say. "And it's clear that you actually mean it. But he still has decided to hold my dad in debt. I personally don't think that is very nice."

"He took an immediate liking to you," Jim says in reply. "I've never seen Damon be like that before, especially not with a girl."

I scoff. "He's disgusting. Asking me to be his mistress. Blackmailing me to sleep with him."

"That's one way to look at the offer," the man replies. "But there are other ways to view it."

"It's the *only* way to look at it, Jim."

I settle back into my seat, annoyed with Jim and especially annoyed at Damon Penmayne. He really was being deadly serious with that insane offer.

What would Damon's offer entail, exactly? Two months

spent with that man in exchange for my father's freedom? Eight whole weeks in his captivity? *Sleeping* with him?

I did say I would do anything for my dad...

But this? In a criminal's custody?

I take another sip of the champagne as the plane rises through the clouds above New York City and resolve to myself to not even entertain the offer. Not even think about it.

Never ever.

6

DAMON

I'm BEING DRIVEN through New York City when I get the text message I've been waiting for all day.

It's Jim.

> The package has been dropped off. All safe and secure.

THE PACKAGE he is referring to is Ava Matson. She's home. She's safe and secure.

A sigh of relief wells up from deep within me, an unexpected and unfamiliar sensation. Receiving this message has brought about emotions I hadn't anticipated.

I shake my head at my reaction to the message.

What the fuck is going on between you and this girl, Damon?

I look out of the window of my limousine, expecting to see the skyscrapers of downtown Manhattan, but instead, we are further from the bright lights and crowds than I would've thought: the outskirt suburbs of New York City, unaccustomed to me. I'm only out this far from Manhattan for a business meeting, otherwise I would be back in the main drag of the city or, better yet, at home in Crystal River.

We stop at a red light. At the corner of the street opposite, I spot a group of young men, all in their early twenties, standing around. *Loitering.* I would never ordinarily pay much attention to a sight like this, but what catches my eye is a child who approaches the group.

I see it all so clearly. One of the guys starts talking to the little boy, as if he's familiar to him. He puts something in the boy's hand. A bag of something.

I don't need to be Sherlock fucking Holmes to deduce what's happening here.

A street gang using a kid as a drug mule.

For fuck's sake.

My driver has noticed it as well, but his eyes are firmly on the traffic lights. He's turning his focus away from the horrific sights in front of him - making himself willfully blind to this shit out of fear or some other fucked reason.

But I am a man who doesn't let something like this slide.

I am a man who doesn't operate out of fear.

"Pull over," I growl from the back seat.

The driver hesitates. "They're just... petty criminals. Don't waste your time on guys like them."

Fuck this. This man is being paid to drive me. Not to give me advice.

"They're using children," I say slowly. "I won't put up with that. Not in *my* city. Pull the fuck over."

The driver nods apprehensively but pulls over alongside the sidewalk anyway. He wouldn't dare disobey an order from me.

Car parked, I straighten my tie and get out of the limousine.

And I approach the street corner.

I know I must look very strange; a man in an expensive black suit striding toward these low-level street thugs with the confidence of someone looking for trouble.

But I *am* looking for trouble.

And I wonder if they will bite.

One of the young men in the group notices me when I'm only a few yards away.

"Who the hell are you?" he asks.

His voice cuts across the street. Uneducated and cruel. A man with no depth to him. No value to society at all.

Makes me sick.

The other gang members turn. I stop in front of the curb and slowly stare them each in the eye. A few stare back menacingly, and also with a touch of confusion. They are not used to someone acting this way in front of them.

One seems to immediately notice who I am. A lot of people in this city know who Damon Penmayne is, and I guess he's one of them. His eyes widen in fear at my stare, and he starts to take a step back before he's practically running in the opposite direction away from me.

I do tend to have that effect with people who recognize me.

But the other three guys remaining seem to not identify my famous face.

Shame.

I was hoping to avoid conflict today.

I really do hate getting my tailored suit dirty.

"Fuck off," one of the gang members snarls at me,

shaking off the fact that his friend just ran away in pure terror.

I just continue to stare for a long moment before I take another step toward them. Now I am on the sidewalk, practically in their space.

I bet they won't like this.

And they don't. The thug shakes his head and then reaches inside his jacket. He pulls out a handgun and points it directly in my face. The nuzzle of the weapon is mere inches from my nose.

"Fuck off," he snarls. Again. He's got the confidence of a man with a very real weapon in his hands. A fitting substitute for his tiny cock.

Now *I* really don't like this.

I sigh. "I hate the use of guns," I say unhurriedly and calmly. I don't even flinch at the action of a gun being aimed between my eyes. "I prefer blades to take care of business. I like things up close. Guns are a coward's way out."

The guy holding the gun frowns. "You can't get close to me. And what the fuck are you talking about daggers for? You can't take a knife to a gunfight."

In response, I simply reach behind my back to the submachine gun I have strapped on, concealed from view of these guys as I approached, and I coolly hold it up. I aim the big threatening weapon at the guy aiming his pathetic little handgun at me.

Everyone, except for me, is in total shock.

I really hate using guns. And I hate this guy for making me use my own.

As the cluster of inexperienced thugs grapple with this abrupt twist of fate, I assertively press the nozzle of my submachine gun against the gunman's shoulder, sending him sprawling to the ground. Swiftly and fluidly, I allow my weapon to drop, suspending it from its strap by my side, and

I pull out my knife, smoothly placing the blade against the fallen thug's vulnerable neck - a maneuver I've honed through countless practice. His gun scatters across the ground, safely away from us.

This is how I like things done.

"What do you think?" I ask the squirming man as he looks up, terrified, into my eyes. "I think I am pretty fucking close to you now, don't you?"

He can't escape. The coldness of my steel reminds his neck of who's boss here.

"You don't know who I am, but you should," I continue. I don't blink. I don't show weakness. I can tell this low-level thug now totally understands that he is dealing with someone far above his station. "Don't ever fuck around with kids again, you got that?"

He nods.

"Tell all your friends to do the same. No fucking drugs with fucking kids."

He nods again.

Honor is more important than anything else in this world.

"You should've followed your smart friend and ran away like he did," I whisper with a sharpness in my voice. "I'm Damon Penmayne. And this is my city, you got that?"

And, for the last time before I set him free, the gang member nods.

* * *

I ADJUST my cufflinks as I close the door to my limo. I glance out of the window at the now-empty street corner where those gang members used to hang out.

That was a big distraction.

A time-wasting one. Something I logically should not have indulged in.

But I couldn't keep these thoughts that are raging through my head bottled up any longer, especially not today. That stunning girl from my hometown stirred something within me this morning, and I was determined to find a way to free myself from her constant presence in my mind.

But it hasn't worked. Nothing has worked.

If only Ava Matson could see me just then. Then she would see that I'm not the cold-hearted killer she thinks I am...

She would see that I am a man who keeps to his word. A man who, despite my business, is respectful and loyal and keeps to a code of honor.

I am a man who doesn't operate out of fear.

I exhale softly and shift my gaze away from the empty street corner and toward my man in the front seat of my limo.

And I say one word.

"Drive."

7

AVA

ANYTIME I WANT to recall the best moment of my life, I think of that day in the meadow.

One of the most magical days of my life.

The meadow itself is not far from my family house, just a block back from our backyard.

That day I was seven years old. Old enough to think I was mature and ready to be an adult already – enough so I could walk through an empty meadow on my own - but young enough to really want my Daddy beside me.

Well, I wasn't exactly walking, more like *twirling* through the meadow. It was a sunny summer's day - one of those long, carefree ones you can only ever experience in the golden haze of an innocent childhood.

Daddy watched me as I danced in the meadow. I was happy. Feeling safe in his presence.

After a time, he wandered over to me, crouching down to be at my height.

"Let's make a wish," he told me, his voice soft. "I'll show you how to make one in the way my mom showed me."

"How?" I asked, so curious. There were a lot of things I could wish for. A pony, a big house, a talking unicorn, a castle, magical powers, a puppy. The list in my little head was endless and Very Important.

"Close your eyes and hold my hand," Daddy said, reaching out. "This is how we make a wish. This is exactly how your grandmother told me. But you've got to be super sure your eyes are closed, okay?"

I let him take my fingers in his.

And, following his example, I closed my eyes. I *really* closed them, just as he told me to.

"Now we wait," Daddy instructed. "And keep those eyes closed."

Yep. I squeezed my eyes as closed as I could possibly make them. I didn't want to disappoint Daddy, and I really wanted to make sure my wish would come true.

"What are we waiting for?" I asked, starting to feel the strain as I forced my eyelids shut.

A slight breeze wafted past us. There was gentle bird-song in the distance. No one else was around in the meadow except for us two.

Dad's hand squeezed around mine.

"Wait one second," Daddy said.

"Do we have to?" I asked.

"Just take a moment and be still, Ava. Really listen to the peace and quiet."

And I did. I made myself feel the breeze. I made myself hear the birdsong.

"Now," Daddy finally said with a chuckle. "Make a wish."

And I did. But this wish wasn't one of the many on my

Very Important list; this wish was much more simple than any of those.

Be happy with Daddy forever.

My lips moved with the wish in a silent mutter.

I held my breath as if that would somehow help the wish work.

"You can open your eyes now," Daddy whispered.

And I did.

My eyes met Daddy's. He was looking at me with all the affection in the world. I gripped his hands tighter.

"I love you, Ava," he said.

"I love you, Daddy."

And then, as if responding to the wish I had just made, a butterfly fluttered between Daddy and me. One wing was blue, and the other green. It spun and twirled between us, just like how I had been doing in the meadow moments before.

I gasped at the sight of the multi-colored insect.

It was magical.

"Daddy, look!"

"I can see it. Look at its colors. It's just like you, Ava. Your own special butterfly."

"Yes, it is just like me."

"You must've made a really special wish, Ava."

I smiled.

Yes, I did make a really special wish.

Be happy with Daddy forever.

I STUMBLE through the front door of my dad's house and immediately announce my presence by dropping my bag with a very long groan, and not without good reason.

All that way for nothing, just to come back home empty handed like a total idiot.

All that way for just some crazy-ass proposal from a scary gangster businessman that I will never - *not in a million years* - accept.

I hear movement from the kitchen before Dad's head pokes around the door.

"Ava? You're back?"

There's so much relief in his voice. I bet he was thinking Damon would've cut me up into little pieces and fed them to his sharks by now. To be honest, I think I would rather prefer that to being forced to be the crime boss' mistress for months.

"Hey, Dad. Big freaking day."

"How are you? You've been gone for so long."

I groan again. "I'm fine."

I'm very much not.

And Dad can see that.

"Come in and tell me what happened. Did you make it to New York? What was it like?"

Like a grumpy hormonal teenager, I drag myself into the kitchen and slump down in a chair.

"I met him," I say, all energy drained from my voice.

Dad sits down opposite me, clearly very interested.

"Who? Damon Penmayne? You did?"

"Yes. *Him.* I tracked him down. I actually met the bastard."

"And what happened?" he asks.

I roll my eyes. I really don't want to recount what went down in that fancy office, especially not to my dad.

"To put it bluntly, he's an *awful* human being," I explain. "He tried to humiliate me. Things didn't go anywhere. It was a total waste from start to finish."

It's a very uncharacteristically short and unelaborated

tale from me. I normally run my mouth off until the cows come home.

Dad nods. I can tell he's trying to hide his disappointment at the lack of success or even a result that isn't nothing.

Other than the dorms at college, I have only ever lived in this house. It's your typical two-story suburban house. Nothing that stands out at all. But there have been a lot of memories between these walls.

It's just Dad and me now. Mom left when I was fifteen. One random day – I think it was a Tuesday – she announced to us that she was sleeping with some guy from work and then just... *left*. She moved with the guy to the other side of the state. I've made a decision to cut off all contact with her. It was easy for me to do so. She doesn't deserve us.

That shit stayed with Dad, though. It's pretty clear he's not over what happened; the house still has old family photos on the wall from when I was younger. Photos with Mom. Nothing about the place changed when she left. It's still the same furniture. Still the same beds.

I guess it was that shit that has driven Dad to his addictions.

And I feel like an idiot for not guessing that earlier. When it could've helped. When we could've done something about it and not ended up in the mess we're in.

I got the whole mixed-color eyes thing from Mom. She had it too. I hope it's the only trait we share.

I look at Dad sitting opposite. He's really starting to look old. All this stress has not been good for him. Grey hair that thins by the day. There is no more of the vitality he used to have in his eyes, just weariness. Each new line on his face reminds me of the pain we've been under, and my total inability to solve it.

I feel like a punch has hit me in the gut. It's as if I've let

Dad down, as if I couldn't extract what we required from Damon. All we ended up with was that bizarre batshit proposition.

This is all just... crap.

I went all that way to New York for nothing. I risked my neck just to get practically spat back in my face by one of the most powerful men in the country. To be viewed as some... *fuckdoll* for temporary entertainment by a horny big-shot criminal with too much money to throw around.

And then, sitting opposite me, Dad suddenly starts crying. He's overcome with tears. I know he really doesn't want to break down in front of his daughter, but he does. I'm so aware that he's been trying to hold back his emotions, reluctant to let his vulnerability show in front of his daughter, but it's a battle he has lost. Before all this whirlwind chaos with Damon and the debts, I had never witnessed Dad cry before. Not once in my entire life. Yet now, in these last few weeks, it is almost routine. His breakdown barely registers with me, a fact that makes me so damn sad.

"I'm sorry," he burbles between sobs. "I am so sorry for all of this."

I lean over and wrap my arms around the man who raised me.

"I'll find a way out," I whisper as my dad cries. "I will. I promise you. We will work this out."

But I know it's impossible.

There is no way out.

We're screwed.

8

DAMON

At least once every day there comes a point when I can recall the worst day of my life, and I relive it to the point when I can feel the moment in my veins - where I feel the moment burst through me like fire erupting through a volcano.

And it makes me so very fucking *angry.*

It was not just the worst day of my life; it was also the day that upended my entire world and changed everything.

But, at the time, it did not feel like one that would be so monumental: it was simply a nice, sunny, summer's day. Warm. *Inviting.* Chicago was looking its best. All brightness and smiles. Tall skyscrapers glistening in the sun. There wasn't a cloud in sight. Everyone in the Windy City seemed so damn cheerful.

I certainly didn't expect the danger coming my way.

But it came for me, nonetheless.

Joshua and I were walking out of our luxury downtown hotel. He'd flown me out to Chicago on his private plane, promising his godson a weekend away from Crystal River and my family mansion. We had planned on watching the ballet out there. Arts and culture were never my kind of thing, but Joshua lapped up that shit like it was gold. He was a true *cultured* man. And like with anything he did, I wanted to be part of it.

Even if it included watching random men in leotards prance around a stage.

I wanted to make him happy. I wanted to be with him, no matter what or where it was.

I had always been close to my godfather; ever since he helped baptize me as a tiny baby, I guess. And I would like to say the man was fond of me.

While I might have been the black sheep of the Penmayne family, Joshua Hall took me under his wing and made me very much feel like I was *somebody*. Like some wise old mentor in a movie, he taught me everything I needed to know. Everything about life, business, relationships, and how to be a man and make sure other men respected you. Every fucking thing a strong man should know as a tearaway, shy boy emerging from the acne-ridden, awkward teenage years. Joshua Hall basically became my surrogate father when my own family ignored me.

I looked up to him.

I *loved* him. In the same way an adoring son might love his own father.

And, sure, he was a bad man: he ran a criminal organization in New York City. He did terrible things to build the life he had. He was close to my father and his media empire. They worked together to help each other build their organizations.

But Joshua was the man I trusted above all others. The man I would do anything for.

Joshua and Father were best friends when they were

boys in Crystal River. They rose up together. My father went into media and news ownership whilst Joshua took charge of a gang in New York, reforming it and shaping it until it became a powerful city-wide organization. He owned nightclubs and bars and gambling dens. An empire under his control. He had nothing dealing with children. He never harmed anyone innocent. Sure, what he technically did as a business was *illegal*, but the man still held onto a strict code of honor and values that shaped who he was. Something so important to him that he passed it on to his godson.

He had a code of honor and values that shaped *me*.

The same honor and values that I've tried my utmost to take with me throughout my entire life.

He was my guide for *everything*. There was no issue too small that I wouldn't have gone to him with and could rely on his expert advice. He meant the world to me.

And my world came crashing down that day. The worst day of my life. The day I have thought about every day since. The day that still lives as pure emotion through my bones.

"Tonight we'll head to the theatre early," Joshua was telling me as we stepped out from the hotel into the Chicago sunshine. "I know the artistic director of the ballet company, and he's promising us a private tour of the backstage before the performance. We have a private viewing box lined up to watch it. And after the show, we'll go out for dinner with the principal dancers and my friend and also the director of the production. Don't worry, you'll be given ample opportunity to tell them how boring you found the show."

I looked up at my tall godfather. He had an elegant poise to him. So confident. Always wearing expensive black suits.

Sometimes I imagined myself as him - that perfect posture - that inherent confidence that I felt like I was lacking. That ability to run such a complex organization without seeming like it stressed him in any way.

He was a perfect role model for me.

"Sounds great," I replied to Joshua. "And, yes, I will *definitely* let them know how boring the show was."

"I wouldn't expect any less from you," Joshua replied with a knowing smirk.

"Thank you for bringing me here," I said to him quietly. I was being honest. Sincere.

And my godfather could see that.

"My pleasure," he replied. "Anything for you, Damon Penmayne."

I glanced around the busy street. Here we were, right in the middle of downtown Chicago. My godfather was treating me as an equal. He had money, influence, and power, and being in close proximity to that made me feel part of his world.

I felt on top of the fucking world.

A car trundled past us, close to the sidewalk. It was going slow. Too slow for the traffic of a busy city.

Black and sleek. Tinted windows. Unassuming. Secretive.

I should've paid more attention to the car. I should've been alerted to the suspicious vehicle.

But I wasn't.

And I still blame myself for it.

As it came within yards of us, the tinted window of the car rolled down. A gun emerged from inside.

It all happened so fast, and yet so slow. Almost in slow motion.

I saw the black gun aim at us.

I saw the man holding it.

I saw his face. I saw it as clear as day. Like someone had taken a snapshot of it.

I saw the snarl on his lips and the triumphant, feverish look in his eyes as he looked at Joshua and me.

And before I could react to all this, I saw a burst of light from the gun. And I heard the sharp bang that deafened me and that shattered the perfect day.

And, next to me, Joshua crumpled as the car sped away, now a hell of a lot faster than any of the other cars on the road.

No, no, no.

And I was turning toward Joshua.

And I saw the blood pouring from his chest. I saw the bullet-shaped hole in the place where his heart would be.

And I realized that this was a drive-by shooting. This was intentional. The man in the tinted car was intent on shooting my godfather.

And he had succeeded.

A scream emerged from deep within me as I looked at the man who I adored.

"Joshua!"

But it was too late.

Joshua was lifeless. His eyes were wide open. His mouth was slack. His breathing had stopped.

My godfather was dead.

And I saw it all.

That was the worst day of my life.

The day that everything changed.

The day I can never forget. The day I remember every single fucking day.

* * *

I STRIDE into the hotel's entrance, flanked by my bodyguard. This establishment ranks among the finest and priciest in New York City, catering exclusively to the wealthiest and most influential clientele.

And I am their most valued guest.

In the lobby hangs a chandelier whose value surpasses that of an entire row of houses on your average street. Gold is everywhere. Security is everywhere. You can't just simply walk into a place like this from off the street. It's a long way off from when I used to beg for scraps just around the block from here. Even though I am rich beyond my wildest dreams, I still will never take all this luxury for granted.

You never can do so when you've lived on the streets.

I make my way to the front desk. The gorgeous receptionist has already recognized me before I even get to the counter. My name and my famous face go far in this city.

Without a need for me to utter a single word, the receptionist hands my bodyguard the key to my exclusive suite.

"The top floor presidential suite. As always, Mr. Penmayne."

I'm turning to head to the private elevator when I'm stopped by a woman. She stands in my way, barring my progress.

I don't stop.

And she doesn't budge.

She wants something from me.

I recognize her face - some European supermodel making big waves in the fashion industry. I recall reading that she's been voted the world's sexiest woman twice in a row in one of those trashy magazines my father owns.

Tall, slender, flawless complexion, glossy black hair. Poised. She is the epitome of a stereotypical supermodel.

"Damon Penmayne..."

She practically *moans* my name as she steps in front of me.

Oh, she's good.

"Hello," I say calmly. My bodyguard comes to a halt beside me. The poor man probably can't hold back his erection at the sight of the supermodel.

The girl takes a step back, and I take a step forward. I still have my eyes on my private elevator. I have no patience for games.

"I didn't know you were staying here," the model says. She reaches out and traces her long fingernail up along my arm seductively.

I am unfazed.

"I frequent this place quite often," I respond. "Consider me a regular."

"I have no doubt you can afford it," she says. "I bet you could even buy the whole hotel if you wanted to. I bet you have so many girls coming in and out of your room, what with your reputation."

I raise an eyebrow. "Really? My reputation? Where have you heard that?"

"Just rumors," the supermodel moans temptingly. "How about you change your reputation? How about tonight you just make it the one girl going in your room? How about you make it *me*?"

I would normally say yes to her, and I would be completely unattached to whatever happens next. It would be fun, sure, but nothing that would make my cold heart stop. I've only ever used girls for sex, nothing more. I like to be in control, especially over my emotions. I have come to understand that getting too attached, in my world, means certain doom for the ones I love.

"Nobody is coming in or out of my suite tonight," I say,

brushing off the supermodel's hand before she can touch my face.

She batters her perfect eyelashes at me. "*Really*?"

She's putting on a seductive baby voice.

"Really."

And then I turn and walk away. I'm not wasting my time here.

Not when there's other girls on my mind.

* * *

I DON'T EVEN CARE about the amazing view from the hotel over Central Park, but I should: my suite has the best view in the entire building, but I shut the window as soon as I'm in here.

And I pour myself a large glass of whiskey from the private bar.

This suite is undoubtedly among the most luxurious in the entire city, yet my regard for its material status remains totally unaffected.

And it's because I don't care for any of this. Not the fancy hotel, not the supermodel purring for a night with me, not the killer view.

Tomorrow I'll fly from New York back to Crystal River. I don't want to spend a minute more in this city than I have to. I just want to be home.

I cheer myself in the mirror, lonely holding up the glass of whiskey to my reflection. Sometimes I can't even recognize the man I've become when I look into a mirror. The *beast* I've become. There was a time when I was an innocent boy, completely naïve about the world, but my years in New York City utterly transformed me like a man would turn into a werewolf in those stories our father would tell my brothers when we were boys.

The power struggles that have scarred me, both physically and mentally. The battles for influence, the journey to construct my empire from scratch, starting from the very streets themselves.

Since then, I've established a legitimate enterprise as a cover for my less reputable undertakings—a sprawling alcohol empire that has asserted its dominion on a global scale, with a brewery I purposely built in my hometown.

Even though I come from a billionaire family, I've never relied on my father's money to survive ever since the day I saw the man I loved most in the world get gunned down in front of me. That day was the catalyst that made me come here to this city in the first place.

That day made me realize I have to rely – wholly *depend* - on myself, and only myself, to get through the cruel world.

I place the empty whiskey tumbler down on the table and pull out my knife from inside my jacket. The same knife I held to the throat of that stupid thug on the street corner. It's my most precious possession. I keep it with me at all times. It has never let me down.

It's a sleek, blackened blade. Its handle fits perfectly in my hand. Engraved along the blade is the name *Joshua Hall*, after my godfather. It is razor-sharp, high-quality stainless steel. Discreet and dangerous. The perfect weapon for a killer who prefers to eschew guns and instead gets up close and personal with his enemies.

I strip down and run myself a shower in the suite's expansive restroom. I take a moment to look down at my body and run my eyes over my many tattoos. I have inked quite a collection into my skin over the years. Black markings of a dark history. They are memories I have wanted to keep on my skin as a permanent reminder of where I've come from. Words I've wanted to etch into my flesh...

As I stand under the hot water of the shower, I allow my emotions to wash over me like a waterfall of pain.

I close my eyes and simply let myself, for once, *feel*.

In my everyday existence, I maintain a stoic facade. However, in these private moments, I grant myself the space to genuinely confront my deepest emotions - even if it's just for the briefest of moments.

And I feel so very alone.

And, standing here in the shower, my thoughts instinctively turn to Ava Matson. I don't know why.

Offering her to be my mistress was very much a *spur-of-the-moment* kind of thing. It was the only strategy I could think of to get her close to me. Somehow, I *want* her close to me, no matter how convoluted it might be.

Maybe I'm becoming obsessed.

For fuck's sake, Damon. That's the very last thing you need.

The intensity of my fixation on the girl with mixed-color eyes scares me.

Nevertheless, my dick is hard. Under the heat of the shower, I start to stroke my thick member, thinking of that girl from my hometown. Thinking of her plump lips. Of the way she looked at me with that fire in her eyes. How she bravely called out my name in my office.

How she fucking rejected me with all that sass.

Me.

Such spunk. That's a girl I would like to know, no matter how.

I lean back into the streaming heat and grunt hard as I cum, thinking of the former cheerleader.

Fuck... to taste her lips... to have her in my bed...

Yeah. Okay. I might be fucking obsessed with her.

9

AVA

I NEED TO ESCAPE. I need to get out of my dad's place. I need to get away from the worry and pain of the debts and the struggles, even if for just a morning.

And so I go to my favorite place in the whole of Crystal River - the coffee shop I can always rely on for a good beverage and a moment of blissful solitude and just, like, good *vibes*.

The Oak.

Stepping inside the coffee shop, I'm overcome with exactly what I'm searching for this morning. The air is filled with the delightful mingling of freshly brewed coffee and the inviting aroma of freshly baked treats. It's all so cute and cozy.

Yeah, there's the good vibe I'm looking for.

There's a rustic feel to the place with the brick walls and artistic shelves meticulously adorned with an array of random knick-knacks. A sweeping counter proudly showcases the array of delicious pastries, invitingly laid out for all to see.

I really, *really* love it here.

"Hey, Josie," I greet the barista. She and I went to the same high school – the *only* high school – in Crystal River together. I've barely seen Josie since then. I mean, we were never close at all in our year, just on first name terms and nothing more serious. Not super friendly, but not high school enemies or anything like that. She got married to her high school sweetheart, but I've since heard that there's been relationship trouble between them. I don't really know what's gone on, but I suspect it's been serious.

To be honest, I've felt out of the loop of the gossip around town since everything started with Dad.

Josie flicks her curly black hair back, regarding me with sad brown eyes. Maybe the rumors are true and she has had issues with her husband. Maybe that's what she's sad about. She softly smiles at me, but I can tell she's putting on a brave face, whatever is going on inside. I feel sorry for her.

"Hey, Ava," she greets. "Long time. How are you?"

I smile weakly back.

Like her, I am also putting on a brave face.

"Things are good," I say, feigning cheerfulness. I'm nearly stammering. It's so unlike me. Dad's misfortunes have really rattled me these past few weeks. "Just coming in for one of your famous almond croissants and a coffee, please."

Josie makes me my coffee and fetches me a delicious croissant with a quick professionalism. These croissant delights truly are my favorite things this coffee shop sells here. I first had them when I was a kid. Every time I have a bite, I am taken back to a much simpler and more fun time of my life - a time before worries about debts and gangsters.

Dad used to take me here when I was a little girl. We used to get a coffee for him and a hot chocolate for me and one big almond croissant to share, and we would sit in the park in happy silence every single Saturday.

He hasn't taken me here for years. We haven't sat in the park together in happy silence for such a long time.

It's one more sad thing to add to my growing list.

After saying bye to Josie, I settle into a seat beside the window, gazing out at the central park of Crystal River. Kids are playing in the playground. I spot the bench Dad and I would sit on. Everything seems so... *peaceful.*

But things are not so peaceful in my mind. I think about Damon Penmayne. His scarred visage materializes in my mind like a haunting nightmare that I can't shake.

That damn offer of his...

He is a violent man, that's for sure. Everyone in this town knows he is. There's no way I would even dare enter his life. The man lives in a dark and dangerous world, and I certainly don't want to end up all tangled up in that. *No, sir.*

I take a sip of my coffee.

I remember how he looked in that office in that black suit: all enigmatic and mysterious and brooding, just like his reputation would suggest, but also so damn confident and handsome. His calmness. His stillness. The way he watched me like a lion in charge of his domain stalks its prey. And the way he talked – so smooth and calculated, each word measured and suave. He was not your typical gangster. This was an intelligent man with an old-fashioned sense of chivalry, despite his insane proposal. He offered to fly me home on his private plane. He did not seem like a cruel man who could choose to have such an ominous hold over Dad.

But he is still a monster. He still has chosen to screw Dad over. He gave me an impossible offer just to rile me up...

The bell for The Oak rings. Someone new has entered.

My eyes flicker up to the door absentmindedly.

And that's when I see him - the man entering the coffee shop.

My ex-boyfriend.

Oh. *Fuck.*

10

DAMON

I WAKE up with thoughts of Ava Matson flooding my head.

Those sparkling, expressive eyes. That cascading silky blonde hair. That infectious smile. That poise. That playful sass.

That indescribable, inimitable *beauty* of hers which makes me so fucking *weak*.

I cannot get her out of my head, no matter how hard I try. She has been a constant presence in my life, refusing to be ignored like some kind of ghost haunting my house, ever since I first saw her and she shouted my name in my office.

Fuck. This is not good.

I turn over and reach for one of my many phones by my bedside. It is a necessity, in my dangerous and clandestine line of business, to have multiple devices always on standby.

And I call Jim.

He sounds like he hasn't even fallen asleep. I've joked with him before that he is such a workaholic, that he is clearly a half-robot who works through the night. He does not like that comparison in the slightest, but I swear it's true. The man just keeps going and going and going and going.

"Damon?"

"I want you to arrange someone to keep track of that Ava girl," I say.

Jim and I converse fast and short to each other, always have. We've worked together through enough hardship and trouble that we've developed a kind of shorthand between us. There is no need for any lovely little pleasantries between us when there's business at hand to deal with.

To my early morning request, there is one of Jim's stereotypical sighs in response. "You're being possessive, Damon. Ava Matson does not need to be followed."

"I just want to know."

"You should not be doing this," Jim says. "It's not logical."

"Fuck logical," I reply. "Find someone good and trustworthy."

Jim sighs one more time and then hangs up. I would not tolerate such rudeness from anyone else apart from Jim, but I know that right now, qualified men are immediately being summoned to Crystal River to obey my request, and that's all because of his speed and professionalism. Jim will always be loyal. He will always follow my commands, no matter how possessive they might sound to him.

I quickly shower and change into one of my black suits that has already been brought up by my bodyguard.

There's a knock on the door just as I'm running a hand through my messy jet-black hair. I answer it to one of my men with a letter in his hand for me. I know the envelope has already been scanned for suspicious substances by my team downstairs. They do it with all my mail or anything else that comes within my orbit. I can't be too careful when being paranoid is a positive trait in my profession.

In the privacy of my large hotel suite, I open the letter. I recognize the handwriting immediately.

It's Jack Ricca, also commonly known as *Handsome Jack*.

My rival in this city. A man after my assets. A man who would kill me in a heartbeat.

I don't like to admit that I have adversaries, but Handsome Jack can certainly claim such a position. He and I have dirty business that goes back years. He's the head of his own gang that wants to take over New York City, always biting at my heels like some dog.

He has eluded my attempts at dousing out his fire too many times to count. He's a wry one, I'd give him that.

But so am I. I've also eluded plenty of the man's own attempts myself.

I certainly think it would be fair to say we gleefully would slit each other's throats if given half the chance.

Whatever he's written to me, it's probably not good. Letters have been the only way he and I have ever communicated, and we don't send many. This will be something serious, I'm sure.

I fold the letter without reading it and tuck it securely away in my suit pocket. I will deal with Handsome Jack and his little theatrics later, but for now, I'm heading back to Crystal River. I want to be home.

I want to be near Ava Matson when she changes her mind.

Because I *know* she's going to change her mind. It is just a matter of time.

"Come on," I say to my bodyguard as I step outside. "We're getting the fuck out of this city."

* * *

Enroute to the airport in my limousine, bound for my private plane, my phone rings - it's Spencer calling.

One of my five brothers.

Spencer and I are close, but we're not ones to call each other out of the blue. I wonder what the motive is for him reaching out like this.

"Spencer."

"Damon."

"What's the call for, brother?" I ask.

Spencer is one of the leading English Literature professors in the country. He can boast an impressive educational background, having studied at esteemed universities both here and in the UK. Despite numerous offers from prestigious institutions, he bucked all common sense – according to our father and most of academia – and chose to return to Crystal River, opting to impart his knowledge at the local university in the small town where he grew up.

But me? I find that deeply honorable. We Penmaynes respect our roots.

And, like us Penmaynes, he is incredibly good looking. That doesn't harm things.

"Where are you now, Damon?" he asks me. "Off shaking down some low-life thugs?"

"Nothing of the sort, brother. I'm in New York heading back to Crystal River now on my plane. Take-off is in ten minutes."

"Perfect timing," he replies. "I'm inviting you for drinks tonight at my place. I'm assuming you'll be free to come, no? It has been too long since I've seen you."

Ah. *That's* the motive for the unexpected call.

I would normally reject such an offer, but I do know that Spencer has actually met Ava in the flesh a few times. Maybe I will be able to glean some information about the girl that even Jim hasn't been able to sniff out. Olivia, the girl that Spencer is seeing at the moment, is – *was* – Ava's roommate at Crystal River University before all these events with her father started. She and Spencer are certainly well-placed to give me a behind-the-scenes look at the girl who occupies my sleeping and waking mind.

And seeing my brother will be nice, I have to admit.

"Consider me coming, Spencer," I reply. "I'll cancel my plans to shake down some low-life thugs."

"Lovely."

Hearing about Ava from a man as trustworthy as my smart professor brother? This will be perfect.

11

AVA

My former boyfriend strolls into The Oak, trailed by his father, while I remain seated in complete and total shock. Frozen stiff like a block of ice.

Sure, Crystal River is a small town, and therefore the chances of running into someone you know are incredibly high, but I really did not expect to run into Luke Abbott when I woke up this morning, and I wouldn't particularly want to. I would've even put it down on my list of *things I would least like to happen today*.

Him walking in like this means that I'm coming face-to-face with my ex for the first time since he dumped me over the entire ordeal with my dad's debts and all that crap. He seemed to think that, with everyone knowing about our family's dirty laundry around town, being seen with me would mess up his perfectly cultivated pristine boy-next-door image.

Yep, Luke didn't want me ruining his reputation, and so he discarded me like a grown puppy after Christmas.

He looks the same as he did the time he broke my heart. Well, it's only been a few weeks since I last saw him, so it's not like he would drastically change or anything. It certainly feels super weird seeing him from far away, and not up close like I'm used to. *Kissing him.*

Seeing Luke from across the coffee shop makes me reconsider him again. I see him completely anew. He's broad-shouldered: a big, muscular physique befitting a former high school quarterback. That trademark short, spiky blonde hair of his seems to sparkle with charisma. He's got that all-American hero aura around him.

No wonder everyone takes a shine to him.

Luke Abbott looks like he's in the prime of his life. No one can touch him. He commands everyone's attention when he enters a room. I wonder what goes through the heads of people in town when they see him...

There's the handsome, popular guy everyone knows. Whatever happened to that blonde bimbo girlfriend of his?

I had thought I had put all my emotions about the breakup past me - that I had set aside the time to let myself fully heal - but seeing the former star high school quarter-back in the flesh again immediately makes me want to tear up and revert back to a teary mess.

Great. Just freaking great.

I truly am a walking bimbo cheerleader cliche.

All the memories of our relationship come flooding back like crashing waves of pain as I lay eyes on him again.

That first kiss we shared right in the middle of the field the moment after he threw that game-winning ball. How he lifted me high and easily in the air, allowing me to wrap my legs around his muscular and sweaty torso, to kiss him passionately in front of an adoring crowd of our friends and spectators...

That was the greatest moment of my life; when it

seemed like all of Crystal River was there to witness our love. He was a hero of the town that day, and I was his girl. I was so proud of my man. I really, really was *his* girl, and I wanted to be nothing else.

I thought that shining moment would last forever.

I remember how he would drive me around in his car for no reason except as an excuse to spend time together in this small town. We'd go around the empty dark streets at night completely aimlessly, but it was those moments alone with him that I truly lived for.

I really thought I was going to be his girl forever. His future wife. The mother of his children.

It was all mapped out, in my mind and also in the minds of our family and friends. It was the surest thing there could be.

It was *always* Ava and Luke. We came packaged as a combo deal.

And then it all came crashing down over someone as stupid as my dad's debts.

In the coffee shop, both Luke and his own dad head straight to Josie at the counter, not spotting me sitting by the window. That's a minor relief.

I mean, should I talk to him?

That sounds baffling, but it could be a way to get some of my dignity and self-respect back. Confront the boy who broke my heart in the middle of a public setting. It would send tongue waggling, that's for sure.

Ugh. I don't know what to do.

He's the one who ended things. He's the one who wanted me out of his life.

I watch the two men get their coffees from the safety of my seat on the other side of the coffee shop. I feel like some kind of stalker, staring at my ex-boyfriend as he chats to his dad completely oblivious to my presence by the window.

They see a friend, some guy the same age as Luke's dad. They all shake hands. Smile. Chat about nothing and exchange pleasantries. Everything's all *hunky-dory*.

And then Luke and his dad leave.

And I breathe a sigh of relief.

He didn't see me. I don't have to confront Luke. I don't even have to talk to him. He doesn't even have to know I'm here.

But then, as he opens the front door – about to step out - he turns toward me across the coffee shop, and we instantly lock eyes.

And he most *definitely* sees me.

A lump forms in my throat, and though I have the urge to rise, I'm immobilized right where I sit. I still remain utterly *frozen*, unable to move a muscle.

Luke regards me for a moment and then scoffs at me in utter distaste.

And then he leaves.

Oh.

It all happens in the quickest of moments, but that's all it takes to ruin my world.

My hands ball into fists under the table. I was helpless. I was *scoffed* at. I was treated as something to be reviled at by the man I once loved.

And I am so, so angry.

But I feel so utterly crushed.

And I want to cry all over again.

Everything has gone to shit.

* * *

I'm LYING in my old childhood bedroom, attempting to drift off to sleep, but I can't. A sharp, disturbing noise is loudly filtering in from the adjacent room. My dad's room.

He's crying. Again.

It's late. Nearly midnight. Outside is pitch black, and Dad clearly reckons he can cry without me catching a sound.

But I *am* hearing him. And I can't go to sleep because of his pain.

He's so upset. I just want to go in there and hug him, but that would be a step too close and personal for my proud father.

And so, I close my eyes and try to drown out the noise of my Dad's heart breaking.

But it doesn't work.

I can't live like this.

Dad can't live like this.

He was already broken by what Mom did. This might very well be the last straw for him.

Crap. Here goes. I need to do something. I'm at the end of everything.

I finally give in.

And I turn over in the bed and reach for my phone and the card that Damon gave me with his personal number on it.

I'm going to call the man right now, accept his stupid offer, and end all of this.

Right now, I would accept anything to stop my Dad from crying at night.

Be happy with Daddy forever.

12

DAMON

SPENCER RESIDES on the most picturesque street in Crystal River. My brother's townhouse is incredibly convenient for him, especially in relation to the university campus. It is also – *especially* conveniently - a stone's throw away from a certain Olivia Weldon: the Crystal River University student who has somehow managed to capture his cold Penmayne heart.

I arrive at his home on the leafy street earlier than we planned, parking my sportscar directly outside. I always prefer to roll up at my appointments just before the appointed time. I may do bad things, but I still consider myself a punctual gentleman.

I turn off the engine and take a moment to spy my brother's place.

On the outside, Spencer keeps his home well-maintained. Impeccably trimmed shrubs line the outer walls, and the lawn is meticulously manicured. This is my first time here; Spencer only returned to Crystal River from Boston a few months ago to start at the university as a professor. I am very much looking forward to seeing what's inside these elegant townhouse walls. Knowing my brother's taste, I am expecting pure class, in true Spencer style.

"Welcome, Damon. Here's hoping you'll stay and not disappear like you are wont to do."

My professor brother opens the front door, expecting me. I've come alone. No need for bodyguards or followers here.

Catching up with my brother is an almost sacred act that remains private.

"I'll stay if you offer me a glass of good whisky," I say to him as I cross the threshold into my brother's place. Spencer merely smiles.

"I wouldn't offer a sophisticated man like you anything less, brother."

We're both dressed in suits, as we always do. T-shirts and jeans aren't *exactly* our style, even when we're not working. I've gone for an open-collar black suit – a hint of my muscular chest on display - while Spencer sports a perfectly knotted tie with his dark brown suit. We easily slot into our roles: the gangster and the professor.

I note he gets his suits tailored in London. I prefer Italian. Another point of difference between us.

But no matter the country of origin, we both share an expensive taste in clothes. Two brothers who are so different, and yet have the same desire for simply *the best*.

I follow him into his reading room. This is definitely his favorite place in the building. There's a real *classic library* vibe emanating from this room. It's so typical Spencer - all resplendent mahogany paneling in rich coffee-brown hues and subdued, atmospheric lighting. My attention is instantly drawn to the large bookcase cradling many famous and great tomes of literature.

Spencer and his books.

The bookcase is certainly not just for show; I know my brother has read every single one of the thick tomes that line the shelves. That's the kind of sophisticated man he is. I've always harbored a tinge of envy for my brother's vast intellect and prowess with the written word. It all comes so effortlessly to him.

Spencer - the *intellectual* Penmayne.

From a small bar in the corner of his library, my brother pours me a drink and offers it with an outstretched hand.

"It's not *your* whiskey, unfortunately," he says. "I hope you will forgive me."

He's mentioning my alcohol company - the global business that I've set up with the purpose of presenting a legit façade to the outside world.

"I'm sure I can manage another brand of whiskey, Spencer," I reply. "As long as it's good. It does feel like a betrayal of my company to dare taste it, though."

We cheer our drinks.

"What do you think?" my brother asks, raising an eyebrow at my sip of whiskey.

"It is respectable."

"That is certainly high praise, coming from you," he replies. "You are a man who knows your alcohol. Please sit."

I gladly do in one of his comfy leather reading chairs. My brother takes his spot opposite me.

"Tell me, how is Crystal River University life treating you?" I ask him with a wry smile. Spencer smiles back at me.

"It's treating me very well," he replies.

"And this girl that you're seeing?" I ask. "How is she?"

I am characteristically blunt.

"Very well, Damon. She is very well."

"Ah, so you're going to remain coy about her?" I ask

cheekily. "Keeping her a little secret from me? You were fine divulging all about her to me that one time I got you drunk on my alcohol."

My brother and I attended a family event a few weeks ago and had too many drinks: a yearly tradition for our late brother, Arthur Penmanye, who was involved in a fatal car crash two years ago. Arthur was the life and soul of our family – the lovable, adventurous, optimistic, popular Penmayne. His twin, Royce, has not taken things well. Every year, it is customary for us to rent out a bar in town for the night and drink and celebrate the life of our beloved brother in seclusion. That was where I brought along some samples of my alcohol. That's where I got Spencer drunk, and where he told me all about his little dalliance with Olivia Weldon.

Despite my infamous cold heart, there is a place there reserved for Arthur. His passing is still so raw.

We all miss him.

I miss him.

"I think it's best I keep Olivia from the rest of the family at this present stage," Spencer replies coolly. He's smart enough not to take the bait of my teasing. "I can see... *issues* arising if she were exposed to that level of chaos just yet."

"True," I reply. "The very last thing you need right now is Mother getting her hands on the poor girl."

"Definitely."

"And what about the university?" I ask. "Do they know about your little affair?"

"I think it's best we keep that from the university as well," Spencer says.

"Ah. I see," I reply. "You know, behind all that book smarts of yours, you truly are a little mischievous devil as well, Spencer. And what would you call your fling with this girl? When will you drop her?"

"It's not like that this time. Things are... *serious* between Olivia and me," my brother replies cryptically. I raise an eyebrow in response.

"What's this? The great Spencer Penmayne actually... *lost* for words for the first time in his life?"

"Tell me about your business, Damon. How's it all going? You like to keep all that side of your life secret."

"Trying to change the subject, are we? Tell me more about this *serious* relationship..."

"What's your latest crime, Damon?" my brother asks.

"Oh, we're going there?" I ask. "You really want to tread on my toes?"

"I've heard how you're involved with a mutual contact of ours," Spencer says.

I shift in my seat. He's being sneaky. "What mutual contact? Who are you talking about?"

"Olivia's roommate at college," Spencer replies calmly. "*Ava Matson*. Surely, to you, that name rings a bell?"

Oh yes, it certainly does.

But I keep my cards close to my chest. Even with my brother.

"No idea in the slightest."

My brother looks at me in a way that echoes back to how he looked at me in childhood. He knows when I am concealing something, more than anyone else on this planet.

"Her father owes you money," he says. "A *significant* sum of money. That's what I've heard."

"Maybe he does," I reply. "A lot of people owe me money."

"Drop those debts, Damon."

I grip my whiskey glass tighter.

"It's not as simple as that," I say.

"Why not?"

My brother is really starting to get on my nerves.

"It's not about the money, Spencer, you know this."

My brother sighs.

"What is it about, Damon?" he asks.

"The principle," I reply.

"What *principle*, Damon?"

My brother is really hiding his exasperation poorly.

"It's about honoring your commitment," I reply. "Your word. I'm all about honor. And honoring your commitments."

"Damon..."

"What would my enemies think if I were to simply drop these debts and they heard about it, as they surely would? Without a doubt, I would lose my reputation. I would lose my *honor*. I will never allow that to happen."

"What can be done, then?" Spencer asks. "You're going to murder the poor man simply on principle? You're a bad man, Damon, but you're not *that* bad."

"Ava will help repay her father's debts," I reply curtly. "That's it."

"I know Ava," Spencer says softly. "She's loyal. A *good* person. We both know how rare those kinds of people are, especially in our world. I'm worried about what you will do with her. Tell me, how will she pay off her father's debts?"

I take a long pause.

"I'm simply getting a debt paid. It is the right thing for the Matson family to do," I eventually say.

My brother goes quiet and dark.

"What are you considering, Damon? Tell me."

I shake my head. "Nothing that you wouldn't do, brother."

He regards me for a very long time before he speaks again. I hold his unwavering eye contact.

"I hope to God you know what you're doing," Spencer

eventually says. "You're playing with lives here. This isn't a game."

I scoff. "I've taken lives, Spencer. I know what's at stake."

"*Innocent* lives?" he asks.

"Never. Only guilty ones."

"You certainly are an enigma, Damon. I feel sorry for the poor girl who has to deal with you."

I smile.

"I could say the same for you, brother."

Spencer cooks us both dinner, and we no longer mention Ava. It's like a silent truce between us. We instead talk about his work and other issues. We discuss politics and world events. It's always good to have a conversation with someone on your level.

And then it's time for me to leave.

"It was good to see you again, Damon."

"Good to see you too, Spencer."

"Don't be a stranger now that I'm back in Crystal River," he says.

"Anything you want," I reply. "Anything at all. Just ask."

"Drop those debts, Damon."

He's back on it, is he? What has Olivia told him?

I exhale. "Only when those debts are repaid. Trust me, Spencer, they *will* be repaid. I have offered Ava Matson a very good deal that I know she will accept."

"Yeah, I really do hope you know what you're doing, Damon."

As soon as my brother's front door locks shut behind

me, I receive a call on my personal phone. Only a few people have this important number.

And it's exactly who I'm hoping it will be.

A very good deal...

I pick it up and smile with victory before I speak.

"Hello, Ava. Ready to reconsider my offer?"

13

AVA

Despite my insistence that I can drive myself, Damon still gets his driver to pick me up from home. I don't even need to tell the crime boss my address; he is already somehow well aware of where I am currently living.

And that makes me so freaking scared.

I guess his possession of me has already started...

"I'll send my man to collect you now," Damon tells me just before he hangs up. The certainty behind his deep voice, and the urgency it fills me with, instantly compels me to spring out of bed and start to get ready for whatever I'm about to let myself in for here.

I was not expecting all this to happen so fast.

What the hell do you even wear when one of the most powerful men in the country orders you to his house at midnight?

I guess I gotta wear something that is a strong combo of professionalism, authority, and confidence; I am meeting a man to negotiate a deal, after all. A very *scary* man.

I opt for a pantsuit I have in the back of my wardrobe.

I really, really hope I don't look like Hillary Clinton in this.

Despite my concerns, the pantsuit is modern and stylish. The blazer makes me look like a qualified woman. A light blue blouse, which matches one of my eyes. I have to say, it's not too bad.

Okay, Ava, you can do this.

Negotiate. Stand firm. Be professional. Don't let him roll over me.

Help Dad.

The driver comes promptly and, before I even know it, I'm sitting in the back of another one of Damon Penmayne's limousines.

Okay, all I'm going to do is talk to the man. Talk over the offer. Nothing has been agreed. Yet.

I'm definitely *not* going to commit to anything without a hell of a lot of thought, and I am especially not going to agree to something that might mean I'm effectively signing my body over to the criminal.

I know that's what he wants though, and it certainly seems like Damon Penmayne is someone who always gets what he wants.

He's told me exactly that in no uncertain terms...

The limousine takes me out of the main bit of Crystal River and onto unfamiliar roads into the thick woods that ring my hometown. All the winding way to Damon's mansion. I've only heard about this place before but have never actually seen it with my own eyes. It's spoken about in whispers in Crystal River.

It's very dark outside the limo.

Now I am really scared.

"We're here," Damon's driver announces to me as we turn a corner, everything outside the windows obscured by trees. They are the first words he's said to me since I hopped into the limo back at Dad's.

A chill runs through me.

Here we go.

We pass through the imposing wrought-iron gates that lead inside Damon's property – the only aspect you can see of the complex from the outside. The gates swing open automatically as we approach, which means that I am *expected*.

God, that thought really sends me over the edge.

What am I letting myself in for here?

Just remember Dad. You're doing this for Dad. Forget about everything else.

I look around like a tourist at a theme park when we slowly drive inside the compound. Thank God there are some lights to illuminate the surrounds. Even in the night-time, I notice the garden here is immaculate. I didn't suspect that Damon Penmayne would be interested in horticulture. He must hire an army of gardeners to keep it in pristine condition.

We pass by an outdoor swimming pool. I can clearly imagine the gangster here in the middle of summer as dawn breaks, swimming laps with ease; his muscular, athletic, tattooed body gliding through the clear blue water.

The main building itself rises up in front of us intimi-datingly, just like the man who owns it. The architecture is a fusion of both traditional opulence and contemporary elements. The outer façade has white marble columns that give it some kind of classic statehouse look.

I am impressed, to say the least.

I even spot a helipad tucked away in the corner.

Of course Damon has a freaking helipad in his garden.

Wow.

And there's a garage too. I bet he keeps his collection of high-end luxury sportscars in there.

There is an air of caution inside these walls. I know I'm being watched at all times by an army of security hiding somewhere like sneaky little leprechauns. Damon really has a handle on this aspect of his life, making sure it's all tightly controlled.

The man certainly loves his dominance...

His paranoia must be off the charts.

Damon has evidently built this mansion in order to show off his power to visitors, and it is *definitely* working on my poor little scared ass.

"I bet this place doesn't come cheap," I remark with snark to the driver – trying to mask my fear - hoping for a response from the man.

But he doesn't reply.

None of these guys like a conversation, do they?

Damon opens the front door when my limousine pulls up. He's standing there in one of his trademark black suits, unsmiling. His dark eyes watch me as I emerge from his vehicle. I smell his expensive aftershave immediately. His scar is defined by the floodlights around the property.

I can't help but get weak in the knees when I see him again. The way he's looking at me... his confidence, his cool composure, and his sheer physical strength – it all hits me like a tidal wave of mixed emotions. This guy's got the world wrapped around his finger. Everything bends to his will.

Including me, apparently. Coming here like this tonight.

"Hello, Ava."

That calm, resonant voice that shoots straight through me.

That cocky confidence.

That coldness behind his handsome face.

"Damon. Good evening."

"So, you finally called me," he says.

"You were waiting for me?" I ask with a frown.

"I might have been."

"I don't know what to say to that."

Damon ignores that comment.

"Follow me," he says.

He leads the way inside his mansion.

I can't help but swivel my head in all directions once I step into his inner sanctum. The foyer in here is *striking*. An ornate chandelier dangles overhead, casting its glow. A marble staircase stretches upwards into the expanse above our heads. Elegant artworks grace the walls, while a selection of plush upholstered furniture imparts the foyer with a lived-in feel.

I've definitely, without a shadow of a doubt, never been in a house like this before.

Damon certainly has a taste in the fine things, it seems...

"This place is... *big*," I mutter, glancing around the stronghold of a building.

Damon nonchalantly points down a hallway. "Down there is the gym I've built," he says before pointing down another hallway. "And there's my indoor swimming pool with a spa and sauna. Beyond that is my private cinema and bar."

He reels them off as if *everyone's* house comes with a nightclub-level bar tucked in another wing.

"What's this?" I ask, gesturing at a steel door.

"My gaming room," he explains. "I like to run illegal high-stakes poker nights."

"Of course you do," I reply with a roll of my eyes.

"Don't tell the police," he says with a smirk.

"Oh, I'm sure there are a hell of a lot more things they'll

want you for before they move onto the topic of illegal poker nights."

He takes me up a flight of stairs and into his private office. He scans his thumbprint into a biometric detection thing on the wall next to the office. It beeps in recognition.

"I've only ever seen that in movies," I remark, nodding at the scanner thingy.

"I value my privacy," Damon says. "Every security measure in this place is top-of-the-range."

"Yeah, I guessed that."

"This is where my most vital work gets done," the man tells me as we step into his office. I want to laugh at how serious and somber he is. No one speaks like this outside of movies. But I quickly stifle the laugh. I have a feeling that Damon Penmayne does not take well to people joking at his expense.

The office is dimly lit. The dark wood walls are adorned with ancient weaponry. There are large bookshelves filled with books. I wonder if Damon's read them all.

The main part of the office is the large desk. Behind it is a leather chair, and behind that chair is a minibar stocked with whiskey and Scotch. I can also see a collection of cigars on display. Above the minibar is a massive world map that takes up the rest of the back wall. Thick black lines mark out countries and borders.

It's like Damon wants to conquer the world, and I wouldn't put it past the man to actually do it.

The room simply screams authority.

And it also feels so private. This is Damon's inner den, and he's invited me inside.

Me.

"Nice room," I remark.

"Only a few people are ever allowed in here," the gangster replies.

"So it's like a *boy's only* treehouse club thing?"

Damon gives me a stern look.

I guess my impeccable sense of humor goes straight over his head, then.

"This office is reserved for my most... *intimate* negotiations," Damon continues, ignoring my snarky remark.

"Intimate?"

"You should feel honored that I've let you go behind the curtain, Ava."

"We'll see about that."

Despite the fear still thudding away in my tight chest, I refuse to bow down to the crime boss. I ain't about to bend over backwards just because this man has a lovely indoor swimming pool.

Suddenly, the door behind me bursts open, and in comes a large German Shepherd. The dog bounds over to me and starts to lick my hand. I can't help but giggle now. I pet the cute dog, completely forgetting about Damon and the freaky situation I've found myself in.

"What's your dog's name?" I ask the man, giving the German Shepherd a good scratch behind the ears.

"He doesn't have a name," Damon replies. There's a strange look on his face. Is it... surprise? I can't tell. I wouldn't imagine stoic Damon's ever been surprised.

"Your dog must have a name," I say. "You can't just call it *Dog*."

"I do, actually," Damon says, still with that strange look on his face. "He's my guard dog. He doesn't like people, and deliberately so. He's solely trained to attack strangers, not lick them."

"Well, he's licking me," I reply. "He mustn't be *that* well trained."

"That dog loves no one except for me," Damon says. "I made that so. Why is he like this with you?"

I continue to scratch the adorable pup.

"Well, it seems like he loves me too, then."

"I really don't understand..."

Damon's voice trails off. It's the first time I've seen him momentarily lose his self-assuredness.

Oh. So he is surprised.

He never expected his dog to love someone else.

Ha.

I take full advantage.

"Your dog is *adorable*, Damon," I coo. "You may want a big scary dog, but you've instead ended up with a super cute one. And he loves me."

"This is indeed strange..."

"Come on, you can admit you're a doggy dad," I tease. "Go on, Damon."

"Dog. Out."

Damon's sharp command echoes around the room. The dog immediately obeys. It scuttles out of the room.

It's another example of how Damon is a very commanding man, and another example of how everyone follows his orders.

With his dog out of his office, Damon gestures at the chair opposite his desk.

"Sit," he commands to me.

"You may talk to your dog like that," I reply with a flick of my blonde hair. "But not with me. I'm not going to be ordered around like an animal. Give me the respect that I will give you."

"*Please* sit, Ava."

"That's better, Damon."

The man takes his place in his chair behind the desk. His eyes don't stray from me.

I stare back at him.

He's taking me in, I can tell. Scanning me. Trying to

figure me out. It's very intimidating, but kinda also turns me on. The way this man's entire focus is on me. It's like he's *deciphering* my soul.

"I know your roommate is sleeping with my brother," the man says eventually.

"Olivia?"

"You know about it?" he asks.

"Of course," I blurt out. "I sort of... *walked in* on them."

"What?"

"Yeah. It was not a great sight," I reply. "And I wasn't expecting it. Very nearly had a heart attack."

"Tough way for you to find out," Damon replies.

"Yeah, it wasn't pretty," I say.

A slight sparkle crosses Damon's eyes. "I had to wrangle that information out of my brother. We don't get involved in each other's lives."

I scoff. "I warned Olivia about you Penmaynes."

"Oh, really?"

"But she clearly didn't follow my advice. Olivia is new to Crystal River, but everyone here knows you brothers' shared reputation. *I* know your shared reputation."

"Pray tell, what kind of reputation is that, Ava?" he asks.

"You know what I'm talking about, Damon."

The man finally smiles. He likes this back-and-forth between us. He's a man who likes conflict.

Well, if he's after conflict he's certainly called the right woman to come to his office in the dead of night.

"People like to judge us on our reputation, Ava, and not on who we actually are."

"I want you to know, Damon Penmayne, that I am going against all my natural instincts to come here today," I reply slowly. "To speak to you. I am going against every freaking fiber in my body simply being in this room with you."

Damon leans back in his chair, clearly enjoying this.

"What are you here for then, Ava? Must be pretty important."

"I want to put an end to my dad's debts," I reply. "Any way I can. I want to talk about it with you. I want to talk about the offer you made to me back in New York."

"I'm not a man who likes to talk," the gangster replies darkly. "I am a man who likes action, and there is only one way to erase your father's debts, and it has to happen right here. Right now."

"I know what you want, Damon," I say, practically whispering. "And I am here to negotiate. I'm not playing around. *Negotiate.*"

The man smiles again.

There's a devil behind that smile. A very handsome devil.

He leisurely takes a long pause before he speaks.

"The very word I want to hear," he says. "Let's make a contract. Let's negotiate, then."

14

AVA

I just take in a deep breath and reiterate to myself, in my mind, of the reason why I am standing here in this office in the first place. I repeat it over and over and over, just so that I don't lose my freaking mind.

This is the only way to free Dad. This is the only way to end all this. This is the only way.

"Let's review all aspects of this offer," Damon says to me quietly as I'm silently trying to reassure myself. "Let's make sure we're completely on the same page when it comes to everything I'm proposing, and then I'll summon my lawyers to draft a contract up immediately."

"Wouldn't that take a long time?" I ask. "I mean... calling up lawyers and writing all that surely will take forever..."

The man chuckles darkly to himself as if I've made a joke. "I have my legal team available around the clock, Ava. Every hour of the day. I guarantee you that as soon as I pick up my phone, they will swiftly coordinate any necessary arrangements to my liking with the utmost speed. There will be a contract delivered to us within the hour, I'm sure of it. Now, let's talk about what we're both hoping to get out of this agreement."

"Hang on one second, please. You're really going to negotiate with me over this?" I ask, incredulously. "With a contract and lawyers and everything? Like it's some big-shot commercial business deal?"

Damon nods. "We are both adults here, Ava. And we are both entering a consensual contract. I want this to be all protected legally. I want us both to feel as comfortable as necessary before we proceed."

Proceed? Jesus, he now even sounds like a lawyer. This now sounds like some Wall Street takeover arbitration and not something a lot more... well, *sensual*.

Damon pulls out a notepad from a drawer in his desk, ready to write down our negotiation. I watch him as he does so. And *now* - seeing him about to actually physically write down his insane offer - it really becomes real.

I take in another deep breath. "So, you really want me to be your mistress? For two whole months?"

The crime boss regards me with his dark eyes.

"That part is non-negotiable," he says.

"Oh."

"I really want you to be my mistress," he adds.

As if I didn't know.

"Yeah, I'm starting to see that..."

"You are to be willing to indulge in my pleasure without a single hesitation," he says. "Cater to my whim. That's the way I want it to be."

I wonder what those whims might be. A man like Damon would have plenty of dark and terrible desires for sure...

"Okay..."

"You will make yourself completely accessible to me," he continues.

"Right."

"But you will be able to negotiate with me before we engage in anything. This may be a contract, but consent takes precedence over everything. Plus, I will not harm you, or do anything that may cause you distress. If I do, then the contract is terminated."

"Good to know," I reply.

"You have my word. No harm will come to you."

"Good."

I don't know if I can trust the word of this man. I don't have to be a detective to understand the word from a gangster is worth literally nothing.

But this little interaction has gone a hell of a lot more different from what I was thinking when I came here tonight. He seems to actually be serious about all this, and is actually listening to me. He seems to be... dare I say, *respectful*.

Yeah, as respectful as a man who kills for a living can be.

Damon continues to stare at me from across his desk as I slowly take in his words. "But I am... *open* to the other terms of the contract," he continues. "Just name me what you will and will not do and I'll see if I'm reciprocal to your demands."

Huh. Okay. Let me hit you up with my own demands, then.

I'm quick in with my first request.

"Well, I'm not going to witness any violence, from you or anyone else. Never ever."

"Violence?" he asks.

"It's a deal-breaker," I say, jutting my chin out in my best impression of being steely. "No violence. No fights. No blood. I draw the line there. *That* part is non-negotiable for me."

"Understood," Damon replies, his expression unmoving. "Anything else a deal-breaker that I need to know of before we proceed?"

"You don't have a wife or girlfriend, do you?" I ask. "I'm certainly not entering this if there's another woman around, that's not who I am. Cheating is a *no-go*. Please be honest with me."

Damon shakes his head. "No, there is no other woman."

"Really?"

"I am a man who honors his commitments to any contract. There is no one, Ava, except for you."

Damn. That's kinda hot.

"And I will be under your protection?" I ask.

"You will be my girl," Damon whispers. "And no one touches what is mine."

Those words sink in deep. And, I have to admit, an enticing shiver of excitement runs through me.

I will be his only girl. Even if for a few months.

He's going to all these lengths to have me as his.

"And you will wipe off all of Dad's debts after this?" I ask. "Completely forgotten and forgiven?"

"Yes, Ava Matson. After exactly two months, you and your father will be free from me forever."

"Really?"

"Really," he says earnestly.

Yeah, he really is serious about all this.

Fuck it.

"Okay, I will be your mistress," I reply, "but I will tell you if there's anything that makes me uncomfortable, and I would want you to stop. Anytime I ask. Do you promise you'll do that?"

"I promise I will remain a gentleman throughout all of

this," Damon says. "I want you to know that I get the most pleasure from *your* pleasure. And I want everything to be consensual. Despite what you may have heard of me, I can be a thoughtful lover."

Am I really seriously considering going through with this? Am I really seriously considering signing a pact with the devil?

I can't deny that there is a part of me that's so freaking turned on by the thought of submitting myself to this man. But this is going to be an agreement where I practically turn over my body, and all the obligations that come with that, and I am terrified of what that might possibly mean.

But. Still. It's kind of *erotic*. In the most fucked-up way.

"And one more thing," I add. Damon is intently listening. "I want you to promise not to touch my dad. Not during this whole thing. Not one hand on him."

"I'm a man of honor," Damon replies solemnly. "I wouldn't do that. Consider your father completely off-limits. Again, you have my word. When you are my girl, you are like family, and I allow no one to go near my family."

"Okay," I say, nodding. "Give me the damn contract. I'll sign it. Get this over with *asap*."

"Let me call my lawyer," Damon replies. "They'll have it all drafted up in an hour."

* * *

TRUE TO HIS WORD, Damon's lawyers come back with a copy of the contract within the hour. He really does have that kind of power to just call up a team of law professionals in the middle of the night to cater to his crazy whims. It's weird seeing the actual written-down document in front of me. It all looks so... *legal*.

Damon was on the phone with his lawyers as they

wrote it up, and so I sat here in his office feeling very left alone, still trying to process what the hell I've signed up for.

I want to bite my nails down to nothing. I feel itchy all over.

Even though I'm wearing my professional pantsuit, I don't feel very professional at this minute.

I feel desperate.

And a tiny bit turned on, I have to admit. It's kind of alluring seeing Damon so businesslike and commanding. Seeing him so adept on the phone. Hearing the lawyers bow down to him like he owns their ass.

He sure is a powerful man.

"Before you sign it," Damon says to me once everything is completed and there is a contract being printed, "I'm going to need you to sign something else. A non-disclosure agreement."

"An NDA?" I ask. "What for?"

"It's just something we Penmaynes have to be careful about," the gangster replies. "Our lives are very... *exposed*. We don't like our privacy aired out in the open like dirty washing, especially me. Every single one of my employees has to sign an NDA."

"So I'm one of your *employees* now?"

"Ava. Sign it."

I sigh. "Okay, let me see it before I put my name to anything."

Damon pulls out another form. Reading it, I can see that it's a watertight NDA. So much legalese it makes my head spin. I wonder how many people he's made sign one of these binding documents. Reading it, I understand it really bars me from talking about Damon, his businesses, his family, and basically anything even remotely related to the Penmaynes to anyone else.

Holy shit, this is all so very real. What have I got myself into here?

"You really want me?" I ask the man, my voice quivering on the edge.

Damon stands up and glides over to me sitting in his office chair. He lowers himself down to my level. He gently brushes my hair to the side in order to whisper into my ear.

"I really want you, Ava," he snarls quietly. His breath is hot against my neck. "Isn't that obvious enough already? I want to make you mine."

I nod tentatively.

I'm surprised by how wet I am.

God, this man does impossible things to me.

"Okay, then," I sigh. "I swear myself to silence."

I sign the NDA. Of course I do. This is all for Dad. Just a few months of this and then everything will be over forever. No more gangsters. No more debt. No more threats.

And especially no more Damon Penmayne.

It's the only way to free Dad. It's the only way to end all this. It's the only way.

Damon finally places the contract in front of me. It has all the terms we agreed to.

I sign it.

I exhale.

Done.

That's it. No going back now. I'm Damon Penmayne's mistress. He owns my ass for the next few months.

Damon offers me a glass of clear alcohol.

"What's this?" I ask him, still reeling from what the hell I've just committed.

"Tequila," the man says. "As congratulations. It's my own tequila, made by my own company. It's the strongest alcohol we produce. I think you might need it."

"Well, I do need something strong right now," I remark. "My heart is racing at a hundred miles an hour."

"I know the feeling," Damon says softly.

"I don't think a man like you would."

"I am human, Ava, just like you," he replies. "I can feel things."

"I doubt it."

"Try me."

He chinks my glass with his own before he downs it. He chugs it back like water. I try to follow his example, but the stuff is way too much for me. I end up coughing. It's like fire rushing down my throat.

Yeah, *strong* is an understatement when it comes to that tequila.

There's silence after I splutter through the alcohol, a tension in the air between us. I look at the gangster standing before me, and I can't help but admire how gorgeous the dangerous man is. His strong jawline. His dark eyes. His smooth complexion. It goes against every fiber of my being, but I like it. I really shouldn't be thinking of Damon Penmayne like this, but it's irresistible to let my mind wander into all the possibilities...

"So... what happens now?" I quietly ask him.

"Now we must consummate our agreement," Damon says.

And I blink.

"What the hell did you just say?"

15

AVA

"I don't want to have sex with you."

I stare at Damon. He stares back equally as fierce. If he's mad about my blunt comeback, he sure isn't letting it show.

Is the man moved by anything?

I try to spot anything about him that would give his inner thoughts away: a flicker of hesitancy behind those dark mysterious eyes of his, perhaps? But nada. *Nothing.* The man is so confident in himself that he doesn't even flinch at my snarky attitude.

And you know what's kind of crazy? That steely assurance he possesses somehow adds an extra layer of attractiveness to the man, like it's this magnetic pull that draws you in even deeper. His sheer *certainty* in his manner makes him so damn captivating...

Remember, he's a criminal, Ava.

"That's what you signed up for, Miss Matson," Damon replies quietly, on the verge of a hiss. "Your signature is still fresh on that contract. This is why you're here. Willingly."

"Yes, I know," I say. "But not *now*. Especially not when the ink on that contract isn't even dried yet. I'm not some whore to strip down immediately for you and spread open my legs, no matter what agreement I've signed."

The man's eyes bore straight through me like lasers. "Already trying to break the terms of our agreement, girl? It's not even been ten minutes."

"Let me ease into things," I reply. "I mean, after all, you are a cold-hearted killer."

Damon raises his eyebrows at that. "Cold-hearted killer, you say? That's strong words."

"*True* words," I retort back quickly.

Damon takes in a long breath.

"You have a lot of misconceptions about me, Ava," he says. "I have never ordered violence on anyone innocent."

"Say what you want, Damon... spew as many lies as you want, but I'm not going to let you fuck me right now. It ain't happening, dude."

And then Damon smiles.

"How about you prove how much you don't want to have sex with me, then?" he asks.

I shake my head, confused. "What do you mean?"

The man leans back in his chair opposite me.

"How about you show me how much you *don't* want to have sex with me by coming over here and sitting in my lap?"

He's nuts...

I scoff. "Stop joking around, Damon."

The man's face immediately drops. There's a brooding temper brewing there. Okay, he does not like my condescending tone, that's for sure.

"I never joke, girl," he snarls. "Come over here and sit in my lap. Now."

Oh, God.

"But..."

"Come over here *now*."

There is something in the man's voice that compels me to do his bidding. It must be his control that coerces. His poise. His brashness. His complete sureness that he's going to get his way no matter what.

That sheer annoying *arrogance* of his.

And let's not overlook that unbelievably alluring resonant baritone voice.

I'd do anything to hear him boss me around like this...

But there is also a part of me that wants to disprove the gangster. To defy him. To show him how strong I am, even if I'm here to repay a debt.

"Okay, then," I reply. "Sure. Let me prove you wrong, Damon Penmayne. I will sit in your lap, purely *platonically*."

And so I stand up and slowly make my way over to him, finally resting my ass down on the man's muscular legs. He doesn't buckle under me. He holds my weight effortlessly. His body is a lot warmer than I expect.

I realize I've never been this close to him. There is a tingle on the back of my neck as his hot breath hits me whilst I snuggle in on his lap. He smells so good.

He's so damn close...

My heartbeat quickens - I hope he doesn't notice.

My breathing shallows - I hope he doesn't hear it.

"And how does this feel?" Damon asks me, his deep voice now very much a whisper in my ear.

I shudder at his tone. The man knows how to tempt a woman.

"No change," I mutter, somewhat dishonestly. "Nothing at all."

I might be lying through my teeth, but I am still not going to let him win.

"If we're going to spend so much time together," he whispers, "then I must conjure up a nickname for you, Ava. I think I will call you... *Beauty*."

"Beauty?"

"Yes."

I nearly snort in derision.

"What?" I ask. "If I am Beauty, then doesn't that make you a *beast*?"

"Oh, something like that," Damon replies cheekily.

And then his fingers find my chin. And he's pulling my face around so that we're now confronting each other. So very close. Our eyes lock.

And then, breaking the tension that's been lingering between us like a dark rain cloud, he kisses me.

And, in my head, it begins to rain.

It's not a gentle kiss, that's for sure. It is a kiss of a man who's getting exactly what he wants. He's demonstrating to me that I am his. Totally, utterly *his*.

The kiss is just like his alluring arrogance.

So. This is what it's like to be owned by a gangster.

He's really going to do what he wants with me, isn't he?

Something about that turns me on, despite all the logic in my brain telling me how bad it is.

I let him kiss me. I enjoy it. The fact that he's attaining exactly what he desires – *me* - sends a sharp and delightful rush of excitement through me. Right down my spine to the wetness between my legs.

"You've been such a little tease," Damon growls. "Coming in here today dressed the way you do in that sexy little serious pantsuit of yours. It's like you want to turn me on. It's like you want to make me yearn for you."

"Oh, yeah?"

"Do you know what you are, Ava Matson?"

I blink. I can't take much more of this cocky sureness before I'm melting.

"No, what am I?" I ask.

"My reward," he snarls back.

Hot damn.

Yeah, I definitely like this. I like feeling like a gift for him. Like a little present wrapped up in a bow and delivered to him on a silver platter.

His little willing captive.

You should stop before this gets out of hand. You're rushing into bed with a gangster, Ava.

And, despite all the doubts in my mind, I am fucking loving it.

I don't want to stop.

"You can do whatever you want to me," I whisper, my voice breaking as I imagine all the dirty things he could actually do to me in his big-ass scary mansion. "I've already gone against all my better instincts coming here. I am your reward."

"Well, you have been such a little brat," he says. "I think I better fuck you into being my good girl."

"I've been very bad, haven't I? Finally giving in to your terms..."

"So fucking bad, Ava," Damon whispers. "You are such a fucking little tease, you know that? You really deserve a good fucking from me."

"Well, what are you waiting for?" I ask him. "A written invitation? I'm your reward, remember?"

"You want me to fuck you senseless?" he asks, a stern look on his face.

I nod and bite my lip seductively. I know how much I'm turning him on as I sit here in his lap. I can feel his manhood twitching beneath me in longing.

Oh, I like to tease.

I've truly submitted myself now, and I no longer care for the voices in my head warning me against this.

I just want Damon.

"You're agreeing to this, then?" he asks me. "You've changed your mind? You couldn't sit in my lap without wanting me to fuck you?"

"Hurry up before I change it again," I reply.

"You don't have to ask me twice. I've been fantasizing of making you mine ever since I first saw you."

"I think I really deserve to be fucked by a strong man," I whisper, "if there's one around to claim me."

"I'll claim you," Damon rumbles. "I'm man enough. Goddamn, you are a lot to handle, Ava, but I want to be the only one to handle you."

"Then handle me, mister."

Damon growls deeply and pushes me away from him before he leaps out of his chair. He takes my hands and pulls them behind my back. He pulls me to his desk, placing me face-down on it, my ass hanging over the side.

I squeal in pleasure. I've never been manhandled like this. I have never submitted myself under a man's powerful control, and Damon is so freaking powerful.

But this is not all his power. This is not all his control - I always have a sense that I am *allowing* him to do this to me. I know that all I have to do is utter one word and this man will stop immediately. I know he's respectful of my boundaries.

But that doesn't stop him from lifting my skirt up and yanking down my panties. With his other hand, he continues to pin both my wrists behind my back.

"You're on the pill?" he asks me.

I nod, my cheek resting against his cold desk.

"Good," he triumphantly announces. "Then I am going to fuck you raw."

"Please, Damon. Fuck me raw."

"Beg for my cock," he says.

"Please fuck me, Damon, with your cock."

"You're mine now," he whispers into my ear from behind. "You've signed yourself over to me. You've signed your body away. You're totally mine to do with what I please."

"Please fuck me, Damon. Fuck me good. I deserve it."

"Oh yes, you do."

Something big and long enters me from behind. I gasp as Damon fills me up. I didn't realize how freaking wet my pussy is until Damon slides himself in. I feel my body accommodating the man and his cock.

"You're so tight, Ava."

Oh, I very much like it when he compliments me.

I'm holding my breath as Damon fucks me from behind on his impressive office desk. I'm being used for the man's sexual pleasure, and I secretly *love* it.

This is what I want.

I squirm against his tight grip. Damon doesn't let go of my hands, no matter how much I wriggle. I like to feel myself tussle against his authoritative strength as he fucks me hard.

"You're totally mine," he snarls. He buries himself deep. "Totally and utterly mine."

I nod again. "I've given myself to you. Fuck me like I'm your toy."

Like how I've teased him with my words, the gangster teases me with his cock. He rides me slowly and rhythmically. He's listening to my little gasps of delight and really elongates the waves of pleasure that I feel with each thrust. He's a goddamn pro. Sometimes he's so deep inside me it's like I'm an extension of his manhood, and other times he teases the lips of my pussy.

It's driving me wild.

It's driving me to climax.

And, suddenly, I do.

I let out a cry as I orgasm. My legs shake against the desk as I continue to struggle to break my hands free from Damon's grasp.

Being pinned down like this is such a joy...

And then Damon, too, is finishing. He unloads into me. I feel heat run down my leg as the man growls animalistically.

I pant hard as he finally lets go of my hands.

"You couldn't resist me once you were in my lap, couldn't you?" he asks, breathless.

"No, I really couldn't," I reply, equally as breathless.

"Good."

I feel totally and utterly used like some kind of sex doll, and it somehow feels *great*. It's like Damon has truly demonstrated that he owns me in such a physical way. He wanted me, and he got me.

This is realization enough that I have literally signed myself over to him and his desires.

Holy crap, I truly am his now, aren't I?

He really does own my ass.

16

AVA

Wow. *What have I done?*

Sex with my sworn enemy. Sex with the man who controls the destiny of my dad.

And, worst of all, I *enjoyed* it. And I would do it all over again in a heartbeat.

A shiver runs down my spine. There is something within me. A new sensation that I've never felt before. I feel so dirty. So naughty.

And it feels so damn good.

Damon is already on his feet, already sliding back into his black suit. He turns to me.

"Get changed, Ava."

"What for?" I ask.

Is he kicking me out?

"I have work to do, so I need to get going," the man I've signed my life over to replies.

"Um, it's super late at night, though."

"I always have business," the man says. "I will call you when I am next ready. You're mine now."

"You'll call me?"

I'm left in a dumb mess. *Why am I asking such stupid questions?*

Damon, not fully dressed, reaches his office door.

"You'll be able to let yourself out," he says before he leaves.

He shuts the door behind him, and I feel a surprising pang of desire for him as he disappears.

Did he really just fuck me and then discard me? In the middle of the night?

My head is in a total mess. I don't know what to feel. The man literally just used me, and now I'm actually *feeling* something for him? All from one quick, dominating fuck? What is going on with me?

I am so confused.

But I gather my shit. I'm going home.

17

AVA

Walking through the dorms of Crystal River is a hell of a different experience than what I am usually used to. I've not been back here since I left, a few weeks ago, to rush back home to support Dad. The last time I was here, on campus, was just as I was hearing about the debts for the first time and when Luke broke up with me, and when everything went to crap. A whole terrible whirlwind.

So it's very weird to be back.

But I haven't forgotten the maze-like layout. I still find my way up the stairs to the dorm room I used to – well, technically *still* – share with my new best friend, Olivia Weldon.

I knock on the door. Very unusual to do so as well; I typically used to barge in here without a care for my room-mate's privacy.

Olivia opens the door with a big smile. If you met us in the street, you'd think there is no way we would be friends; we're so different, her and me. I'm the big extrovert and she's the shy introvert with a love of books and reading. I like being with people, and she's perfectly content being on her own.

But somehow we just click. I guess it's *opposites attract* and all that.

"Ava!"

"Olivia!"

I enthusiastically wrap my arms around my best friend, bringing her in for a tight hug. It's so nice to see her pretty face again. I have to say, I've really missed her.

And I know she misses me. In her own introverted bookish way.

She's got this tawny brown hair that falls to her shoulders, the exact same shade as her eyes. Her skin's all creamy and smooth. I've caught on that she sometimes doubts how she looks, but in my eyes, she's just incredibly pretty, no doubt about it.

"Can I come in?" I ask her. "Is that *allowed*?"

Olivia just frowns at me. "Of course. This is your home as much as mine. Get inside, you lunatic."

I shut the door behind me. I can see Olivia has done little to the place since I hastily left: my bed is still there, and so is my trademark chaos of clothes on top. I tried to pack as much as I could when I was in a rush to leave, but I still left a lot behind. I am a messy person, that's for sure.

"Sit down," Olivia says. "Let's talk. Tell me everything."

I snuggle in close to her on my bed.

"First of all, how are you going?" I ask her, eager to avoid any talk of Damon Penmayne and debts and sadness.

"Yeah, pretty much the same," she replies.

"Still re-reading that little book of yours?" I ask.

I'm referring to her battered copy of Wuthering Heights. Olivia *loves* that book. It's a running joke between us that I just always see her reading that thing instead of doing normal college things like parties or boyfriends.

Well, how wrong I was on that whole boyfriend thing...

"Still am."

"And what about your professor?" I ask. "Your *lover*. How's all that between you two going?"

This time I'm referring to Professor Penmayne. Spencer Penmayne. The hot new professor on campus who Olivia has started seeing privately. I'm the only person here who knows they're secretly dating, mostly because I accidentally walked in on them as they were... *doing* it.

And Spencer is Damon's brother. A whole other freaking layer on top of the crazy cake that is my life at the moment.

This is so very weird.

But I'm sure Olivia knows nothing about Damon and me and the little agreement we've set up.

"Ava, I know you really don't like the Penmaynes," she mutters.

I smile at that. I told her – when she first came to Crystal River - all about that powerful billionaire family. I told her how she should never, in a million years, get herself wrapped up with them.

Oh, how little she knows...

"I might not like them, but I'm interested in you and how you're going," I say. "Penmayne or not."

"Things are going great," she replies.

"Great?" I ask. "As in *great* great?"

"Yep. We're serious."

Olivia says that in the softest and cutest way. How can you not love her when she's so damn adorable?

"Wow."

"I really like him, Ava," she says. "And he really likes me."

"And are you happy with him?" I ask.

My roommate looks up at me with those sweet coffee-brown eyes of hers.

"Yes, I am. So very happy."

I give her a hug.

"Then that's what counts. That's *all* that counts. Love is the most precious thing in this whole wide world."

I know I can't talk to Olivia about Damon, and not just because of the weird-ass NDA he made me sign, forbidding me from speaking about him to anyone, but also because I know Olivia wouldn't understand. She just simply wouldn't understand why I'm doing what I'm doing. I do not have the strength in me to answer all the inevitable questions that'll come, such as *what the hell are you thinking.*

I don't have the strength to answer her because I honestly don't even know *how* to answer that question.

I really don't know what the hell I'm thinking.

"And what about your dad?" Olivia asks me softly. "How's everything going with all that? You okay? I tried to message you, but you never replied."

"I'm sorry I never did get back to you," I reply quietly. "I haven't really been talking to anyone since it all went down. It's been a very hard few weeks..."

"You don't have to apologize," my roommate says, her hand squeezing mine lovingly. "Are you fine, though? Are things getting better?"

I feel myself starting to well-up. I really don't want to cry, not here in front of my best friend. But the weight of the last few days really hit me hard.

What on earth am I seriously getting myself into here? Letting a gangster basically control me?

I bet, even know, he's somehow finding a way to spy on me right now as I sit in this dorm room. Monitor me.

I know that, for the next few months at least, I won't be able to escape his ever-present tendrils.

"Everything is... *fine*," I reply to my best friend. "We're working on a solution. It should all be fine soon."

"Oh, okay," Olivia replies. "I'm always here, Ava. Just one phone call away. I can help. If you want me to."

"Thank you, Olivia."

And then my phone buzzes. I reach for it, just to check it isn't Dad.

But no. It's not him. It's the other man in my life.

It's Damon.

Come back to my place. Right now, girl.

AND I KNOW I must obey him. It's in my contract. I've got to go back to his mansion immediately. His tendrils have reached out and have brought me back under his control.

"Sorry, Olivia, I have to go."

"I understand," she says.

She really doesn't.

"I'll call you," I say to her. "We need to meet up again soon. Maybe a classic almond croissant at The Oak, how does that sound?"

"It's a date," she replies with a soft smile.

And I shoot out of there. I'm heading down the stairs and out the main doors of the dorms, past students milling around.

Yeah, students who aren't in debt to a dangerous gangster and his insane contracts.

But I am surprisingly turned on by the message Damon

sent. His power. His demanding tone. His possessiveness over me.

I'm the only girl he wants...

I know I am forced to obey him, but I also kinda *want* to.

Crap.

Does that make me as crazy as him?

18

DAMON

JIM IS STARING at me from across my office.

And it's not one of his friendlier looks.

"You need to respond," he barks at me.

I stare back.

"I'm not interested in responding to the man," I reply dispassionately.

Jim lets out a frustrated sigh. If it were anyone else, and they dared to breathe like that in response to one of my remarks, I would have them on the ropes before they could blink. But Jim is permitted to be exasperated with me; he's my North Star when it comes to business. He gets a pass.

But, on this one particular topic, I am not budging.

"Handsome Jack wants to have a meeting," Jim explains in a low, grave voice. "And he is being serious. His people have been pressuring us. We should go ahead right now and organize a face-to-face encounter between the two of you before it's too late and tension in New York reaches boiling point. We can't have another major conflict break out simply because you don't want to see the man."

My dog is curled up in the corner. Jim is the only person he doesn't lunge for aggressively. Well, apparently not only Jim now, but also Ava.

What is it about that girl that's calmed my vicious dog?

I was so shocked to see her simply pet the animal when it burst in here while we were negotiating over the contract. I have not trained my dog to do anything remotely like that – in fact, quite the opposite - and I am a strong master.

What is it that my dog can see in her?

She called me a doggy dad. Whatever the hell that means.

She's cute, I gotta say. Adorable, even.

And *incredibly* sexy...

How she looked when I fucked her from behind. The moans she made with her pretty little mouth. The fact she willingly signed herself over to me and seemed so fucking excited for it.

I'm standing behind my office chair. I grip the headrest tighter. My knuckles go white.

"Not now," I say to myself behind gritted teeth, even as my mind drifts back to that time in my office with me pinning her down and fucking her from behind and how much she loved it.

I am not thinking straight. I feel like I can't make a rational decision right now. This is so unlike me.

How can I think about meeting Handsome Jack when there's so much on my mind?

Well, there is actually only one thing on my mind right now - one thing that is distracting me to oblivion.

Ava Matson.

Her and her sexy ass.

"Damon, we must schedule a meeting with the man," Jim continues in his guttural voice. "And we must do it as soon as possible before events move beyond our control."

"I can't deal with this now," I reply.

And, as if the fates have willed it, a notification from my security downstairs appears right on the computer screen in front of me, telling me that a blonde girl has arrived and asking if they should kick her out.

So. Ava's come. At my message request.

For a split second after I shot her a text asking her to come to my mansion, I half-expected her to push back with that fiery attitude I've gotten so accustomed to. To bark back at me. To reject my request.

But she has actually come.

I quickly message my security to allow the girl into my complex, and not kick her out.

I glance up at Jim from my computer.

"Ava's here," I mutter.

The man sighs again. He knows my attention is placed elsewhere.

A soft knock resonates through the room, and a tidal wave of emotions smashes into my heart. I've never felt anything like this before with someone. I find myself grappling with an inexplicable mix of anticipation and suspense, all because I know that she's about to step into my world.

You are fucking crazy, Damon.

"Enter," I command.

And Ava comes in.

There is a whisper of a smile tugging at the corners of my lips as I see her again.

That platinum blonde hair... those mesmerizing, mismatched gems of eyes... that gracefully curvy, fit body...

My dog immediately gets up and rushes over to her,

licking her hand enthusiastically like he's some lap dog and not a trained killer.

Ava giggles cutely at the interaction.

"Such a good boy," she says.

That dog is an excellent judge of character, clearly.

She says a cheery hello to Jim, and the man gives a curt reply before turning back to me.

"You've got to schedule that meeting," he says. "As soon as possible, Damon. Please."

I wave him away, and the man goes, with plenty of side-eye aimed in my direction.

But I don't care. I can't be thinking about rivals and conflicts when there's this woman in the room.

"Why did you summon me here?" Ava asks me once Jim has left and shut the door to the office.

"I can't bear to have you out of my sight," I reply. "If you're going to be my mistress, then I want control."

Ava blinks. Her multi-colored eyes gleam at me.

I just can't stop myself from gawking at those plump, kissable lips of hers.

"Really? Control?"

"I want you to move in here," I announce. "Stay here, in the mansion, for the time being."

"What?"

"Stay here," I repeat.

"I can't," she replies.

"Why not, Ava?"

"Because... of *college*."

She's in a flurry, grasping at straws to conjure any excuse that might let her slip away from this one. She better realize the terms of the contract she signed with me. She's smart enough to comprehend how binding our agreement is.

She's meant to be here. With me.

"I can make the arrangements with Crystal River University," I say. "I can get them to place you on a two-month vacation. A leave of absence. That'll bat away any unwelcome questions."

Ava scoffs. "You can't do that."

"Why not?" I ask.

"The college wouldn't accept it."

"You're sure?"

"Yep," the girl replies. "They wouldn't let that slip."

I smirk. "I can do a lot of things that you might think are impossible, Ava."

"Oh, *impossible*? I think you've been listening to too much of your own hype, Damon Penmayne."

"You think I need someone to bring me back to earth?" I observe wryly. "Is that what you think, Ava?"

She crosses her arms defiantly. "Yep, you most certainly need someone to humble you."

"And you're the girl who will do that?" I ask her.

Ava shrugs. "Someone has to."

"I don't think so."

"You're so damn sure of yourself, Damon."

"Well, how about I show you how I can do the impossible," I reply. "In fact, I'm going to do something rather impossible to you right now."

"What is it?" Ava asks, her lip trembling in nervousness.

Closing the distance between us, I move forward toward her with a purpose. Ava's big apprehensive eyes, a captivating blend of anticipation and uncertainty, lock onto mine as I approach.

She's holding her breath.

It's the same look she gave me when she signed the contract and sat on my lap. The same look that made me go absolutely crazy for her.

I lean down so that my lips lightly brush her ear. She's frozen.

And then I whisper to her.

"Turn around, Beauty, and let me take control."

19

AVA

"I'M NOT GOING to turn around," I say to the gangster, even as he has his lips pressed softly against my ear. His slow and intentional movement down to my height makes my knees weak and my cheeks blush and catches me totally off guard, but I'm still holding firm against the onslaught of his dark and dangerous charm.

I am not someone to be used and discarded, even if it is by the sexiest man I have ever met. Even his overpowering looks and magnetism won't sway me from standing up for myself and demanding the respect I rightfully deserve.

"No one disobeys an order from me," Damon replies in a sharp, hot whisper. "You understand that?"

"I'm an independent woman," I continue. "I get to choose when men get to fuck me."

There's a sigh from Damon. "Oh, that's *hot*."

My knees are positively trembling at his warm breath so close to my ear and his manly scent filling my nostrils.

But, yeah, I'm totally gonna keep my strength up against his weaponized charisma.

The man wants me to buckle under pressure. He wants me to become nothing more than his little fuckdoll. And, yes, that is enticing, but I am a hell of a whole lot more than that.

And I want him to appreciate that.

"You better start getting used to this attitude from me," I reply, daring my eyes to flicker up and reach his own.

Damon is staring at me deeply. Like a man possessed. Like a man barely able to hold back his darkest impulses.

Damn...

That is so hot.

"Oh, really, Ava Matson? I gotta get used to your naughty attitude?"

"Yep," I reply, determined.

Damon growls.

"You need to turn around," he grunts. "And that is an order you must obey."

I smile. "Well, I've got something better in mind."

I will play by his rules, but I'm also going to take control when I can.

And so, I drop down to my knees. My fingers extend toward his belt, deftly working to unfasten the buckle. The metallic click echoes softly in the charged atmosphere.

I look up at him as I eagerly pull out his massive cock hidden in his pants.

By the dazed expression on his face looking back down at me, I can tell that Damon *really* likes this. He *really* likes me taking control and putting his pleasure in my own hands.

This is too freaking spicy...

I give him a cheeky smile before my lips ride over his cock. His entire manhood fits inside my mouth.

He tastes hot. I feel him hardening even more between my lips. He can't resist his biological urges.

I'm making him feel like this.

And, to me, the way I'm making him feel feels so damn good.

Damon reclines, producing a long, strained groan that speaks volumes of his surprise at being dealt with like this. He very clearly wasn't expecting *this* to happen. He wasn't expecting to have a girl who knows what she's doing – a girl who loves getting on her knees and pleasuring him.

"This feels amazing," he grunts as I devour him.

I moan in response and continue to suck him.

Damon's fingers run through my hair as his cock throbs in my mouth. I can sense he's going to cum soon.

And, god, I really want him to cum.

Damon groans again. I look up at him, unable to speak because his thick and long manhood is currently silencing me. His eyes are shut in a state of blissful euphoria.

I love that I'm able to do this to him: to be able to render a man of such confidence and strength utterly vulnerable through the simple touch of my lips.

I keep working him until he's groaning again. And again. And again.

"Fuck," he whispers. "What are you able to do with those lips of yours..."

And then there's the sentence I've been waiting for...

"*I'm going to cum, Ava.*"

I moan.

This is exactly what I want. I am so turned on. I am engulfed in hungry lust.

I want to please him. I want him to feel good.

In one final act, Damon thrusts his cock down my throat before he unleashes himself. He hisses as his hot semen fills my mouth. I close my eyes and succumb to him, moaning as he empties himself between my wet lips.

He withdraws from me. I let out a long breath. My lips are wet with him.

That was so incredibly sexy...

Damon is panting.

"I like how you're like that," I say, my mouth still very much tasting of him. "All sweaty and out of breath. I like how I've made you like that."

The man looks down at me with a hard stare. He looks at me triumphantly, like he's made his mark.

He owns my mouth. He truly owns me.

"Well," Damon says, "if we're doing favors for each other, then now it's my turn..."

And then he's pulling me back to my feet with the strength of just one hand.

Oh, there's that big powerful New York gangster again...

He twirls me around and dumps me down into his office chair. I let out a giggle at being manhandled like this. Unlike just five minutes ago, I've now given myself up totally to his control. And it feels absolutely *incredible*.

I'm in his chair, looking up at him, and wondering what he's going to do next.

I don't have to wonder for very long.

Damon gets down on his own knees in front of me, parting my legs with a single push.

He looks up my skirt.

And he tuts.

"No panties today, Ava?" he asks.

I giggle again and shake my head. "Nope."

"Very naughty of you."

"I thought it would be."

"But a hell of a lot easier for me to get to you..."

Damon reaches out with his hand and slides it effortlessly under my skirt. I let out an uncontrollable gasp.

My body arches back against the chair as Damon's middle finger slips down the edges of my vaginal folds.

He's found my wetness.

And I know he's going to tease me.

The bastard.

"Whoa, that's... unbelievable," I manage to say with a slight stumble, my head tilting back and eyes gently shutting.

I can't believe the gangster is down there, ready to please me. It doesn't seem real. It doesn't seem like something that could happen.

I'm completely lost as the man expertly parts my folds and finds my clit. He begins to rub it gently, only getting faster and harder with time.

I start to squirm.

His touch is so nimble and so careful. It's like he's squeezing an orgasm out of me: a true professional playing my body like a flute.

He's such a strong man in daily life. An all-encompassing and influential man. And yet he's on his knees treating me to such delight. His entire focus is purely on *me*.

"I told you," he whispers. "I told you I get pleasure from your pleasure."

I can't help but let out a little happy cry of delight.

His rhythm increases.

I ride his finger.

And then, when I'm about to climax, he stops.

It's so abrupt.

I moan in despair.

But then I feel his tongue down in places where only his fingers have touched.

Oh shit, the man is going down on me...

Ah. I get it now.

That's what he had planned all along. Ever since I let him fuck my mouth – he's now fucking me with his own mouth.

Damon's lips surround my wet pussy as his tongue finds my clit. He spins the tip of his tongue around my pleasure to work me up into a frenzy.

Every part of me feels on fire in the best possible way as I rock into him.

He's lavishing me with attention, and it feels *incredible*.

I'm straining.

Straining.

Straining.

Until I finally release...

I let out another cry of delight as all the tension melts away from me and I lose myself utterly in the feel of Damon's lips around my yearning pussy.

All because of the man between my legs and his expert tongue.

I can't believe it. Damon Penmayne – one of the most powerful men in the country - just gave me head.

And I fucking *loved* it.

20

AVA

Damon leaves the office, completely stark naked.

"Where are you going?" I ask him, admiring his muscular toned body. His ass is a thing crafted by the gods, and I can't take my eyes off it.

"Shower."

It's his one word reply, delivered without even a look behind at me.

When he closes the door after him, I slump down on his office chair, the man's shirt draped around me like a massive towel.

And I shake my head at myself. This... *thing* has evolved way past paying for my dad's debt and into something else entirely. I can't deny that the gangster who just left this room brings me pleasure. A *hell* of a lot of pleasure. He does things to me completely unprompted that somehow arouse me to a breaking point. Stuff that no man has ever done before to me. It's like he knows my body inside and out and can turn me on with just a flick of his finger.

I drag myself up from Damon's chair and start scanning the room. Might as well seize the opportunity while he's occupied in the shower, right? I doubt I'll ever have another chance like this.

Hm. Damon's a seriously private guy; there's hardly a trace of his personal life in this room. No photos, no diaries, nothing that gives a glimpse into his inner world. It's all just so... dull and corporate - strictly business. The only things in sight are some handwritten notes from mundane meetings related to his alcohol company. Nothing here seems to capture his true essence, no hints of his innermost thoughts.

And that's what I'm looking for: an insight into this strange, gorgeous man and what might be going on inside that handsome head of his.

Seems like Damon's gotta keep things super hush-hush in his world. I bet the constant fear of rival folks or even some fed agency busting in is probably a real concern for him.

I make my way over to the bookshelf behind his desk. There are some real famous classics on here. He's a smart man indeed if he's read these books.

I bite my lip as I peruse the spines of the books. So... he's an *intellectual*.

I smirk at that.

It's completely out of left field.

It seems like I'm constantly discovering new things about this man every day.

I hear movement outside the door, and I quickly dart back to the office chair in time for Damon to come back into the room.

His hair is wet. His towel is hanging loose around his lower hips. I can see all of his glistening tattoos. All those inked stories from a dark past. I really wonder where they come from and what is the tale whispering behind each of them. What secrets do they represent?

I take a moment to savor the black ink on display. There are Roman numerals across his shoulders – I'm guessing it's the date of his birthday. On his chest is a name in bold: *Arthur*. That would be in memory of his late brother. I've heard the stories about his passing. There must be a lot of hidden grief there for Damon. I notice there's a quote running down the length of his right tricep: *embrace pain*. His entire left arm is a sleeve full of various tattoos.

Yeah, it's a hell of a lot of stories that he has inked on himself. A lifetime of experiences that he has on display.

Damon's body is a sculptured masterpiece - a canvas of masculine power and excellence radiating both strength and sensuality.

His eyes lock onto mine with a savage intensity. He stands there, at the doorway, for a long, languid pause.

Looking at me. All his focus is on me.

A fixation.

I can feel the weight of his attention as if it were a real heavy physical object resting on my heart, and it thrills me to my very core.

Is he salivating over me sitting here with his shirt draped over my naked body, or is he preparing to leap across the room to kill me?

I honestly do not know.

The air is charged between us. It's not just the man's pure physicality that is a turn on, it's his closeness. His raw vulnerability to be naked in front of me. His dedication to pleasing me.

Unlike during his normal life, with me he's completely and utterly *unguarded*.

And I still don't know what's running through his head.

Not even after he's fucked me into oblivion.

"That chair is mine," he scowls at me as I lie practically draped in it.

"Come and get it," I reply with a teasing bite of my lip.

My heart is beating a million times a minute.

"You're staring at me, Ava Matson," he growls in a low tone. "Don't think I can't see you checking me out. Do you like what you see?"

I bite my lip yet again, restraining myself from turning into a bubbling mess.

"Would you like to find out?" I ask, my voice breaking by how turned on I am.

"Very much so," he says.

"Maybe I do like what I see," I reply. "What will you do about it?"

"There are a lot of things I would like to do to you, girl."

"Hm. Tell me."

And then, in one swift move, he strides across the room and reaches me. With a single, confident motion, he effortlessly scoops me up as if I weigh absolutely nothing, slinging my naked body over his shoulder.

I let out a squeal as he does so.

And then he spanks my bare ass.

I squeal again.

This feels so good...

"I want to dominate you," he whispers. "Make you think of nothing else but the thought of me fucking you."

"Very good," I reply, still very much teasing the man.

And he immediately rebukes my teasing with another sharp spank on the ass.

"Ouch, Damon."

"Call me Mr. Penmayne."

"Ouch, *Mr. Penmayne.*"

"That's better."

"So, are you gonna dominate me?" I ask, my body still

hanging over the man's muscular bare shoulder. "I'm *really* looking forward to it. If you're man enough."

"As I've told you already, I am man enough, Ava."

"Then prove it, Mr. Penmayne. Prove it to me again."

"I will. I am very ready for round two," the man says, carrying me toward the door. "And this time we're doing it in my bed..."

21

DAMON

AND so, with Ava flung over and safely in my arms, I make my way toward my master bedroom. Her ass hangs in the air over my shoulder. The girl's weight is light. Very light. Easy enough for a man of my physical strength and prowess to throw around.

I wasn't intending on fucking her in here. I intended on resting after our office fun, but the way she was looking at me when I re-entered the office after my shower – the way she was practically *drooling* over me – was totally irresistible to me. I *had* to have her.

The way she looked up at me as she took my cock in between her pretty, wet, plump lips.

Fuck. Me.

I toss her weightless body onto my handcrafted mahogany bed.

This room, my inner sanctum, exudes an air of opulence and refinement. Towering ceilings create a sense of grandeur. It's all rich, dark burgundy hues in here.

This is my space, and I do whatever the fuck I want in here.

And the girl knows it.

She falls against my silk sheets with a smile on her face.

"What are you going to do next?" she asks me.

I look down at her. "Fuck you. Like I should."

I bring her dress up over her head, exposing her bare, supple breasts and her soaking pussy.

There's an irrefutable appeal in the way Ava watches me, relishing the sight of me bare-chested, every muscular contour on display. Every tattoo on my skin.

I want to take her. *Consume* her. Put my mark on her. Make her mine.

I want to fuck her until she's moaning my name in her sleep.

My cock is hard. I start stroking it as I aim it toward her inviting pussy. Ava bites her lip and nods approvingly at me as I descend upon her.

"I need you inside me," she mutters. "I want to feel you inside me."

"I like to tease," I reply. "I like to see what you do when I tease you. I like to see the look in your eyes when I tease you."

"You tease me so bad, Damon."

"I like to see what the thought of me does to you," I say.

"Oh, just fuck me already..."

And, teasing over, I thrust inside.

I lean into her, getting real close, my breath warm against her ear as my lips gently brush against her skin.

"I'm going to fuck you in the way you deserve to be fucked," I whisper. "Hard. And with my complete control. And in the way I want."

She moans and her teeth bite down on those delicious plump lips of hers that were just around my cock.

"Yes, fuck me the way you want to," she groans. "I'm here for you. Your reward."

"Good girl."

I pin her wrists down with my hands, keeping her exactly where I want her as I fuck her the way I told her I'd fuck her. *The way I want.*

Her breasts bounce against my chest as I get deeper and deeper inside her, bringing her moans out with each thrust. The noises she makes are like music to my ears. I'm turned on by how sexy the girl looks with her wrists held back and her body responding only to mine. All succumbed to my hold.

My arousal surges as I take in the captivating sight of the girl beneath me, her entirety giving way to my every touch and need, a perfect picture of passion and surrender.

And it's all for me.

She's mine. My girl to fuck as I please.

And she knows it.

"Do whatever you want to me," Ava moans through shallow breaths. "*Anything.* I'm all yours."

I lean in even closer to her ear. "Tonight, you can't cum until I say you can."

Ava moans and sighs. "No, Damon."

"Yes," I reply darkly. "You can't cum until I allow you to. It's under the terms of our agreement."

"Damon..."

"Not until I allow you to, understood?"

"You are really such a tease," Ava groans.

Perspiration runs down the length of her body, mixing with mine. It's so damn sexy.

"You are such a little treat," I tell her. "A naughty treat that I really shouldn't indulge in. A temptation that is just too damn good to ignore."

"I like it when you say I'm your treat," she replies with another moan.

"That's because it's true," I whisper back. "You are legally mine."

"Yes, I am."

Yes, she is *totally* mine.

Ava breathes deeply as I continue to fuck her hard.

"You can cum now," I growl into her ear.

And then she fucking *squeals*.

"Oh, Damon!"

And it is glorious.

Excitement surges through my body.

And I'm falling.

I'm cumming. Hard.

"Fuck," I blurt out as my entire essence seems to rush through me. I look down at Ava's soft eyes while she takes me in as I lose myself.

Jesus.

That was, simply, incredible.

How can this girl do something like that to me?

I gaze down at her. At her sweaty face. At her hands held back by mine. At her mismatched perfect eyes and red cheeks and those plump wet lips.

How can this girl make me feel things I've never felt before? And not just sex, but in and out of the bedroom?

She was only meant to be a little fun. A little side fling.

But... this... *her...*

Exhausted, I pull myself out of her.

"Who owns you, Ava?" I ask her between breaths.

I need to hear her say this.

Ava shakes her head.

"I said," I repeat as my finger traces down her body, hot from being fucked by me. "Who owns you, Ava? Who owns this body of yours? Who owns your pussy? Who is the only man who is allowed to fuck you?"

"You do," she finally whimpers. "You are the only man allowed to fuck me. You own me, Damon Penmayne."

I like it when she utters my name.

Yes, she knows who owns her.

"It's legal," I say. "You're my plaything. I'm the man who can fuck you, the only man who can use you."

"That's true."

"You like being used by me, Ava? You like being totally and wholly mine?"

She nods and bites her lip.

"I do."

"Yeah?"

"I really do, Damon."

"Good."

"I like how much you want me," she says. "I like it when you look at me with that... *look* in your eyes. Like you completely change into a man who's only focus is on me. It's like you want only me."

"Well, you aren't going anywhere," I reply. "I can have you whenever I want. You're *mine.*"

And the look in her own eyes... she definitely knows she's mine.

22

AVA

"I'm HUNGRY," I tell Damon as I lie in his arms in his bed.

I'm so damn aware of the man's presence. I can smell him: a robust, masculine fragrance, an enticing cocktail of post-sex sweat and the lingering suggestion of expensive aftershave that only a billionaire can have access to. The scent, as it envelops me, stirs the fires of desire within me, and it is so damn intoxicating. It turns me on like nothing else can.

I can even hear his heartbeat. It resonates in my ears: a slow, rhythmic, and deliberate sound. So different to my beating little fluttering heart. Even so, it feels like our hearts – despite being in stark contrast – are beating in tandem, making a connection that I can't begin to explain.

The man turns his head so that his lips are in my hair. He's both tender and electric. Every move he makes is an unspoken assertion of the domination he has over me.

"I can call my private chef to make you something," he

whispers. Even his quiet voice and warm breath send a low reverberation through my bones.

"What? You're joking? You have a private chef?"

"Yes, I do," Damon replies casually as if it's nothing to have staff on hand in your own massive mansion.

"No way," I mutter.

"I do, Ava. You want me to call him?"

I let out an amazed chuckle. "It's way too late to call the private chef. The poor guy is probably asleep."

Damon laughs at that. "He's paid to be on my call any time of the day. I'll just wake him."

"No, it's *way* too late to get him up," I protest. "I'm not that hungry anyway."

"No, you're my guest and you're going to have something," Damon replies. "Okay, scrap the expensive private chef I have on call. I'll make you something."

"You will?"

"I haven't cooked anything in years, but I can try."

"Okay, what can you do?" I ask.

Damon pauses. "An omelet," he says eventually, a little hesitation in his voice.

"Go on, then," I reply with a smirk. "I want to taste your omelet."

Look, Damon's omelet is actually okay.

"What do you think?" he asks me as I take a bite, that same little hesitation in his voice from earlier in the bedroom. We're now standing in the man's massive kitchen downstairs in his mansion. It's so big that you could feed an army from this room. It has got every kind of appliance an actual freaking restaurant would require.

I swallow as I nod. "Let's just say you're not going to

win any big culinary awards anytime soon, but it is a good omelet for a man who relies on a private chef."

"Only good, Ava?"

I laugh. "You really are so competitive, Damon."

"I just always want to win," he says. "I always want to be perfect."

"Perfect isn't real," I reply.

"I believe it is," he replies. "*You* are perfect."

I roll my eyes at that awful comment. "You wouldn't win a culinary award, but you most certainly would win a cringe award, Damon Penmayne."

A rare smile crosses the crime boss' face. "Personally, I think I'm hilarious," he says.

"We have very differing views on that, Damon."

"So, it's *only* good, then?" he asks. "Not perfect?"

"No, not perfect," I reply. "It's not perfect *like me*, but it's good, okay? You can rest easy. Stop trying to achieve perfection."

Damon stares at me. "You and I *are* very different, Ava. I am always trying to achieve perfection."

I shake my head. "Honestly, it doesn't exist."

"Every day I wake up," Damon says, "I look to do the best in my business. I am always looking to be the best in what I do. Every *single* day. That's what has made me get to where I am today."

I look at the man. I can see the conviction in him. He's clearly not lying, and he's certainly no longer joking around. He is a man who would search to the ends of the earth for perfection.

"Maybe life is about more than being the best," I reply.

Damon blinks at that. A momentary flicker of confusion. "What do you mean?"

"Maybe life is about relationships and connections," I say. "Maybe it's about doing the best for your family. Giving your all to the people you love. There may not be a perfection in that, but there is something... *greater*."

Damon scoffs. "Sounds like some trash you'd find on a fortune cookie."

I shrug. "It's a shame you don't believe me."

"Relationships and connections are for people who don't have ambition," Damon replies.

"You seriously don't think that, do you?" I ask him.

"Why waste your time on something you can't perfect?"

"Yeah," I reply slowly. "We are *so* very different."

The man smiles. "Let's go outside," he says. "Let's enjoy the view before we fight."

And he leads me through the doors and onto his balcony.

He is right about the view. We can look out over all of Crystal River from here. The stars twinkle in the night sky above us. I can see the lights of the university – the biggest building by far in the small town – and the dorms where I used to live with Olivia.

As I stand here on Damon's balcony, I feel something nudge my leg from behind. It's Damon's dog showing me some love. I give him a good scratch behind the ears.

"I love this town," I say.

"I do too," Damon replies, his voice barely above a whisper.

"That's something we can agree on," I say.

"Yep. It certainly is."

We take a seat at the balcony table, and I quickly devour the rest of the omelet.

"So, tell me about yourself," I say to the man sitting opposite me.

"You want to figure me out?" he asks me, his eyes dark. "Suss out my inner secrets?"

"I simply want to find out more about you," I explain. "Your... *history.*"

"I don't like talking about it," Damon replies.

He's curt and blunt. Very characteristic of the man.

"Oh. Okay."

"You might think of me as some petty criminal, Ava," Damon continues. "But I have also built a billion-dollar company. I am more than my reputation."

"Ah. The whole *perfection* thing you were talking about."

"Yes."

I roll my eyes. "It's all a front, isn't it? Really, though? The company?"

"What are you saying?"

"It's not legitimate," I say. "You got here through violence and suffering, that's your real business."

Damon takes a moment to process what I'm saying before he simply shrugs. "It's what you have to do to survive in my world. That's the harsh truth. To achieve perfection you have to do some bad things."

"Surely there are better ways than that."

"Business is the same as being in the mafia," Damon replies. "The same cutthroat enterprise, just that one is legal and the other isn't."

"I don't care," I reply.

"You don't?"

"It's still bad."

The gangster smirks. "I don't think I can change your mind, Ava."

"You want to hear the truth?" I ask. "Do you want to know what I really think about you and what you do?"

Damon leans back in his chair opposite me. "Sure. Go ahead. I'm sure you're going to tell me regardless."

"In my eyes, you really are just a criminal," I say. "And

no matter what words you say, I'll never erase that from my mind. I look at you and I see violence."

Damon suddenly stands up and takes my plate from off the table. The movement is abrupt and almost savage.

"Get up," he commands. "I want to show you something. Maybe I *can* change your mind."

23

DAMON

"Get in," I command Ava, pointing at my old-school American muscle car that sits in my mansion garage.

The girl smiles up at me. That same fucking smile that does strange, soft things to me every time I witness it flash up on her pretty face.

"This is yours?" she asks, admiring the vintage vehicle.

"Yes."

"Damn, Damon. You really take care of it."

"She's my pride and joy," I reply. The thing truly is. I've spent a long time in this workshop under my mansion modifying and restoring her. I've spent a small fortune on the car, enough that it would make most poor people furious. I dare not tell Ava how much it costs. It's probably more than three times what her father owes me. "My beast. My baby."

"Boys and their toys," Ava mutters with a smirk.

"Oh, this is way more than just some toy," I reply.

I have to say, the vehicle itself is an unmistakable emblem of sheer power, style, and a longing for a bygone era deeply embedded in our nation's history. It is a testament to American engineering excellence, boasting striking, assertive contours and a hood that exudes impressive menace. The body gleams with a high-gloss coat of cherry red paint, and the interior strikes a balance between simplicity and sophistication. And let's not overlook what's beneath the hood – a colossal engine that wouldn't be out of place in a high-class sports car, emitting a resonant, guttural growl.

Power. Speed. Might.

Just like me.

No wonder I fucking love it.

"Stop looking at it and get in," I say to the girl.

Ava continues to smile up at me. "Don't lie. You *love* that I'm looking at it. You love showing it off to me."

I growl. "Get. In."

The girl practically skips inside to the passenger seat. That *femininity* of hers... so damn teasing, and she knows it. She's right, though. I do love that she's admiring my car. It makes me feel manly. Proud.

I like making Ava happy, and the thought of that sends a cold knife to my heart.

This is not what I'm supposed to be. I'm supposed to be more guarded than this.

"So, what are you going to show me, Damon?" Ava asks when I take my seat beside her in the car. "You took me down here at this time of night to just admire your car?"

"Other than this car," I say, "I'm going to show you my other pride and joy."

"What's that?"

"Wait and see, you curious thing," I reply. "We need to drive there first."

"Ah, a surprise? I like that."

"You like surprises?" I ask her.

"Only if they're good ones," she replies.

"Let me surprise you, then."

And so I take her out of town, on a long and winding road that leads north; a road that takes us all the way to my brewery, just on the outskirts of our hometown.

The familiar building rises up out of the forest – a weathered wood façade adorned with hand-painted signage displaying the name of the place.

Crystal River Brewery.

This place, despite turning over an enviable annual profit, still emits an independent charm that you'll never find with some of my big corporate alcohol competitors.

"This is your surprise?" Ava asks. "This is your real pride and joy?"

"Yes," I reply. "It is. This place is very special to me."

Ava pauses for a moment to gaze at me. "I like that you can be vulnerable. That you feel free to share that with me."

I don't reply to that. I don't have the words.

The gates to the brewery open up for me.

"You're going to give me a private tour?" Ava asks me as we weave through the security checkpoint and into my personal parking lot. Her eyes are lit up.

"I think it is time for you to see my real business," I reply. "Let me take you through what I do. Let me show you who I really am."

"Oh, you're really going to show off? I'd love a personal tour from the CEO," Ava says, a smirk on her pretty face.

Even though it is late at night, there is always security around. They recognize my car immediately and quickly wave me in. Everyone who works for me is terrified of getting on my wrong side. I rarely rise to anger, but when I do, it's a real show.

I park the car and lead Ava through the brewery and toward my private office.

We pass through the array of stainless-steel brewing tanks and kettles. It's where the magic happens in this place. Where the drinks that I have personally designed with my trusted team are mixed, fermented, and crafted.

To perfection.

Just as I want it.

The air is full of the smells of the place. Hops and malt and yeast. Intoxicating.

I could never tire of the scent in here.

This is my passion. This is where my heart truly lies.

What started off as a front for my other business has quickly turned into my obsession.

"This place is pretty damn amazing," Ava says in awe as she glances around. "Tell me the story behind it."

"So, you can agree that what I do isn't all about violence?" I ask her.

Ava rolls her eyes.

"Yeah, okay. I get it," she says with a smirk. "You are clearly more than what your reputation suggests, Damon. Now, tell me the story behind this brewery."

"I started this place with a loan and not a lot of hope," I tell her as we pass downstairs to the brewery floor. "But now it's a business that delivers alcohol to nearly every country on Earth. I employ hundreds of people here. Every suit told me opening this brewery up in Crystal River was a terrible business decision, but I told them to fuck off. I want to serve the people of my hometown over any profits. I want to give back to this community."

Ava gazes up at me, her eyes meeting mine. "Keep going," she says. "Tell me more. Tell me everything about this place. I would love to hear whatever you've got to say."

Fuck. She's genuinely interested.

She actually wants to listen to me talk about my passion.

And something about that *really* sends that cold knife to pierce through my heart and change my soul.

She was meant to be just a fuck, but I get so giddy thinking about her.

She is turning into something *more*.

And I need to be fucking careful.

24

AVA

Okay, so it seems like Damon is passionate about things *other* than killing and collecting debts. I get that now.

With each passing minute I spend in his company, it becomes increasingly evident that there's much more to this man than the stereotypical image of a gangster. It's as if every moment spent with the guy unravels a new layer to him, unveiling facets of his character that defy the clichés. Perhaps, deep within that chest of his, there is something more than just a frigid, unfeeling, cold heart. Maybe there is more than I initially assumed.

Damon is clearly so proud of his brewery. He shows it off to me as if he's never shown it off to anyone before. And I love it. I love seeing the passion in his face and the pride in his voice and the fire in his eyes as he takes me around the building.

Yeah, he's a lot more than just a gangster...

I like this brewery and this building, but I think that's because of the wholesome enthusiasm that Damon has for it rubbing off on me. It's certainly inspiring. I am the first to admit I don't know a single freaking thing about the making of alcohol, but I can see the level of talent and artistry on display here.

And he purposely set it all up in Crystal River to service our hometown. Give jobs back to our community. I'm sure he could rake in a whole lot more cash if he set it up somewhere else more logical in a business sense, but he actually wants to make a *difference*.

That ain't very gangster of him.

And Damon really likes to tell me all about it in a voice that's bordering on actual emotion.

His face lit up like this...

I wouldn't have expected any of this from him.

There is definitely much more to this man than I first thought.

"I really like hearing all about this place," I tell him. "Thank you for bringing me here."

The man merely growls in response.

Okay, so getting him and his cold heart to really open up will take a little bit more effort. I'm fine with that. I can wait for him.

When he drives me back to his mansion in his fancy vintage car, he takes me to another bedroom upstairs on the same level as his own.

"What's this?" I ask him when he opens the door to the room.

It's expansive in here. High ceilings. Soft gray tones. A king-sized bed in the center of the room covered in plump pillows and silk sheets. I spot a walk-in closet entrance in the corner. An ensuite. It's like a really posh five-star hotel room.

"It's the guest bedroom," Damon replies. "It's for you, Ava. I had the maid make it up today."

"We're not sleeping together?" I ask him.

Damon turns to look at me. "You're my mistress, not my wife. No one sleeps with me."

"Really?"

"But then, no girl has ever slept over here in the first place," he says.

"I'm the first girl to actually sleep here?" I ask. "You just throw girls out of here when you're done with them?"

He ignores my amazement.

I don't know if me being the first girl to spend the night in this mansion should be taken as a compliment or as a glaring red flag.

"This room should be adequate enough for you," Damon says as if he's a realtor showing me around. "I can keep an eye on you and still give you some freedom within my home."

I roll my eyes at that stupid comment. "Thanks," I reply, adopting the most sarcastic tone I can. "I'm so glad you can keep me around as a little pet."

Sometimes Damon can make me feel special, like I'm the only girl in the entire world as when we were back at the brewery, and other times he really likes to drill home how little I truly mean to him. Just simply some mistress who signed a dumb contract. That's it.

My comment un-moves the man.

"I'll arrange for someone to promptly collect your things from your college dorm and your father's house," he explains, all matter-of-fact.

"I'm happy to collect it myself," I reply. "I can swing by home and the university tomorrow and grab all my things."

Damon sighs. "I'd rather you didn't."

"I want to see my dad," I reply. "Can I see him in the morning? Does that fit in with your strict contract?"

Damon's face is unemotional. "That's fine. But my men will collect your things from the university."

Ugh.

There's a possessiveness in him. The need for control. It goes beyond the feeling I get when we had sex. I don't think I like it.

"Well, goodnight, then," I say in a sulk.

I storm into the guest bedroom and nod at Damon to close the door.

The man hesitates.

"You liked the brewery?" he asks me.

Is he looking for reassurance?

Well, I'm not giving it to him. Especially not after this weird abrupt turnaround.

I cross my arms.

"Goodnight, Damon."

See? I can be equally as matter-of-fact back.

He shuts the door.

And I crumble onto the soft bed, my mind spinning at a million miles per hour.

Angry. Confused. Sad.

I really don't know what to make of this place. Damon is so hot and cold to me from minute to minute. He shows me his vintage car and his pride and joy brewery like a little excited boy, and then he flicks back to bachelor gangster mode as quickly as possible. I can't read him.

I just feel really alone.

25

AVA

"Hello, Dad?"

My hand gently pushes against the tough front door of my dad's house, and it swings open with a familiar creak. It's only when I step into the place that I can hear him from the kitchen.

His soft, sad voice.

"Ava?"

"Hey."

I head straight for the kitchen, finding Dad standing by the window, gazing out at the backyard. With a quick pivot, he turns to meet my gaze as I enter.

"Where have you been Ava? It's like you've gone completely silent these last few days."

I sigh reluctantly and take a seat.

"I'm working on clearing those debts, Dad. That's where I've been."

He frowns. "Doing what, exactly?"

"I can't say," I reply, shaking my head. "I really can't say, but it's working. I'm going to make sure all those debts are erased completely."

Dad nods slowly and turns his stare back out the window, avoiding my eyes. "Should I know what you're doing?" he asks me in a quiet voice.

"No. I can't, Dad. I can't tell you."

"Okay."

We stay like that for a few more silent minutes until I eventually pick up the courage to leave.

"Bye, Dad. I might be gone for some time."

He doesn't turn from the window.

"Bye, Ava."

As I walk down the hallway to the front door, trying to hold back my tears, I message Damon to send his driver to pick me up. I had thought I'd be here for longer, but now I see that there's a new chasm that's opened up between Dad and me. He doesn't know exactly what I'm doing, but I am *pretty* sure he can fit the pieces together.

And it seems like he's disappointed in me. Somehow disappointed that I'm trying to do the one thing that will help him.

And it makes me doubt myself, and everything I've done.

Damon is cold to me, and Dad is disappointed.

I just want to go.

Damon messages back immediately, confirming his driver is on his way.

I close Dad's door behind me as I step out onto the sidewalk, and I nearly run headfirst into someone.

I look up. It's not just *someone*, it's Luke Abbott.

My ex. Outside my house.

26

AVA

WHAT THE HELL is he doing here?

Luke, I realize up close, hasn't changed a single bit since he broke up with me. He's still the same guy I thought I'd fallen in love with once upon a time, and the very same guy who shattered my heart just a few weeks ago, although that feels like an entire lifetime ago now when I think about it.

I'd noticed all that in The Oak, but it's even more true when he stands mere yards from me outside Dad's place.

That spiky blonde hair. That tall, muscular physique that betrays a childhood spent playing sports. Those green eyes of his.

He hasn't changed, even if our relationship has.

He's handsome, I'd give him that. It's one of the reasons I once found him attractive. But now - as I close the front door of my family home with him waiting unannounced for me - that hulking handsomeness seems a hell of a lot more intimidating than a turn-on.

It takes me a moment to process that he's standing right here, outside my dad's place. This isn't a fluke or a random twist of fate; Luke definitely knows *exactly* where my dad lives, so his presence here is not a coincidence at all.

He's been anticipating catching me here off-guard...

"Have you been waiting for me?" I ask him, my voice wavering as I try to figure out why he might possibly be here.

I don't know what I'm feeling when I see him. This boy broke my heart simply because he couldn't be *spotted* around town with a girl whose dad is known for being in gambling debt. He dumped me simply for his goddamn reputation, but there's still a part of me that loves him. A part of me that loves the time we spent together. There's still a part of me that is that little teenage cheerleader who fell in love with the high school star quarterback.

"Yeah," he says to me. "I've been waiting for you, Ava."

I shake my head. Despite signing that contract with Damon, I still have enough self-respect to not allow myself to get trapped by my ex.

"Go," I tell Luke with as much authority as I can muster. "I don't want you here. I don't want to see you. I *never* want to see you."

Luke's eyes roll, his arms folding firmly across his chest.

Crap.

The telltale sign of a triumphant smirk plays on his lips. He's come here to reveal something. Surely. The signs of a man with a secret to expose are written all over his face, and I can't help but feel a sense of intrigue mixed with trepidation, as I'm certain he's come here with something he's so very eager to share.

"I know about you and Damon Penmayne," he says.

And there we have it. His big grand reveal.

That's why he's here.

Double crap.

"What?"

I'm shocked.

How the hell does Luke know about Damon and me?

"You two are in some kind of fucked-up relationship, aren't you?" Luke asks me coolly. "You two have some real weird-ass thing that you are trying to keep secret from everyone?"

Fuck.

"What are you talking about, Luke? You're crazy. Listen to yourself. Me and Damon Penmayne? Is this why you've popped up here?"

"Come on, Ava," he replies matter-of-factly. "You know me. I've got friends all over Crystal River. Nothing goes on in this town without my knowledge. I know about you and Damon Penmayne. I can see it as clear as fucking day. You always were a shit liar, and here you are again with your shit lies."

"Luke..."

He cuts me off immediately. "There's no need trying to deny it. I'm gonna spill the beans about you two, and everyone will take me at my word. Folks in this town already quaking in their boots when it comes to the Penmaynes, and if I drop the bomb, you and your old man will be even bigger pariahs. You've got it coming."

"Don't do that, Luke."

He is most definitely right in what he threats; he's got connections. He can really ruin Dad and me.

"I really could destroy you," he says. "Just a few words from me and you two are *fucked*. Remember, you've brought this on yourself. You're the one who chose to get involved with a murderous criminal. I'm here to make sure you're held accountable for your actions."

"I don't want a war," I reply. "Damon is very territorial, trust me. You don't want to mess with the guy."

"So, it's true then? You and Damon? You and a fucking criminal? You disgust me, Ava."

"Luke, *please...*"

"I don't care about Damon or the Penmaynes," he spits back. "In fact, I hate them, and Dad's always hated them, and now it's my turn to get back at them. Damon's not a good man, Ava. His brothers are not good men."

"Yeah," I reply, "and neither are you."

Luke melodramatically places his hand over his heart like he's been shot. It's all a sarcastic game to him. "That *really* hurts, Ava. How can you say something like that when your own dad is in debt to one of the worst men in the country? You've got such a terrible sense of perspective. You've truly done this all on your own. You and your dad have fucked yourselves over in your own ways."

"Maybe I do have a terrible taste in men," I retort. "I mean, I did date you for years."

Luke chuckles. "Oh, Ava. So pathetic. How about you run off to your little gangster squeeze now? Go and cry to him about me. Get one of his little goons to chase after me. I bet the man can't do shit himself. I bet he would be scared of getting into a fight with me."

"You don't know anything about Damon."

"Sure, I do. It seems like I know a hell of a lot more about him than you, Ava. I know he is a bad man you would be stupid to get involved with."

"What do you want?" I ask him. "Why are you really here? Do you just want to tell me you're going to ruin my reputation around town? Because guess what? You've already done that by telling everyone about Dad's addiction. What else is there for you to do to me?"

Luke is really enjoying this. It's clear to see. "I truly want nothing, Ava. All I simply wanted was to see the look on your face when I told you I've discovered your dalliance with the Penmayne and, I must say, it hasn't been a disappointment in the slightest."

"Please don't tell anyone, Luke..."

Luke smiles. "You've bitten off more than you can chew, Ava. You always were like this, chasing after money and fame. Even when you were with me. So goddamn superficial. I'm glad I cut you off. Such a waste of time dealing with a bimbo airhead. You would really fit in, being the trophy wife of a gangster. I can picture you with him so clearly now. Nothing but a has-been bimbo airhead."

"Why are you so cruel?" I ask him, a lump rising in my throat.

"Because you're playing around with a man who Dad and I detest," Luke replies.

"Is that all you've come here to do?" I ask him, close to tears. "Just to insult me? Try to make me cry? Because I won't. Not in front of you."

Luke smiles.

But before he can deliver another biting sting, a car comes to a halt by us on the sidewalk. Damon's driver.

Upon laying eyes on the car, Luke exhales deeply. He knows who the vehicle belongs to and why it's here. I can practically see the disgust building in his snarl as he regards me and the car.

"Go on, bimbo," he sneers at me. "Scuttle off to your new boyfriend."

And then, without waiting for an answer for me, he turns and strolls away.

I want to scream after him. I want him to come back

with something that would devastate him. That would rock his world.

But I have nothing. Not a sound.

I'm just a mess. *A bimbo airhead.*

I am totally lost for words as my ex destroys my heart once again and I am left behind in his trail of dust.

27

AVA

I spend the entire night waiting for Damon in his guestroom, but he never comes. I haven't seen him since last night when we agreed I would be seeing my dad this morning.

After Luke walked away from me outside Dad's place, Damon's driver picked me up and took me back to the man's mansion where I dutifully went to the bedroom and waited.

And waited.

And waited.

But there's no sign of the man. I've been anticipating for him in suspended excitement; waiting for the moment he'd come home to claim what he sees as rightfully his - the girl who reluctantly signed his contract. Yet, to my surprise and maybe even my disappointment, he's nowhere to be found.

I know I should be happy that I haven't seen him. I know I should be celebrating the fact I could be spending the night without the gangster, but I really am not.

I'm falling for him, aren't I?

Oh, God.

I really want to see him.

No SIGN of Damon for the next day as well. He must've spent the night somewhere else. Is that a pang of jealousy I feel in my heart?

God.

I spend my morning exploring around the mansion. The door to his office is locked with that biometric scanner thingy that only he can open. Shame. I would've loved to have spent some time snooping in there.

I decide on taking his cute dog for a walk, circling the property aimlessly just to kill time as the dog sniffs around the crafted garden. I try to look for any routes out of here, any places from where I can potentially escape.

But even if I could, would I leave this place? I know I'm not allowed to leave the mansion compound. That's what he told me. I'm sure Damon has instructed his security not to let me attempt to get out of here.

I think about Luke and his vile words outside Dad's place.

He's discovered us.

But would he really go around and tell everyone in town? Would anyone actually believe him?

I guess, after Dad's public humiliation about his debts, people actually *might*.

I want to talk to Damon. I want to tell him all about yesterday.

I want him to comfort me. Hold me. Tell me everything is going to be fine.

Wow, you really are crazy, Ava. Damon wouldn't comfort you. You wouldn't be able to cry in front of him.

He wouldn't understand such a petty thing as *emotion*.

When I get back inside the mansion, I pass by his office one more time. I can hear voices coming from in there. *Damon's* voice. He's on the phone, but I can't make out what exactly he's saying. I put my ear up against the door to listen, but I still can't pick out the words. Only his voice.

He's here, though. He's back home at the mansion.

I'm excited. Against my better judgment.

He's so close.

I wait in my room just in case he does decide to come and claim me. An hour later, there's a knock at my door, and I leap up in excitement, but it's just the private chef bringing dinner.

"Is Damon going to be joining me?" I ask the chef before he leaves.

He purses his lips.

"What I've heard is that he's going to be having dinner in his office," he says.

"Oh, okay. Thanks."

Maybe he's just busy. Damon is, after all, a billionaire very much in demand.

Well, that's what I tell myself.

But then I don't even see him the next day.

Nor the day after.

I go snooping again. This time, I take my chance to look around Damon's private gym. I have a little play on some of the machines, but Damon has his weights set to very, *very* heavy, and there is nothing in this room around my range. I can barely move anything.

I sneak into his mansion cinema. The screen is the size of something at a commercial multiplex. I am still bowed over by the man's wealth.

All this just for when he might fancy a movie?

I wonder what's happening in the outside world. I wonder how Dad is, and I think back to the last time I saw him standing there in the kitchen. How he seemed so disappointed in me. I wonder if he's even thinking about me, or wondering where I am.

I also wonder if Luke has followed through on his threat. Has he gone around telling everyone about Damon and me yet? Or was that all just a tease?

I think about messaging Olivia for some company to help me not go insane, but I decide against that. I wouldn't be able to talk to her about all this anyway - the stupid NDA and all that.

Ugh. I'm such a people person and extroverted; it is totally against my nature to be locked up like this in Damon's mansion.

I just want to see him.

I feel like a princess being held captive by a monster.

A gorgeous, charming, dark, and dangerous monster who somehow makes my heart somersault...

And I get my chance the next day. For only the briefest of moments. I spot Damon walking out of his office, heading downstairs to his car. Probably off to some meeting. I nearly call out to him from the top of the staircase in the same crazy way I did the first time I saw him in his New York office, but I decide against it at the very last second.

In the evening, he returns. I can hear him enter his office. I leave the guestroom door open a little as a kind of invitation for the man to enter, but he never does.

I fall asleep feeling even more empty.

Waiting. And waiting. And waiting.

It's only at the end of the week when something happens. Jim arrives at the mansion. I hear him greeting Damon at the door with that gravelly voice of his. The two men scurry off into Damon's office.

Now's my chance.

I sneak across to the office door, trying to listen to their conversation. This time I can pick up some of the words from inside the room. They're talking about some guy called Handsome Jack, whoever that is. I don't really understand the rest. They seem concerned, though. Thinking things over.

Someone's moving inside. I can hear footsteps.

They're coming for the door.

Fuck.

I sprint away, just in time, before Damon swings open the office door. I've made it back to the guestroom, my heart beating fast.

Too close...

I take a moment to calm myself. I don't know what I think. I was just starting to actually like the man, but he hasn't spoken to me for days now. Why is he keeping me here?

I'm really just being used, aren't I? I've been black-mailed into all of this.

Why did I allow myself to fall into this insane arrangement?

I want to break down and cry.

But then there's knocking at my door.

"Ava."

It's Damon. He's finally come to see me.

28

AVA

I LET HIM IN.

Of course I do.

Damon enters through the doorway of the guestroom, exuding an aura of silent, brooding intensity, and settles down on my bed without a word.

His gaze quickly scans around the space before landing - fixed - on me. As he has done many times before.

That same stare I cannot – for the life of me - decipher.

"Hey," I whisper, anxious as to what comes next.

I tentatively close the bedroom door behind me and stand by the doorway awkwardly as Damon leans forward on my bed.

"You were speaking to Luke Abbott the other day," he eventually says, his voice low and quiet. Deadly freaking serious.

I won't dare lie to him. What use would that be? He seems to know everything, anyway.

I nod. "I did, but not out of choice. He was waiting for me outside my dad's house."

Damon inhales deeply, his broad shoulders moving in a measured rhythm with each breath. Even in this relaxed pose, sitting on my bed, the guy oozes a striking, rugged, dark charm.

"What did you say to him?" he queries, his voice maintaining a hushed and subdued tone.

This time, I shake my head. "I told him nothing," I whisper. "But he's somehow found out about us."

"Us?"

"You and me and the *relationship* we're having," I say. "He's threatening to tell everyone in town about it."

The enormity of what Luke might go and do dawns on me. If he does follow through on his threat, then I am totally freaking screwed. And so is my dad. Crystal River is the only place Dad has ever known, and to be completely cast out from that would drive him even more into depression.

A dark growl emerges from deep within Damon when I tell him of Luke's intimidation. "I'll deal with that boy..."

No, no, no.

I rush over to the bed and sit down next to the man.

"Don't," I plead. "Please don't hurt him."

"Did he hurt you?" he asks.

Damon's eyes are burning into mine. He's only concerned about me.

"No, he didn't."

"You sure?"

"Yes, Damon," I reply. "He didn't even touch me."

Damon is silent for another moment. "Good," he says. "I'm glad he didn't lay a hand on you. I'll still need to deal with him, though. No one talks you like that, especially not when you're under my promised protection. *No one.*"

"Please don't."

"I have no choice," Damon replies. "He's threatened you, and by extension, he's threatened *me*. I won't let that go unpunished."

He really thinks that. He really thinks he has no choice but to hurt and commit violence...

It's scary.

It hits me that this guy is operating on a whole other level than I am. A genuinely *menacing* man.

I touch his arm. "You've always got a choice."

"I really don't, Ava."

"How about, this time, you don't hurt him?" I ask. "How about this time you don't do a damn thing?"

He regards me with those dark eyes of his.

"You don't want revenge?" he asks. His tone... it's like he's bewildered by my nature.

I nod. "I don't want you to do anything to Luke."

"You are so strange," he whispers.

"Damon," I reply. "You have a choice here. You *always* have a choice. I'm asking you not to do anything. No violence."

Damon takes in a long breath. "Sure," he says quietly. "I respect your decision. This time I won't touch him."

"You won't?"

Damon slowly shakes his head. "No. If that's what you truly want..."

And then I'm kissing him. I don't know why I make the lunge to his face, but I'm happy I do. It feels very right to be kissing him right now. His protectiveness... his forbidden possessiveness... his sheer *menace*...

The way he is listening to me.

The fact he made a choice just then not to indulge his natural impulse, and instead simply respected my wishes.

Damon allows his lips to linger on mine for the sweetest of seconds before he suddenly pulls back.

"I was being honest with what I was saying before," he mutters. "If anyone lays a hand – even a *finger* – on you then they die. No one touches my girl."

"You really think that way about me?" I ask him. "I'm your girl?"

"Yes," Damon replies. "You're mine. My girl. And no one but me can touch you."

And then I kiss him again, and this time it's even deeper.

And I feel his hand start to reach down my chest and toward my wet pussy...

29

DAMON

Her pussy is wet to my finger's touch, and her kiss is forceful and wanting.

I like that Ava has taken the initiative to lean out and kiss me. It's sexy to feel her power behind her lips as she pioneers our closeness. It makes me hard to feel her desire for me in my very own guest room that I've kept her in.

She couldn't say no to me – she didn't even want to - and it gives me a real emboldening sense of power.

But I want to prove to the world that she's mine.

And mine alone.

My hands trace up and down her inner thigh. The girl lets out a goddamn sexy sigh.

"I'm going to fuck you now," I whisper into her ear. I've come to realize she really likes this: my lips intimate to her hair and ears.

My murmured comment elicits another sexy sigh from between her pretty lips.

"Take me, Damon," she says.

She really can't say no to me...

I reach around the back of her head to snatch her hair in a tight grasp.

The girl sighs again, submitting herself to me.

Fuck, I am so hard at this very moment. Her sighs do impossible things to me. My cock is twitching to be let inside her wet hot pussy.

I'm in control now.

I guide her toward the guest room bed, throwing her down on the soft mattress with a simple flick of my wrist. The girl gladly lets herself fall down, facing up at me from the bed with her wide expectant eyes.

I can't fucking resist...

I pull out my cock and the girl leans up to take the thick shaft into her mouth, but my hand comes to rest on her head to gently push her back down onto the sheets.

"Not with your mouth," I say, "but with your sweet pussy."

Ava nods, practically drooling.

I love to see her like this; so totally dominated by me. Her lust for me is uncontrollable.

I sink down to between her legs, my erect cock ready in my hands. I enter her with a powerful thrust, strong enough to make the girl's eyes widen further. Her mouth hangs open in delightful surprise, and that sexy look of hers wills me on even more.

I fuck her hard.

Like I'm proving to her that she's mine.

I watch her as I do so, taking in her beautiful face. Those soft eyes of hers that shut close in pleasure as I rock her world.

I enjoy every second of fucking my girl until I'm finishing with a loud and violent roar.

I look down at her. Ava is basking in that post-fuck glow,

and she looks so fucking beautiful. Hot and sweaty and just glistening in delight.

That's my girl.

No one touches her apart from me.

I pull out, my erect cock wet with the juices of Ava's sweet pussy...

And then dark thoughts gather in my mind.

The thought of her talking with that boy. That Luke Abbott. Her fucking ex. That thought drives a dagger into my mind and makes me angrier than I've been for years. Not at her, but at that boy for dragging her back down to his level. She's better than that. I want her to feel power again.

And the best way to do that is to make her cum.

Still standing over her, I reach down and begin to gently stroke the outside folds of her pussy. Ava sinks into the soft bed, gasping with my teasing. Her cunt is wet and burning hot.

I've made her like this with my fucking...

And I'm going to do a hell of a lot more to her.

My middle finger descends into her opening as my thumb coaxes out her clit, tenderly circling her pleasure center as I grin at her.

Ava takes one glance at my menacing look and sighs again in that sexy way of hers before shutting her eyes and submitting herself to my expertise.

I play with her sweet pussy until the girl is quivering and shaking under me. She's out of control, and I love that.

I love how I'm able to do this with just my touch.

With just my middle finger and my thumb.

The girl arches her back and cries out.

"Damon. What you can do to me..."

I really smile then.

No one can touch her except for me.

No one can touch her like this. No one else can make her feel like this.

I have her totally under my spell, and I'm not going to let go until I hear her squeal.

And soon, she does. Her entire body squirms as she cries out my name one last time before she shudders in waves of pleasure. Her pussy is tight against my finger as my thumb continues its tease over her clit.

The girl rocks back and finally opens her eyes to look at me, her breath so shallow it makes her bare breasts shake.

I stare back at her, our eyes connecting.

"Holy shit," she breathes. "That was... *incredible*."

I finally let go of her pussy.

"Good."

Now I feel like myself again.

I LIE DOWN NEXT to her. My hands trace around the outline of her soft lips. I'll listen to her now. The anger about her ex is gone. I was so fucking angry when I entered this room, but she's somehow managed to calm me down.

I'm resolved. I won't touch the boy. But if something else were to happen – if that Luke boy dares cross the line with Ava – then I would not hesitate for even a second. I'd have him before he could even beg.

I picture his face now. Bloodied. Pleading with me.

And I would tell him: *no one touches my girl*.

If he fucks with Ava, he wouldn't even know what hit him.

30

AVA

Damon fucked me like he wanted to own me.

Even though he is like an animal in bed, he knows *exactly* what buttons to press and when to make me reach new heights of ecstasy. And I let him. It feels good being his captive. In his custody.

And - when it is all over and I'm left a shuddering, happy mess - as he leaves the room, he turns around at the door and tells me one simple thing.

"My brother is in town. August Penmayne. Do you want to go to dinner with us?"

And I nod.

Yes, I would very much like to go to dinner with your family, Damon.

31

AVA

"WAIT... WHAT ARE YOU SAYING?" I ask.

Damon takes in my puzzled expression, a casual smirk playing on his lips. He's utterly unbothered by my complete disbelief in what he's just told me.

"I've booked out the restaurant," he replies, his deep voice extra smooth. Extra charming. Extra *sure* of himself. "August has already said he's coming."

The whole entire restaurant?

I casually lean against the wall in the guest bedroom of his sprawling mansion while Damon lingers by the doorway. It's late afternoon, and he's just knocked on my door to tell me about his plans for meeting his brother tonight.

"Slow down, am I hearing you correctly?" I ask, my voice stuttering. I've got so many questions. "When you say you've booked *out* the restaurant, that means you have a table booked for you, August, and me. Not that you've actually booked out the *entire* freaking restaurant, right?"

The man just continues to smirk at me.

And that's when I realize he isn't joking.

"You actually booked out the entire restaurant, Damon? Are you crazy?"

"I don't want to be disturbed," he says. "Come now, Ava, you must know what I'm like by now."

"I didn't know you were this... *gangster*."

Damon nods at me. "Now onto the more important things. I've bought you a dress I'd like for you to wear."

"Thanks, but I've got my own," I reply.

"I want to see you wearing this one," he says.

"You've bought one for me?" I ask.

"Yes. I've had my people figure out your dimensions," Damon replies casually. "And I picked out one that I believe will look great on you."

"I really do have my own, but I'll have a look at what-ever it is you've picked out," I say. "I'm curious now to see what you think will look great on me."

He takes me into his private office, reaching into the closet to pull out something that immediately makes my mouth drop open.

The dress is *beautiful*. A stunning blue, it has a delicate sweetheart neckline. I can see it's crafted from a satin fabric in a rich shade. It cascades into a lighter blue skirt. It looks so... *sophisticated*. It's like Damon pictures me as a refined, high-class woman.

I've never had a guy buy me a dress before, and certainly nothing like *this* dress.

"This has got to be expensive," I whisper as I gingerly reach out to touch it. "How much is it?"

Damon shakes his head. "I'm not telling you that information."

"Oh."

"But I would like you to wear it tonight," he says.

I shake my head. "I really do have my own..."

"I'm not asking," the man growls in that commanding way of his. "You're wearing it tonight."

And I blush. I like it when he's like this.

I see that crazy look in his eyes. His yearning to see me in the dress that he's bought specifically for me.

"Oh, what the hell," I say as if I have a choice. "Okay, sure. I'll wear it. For you, Damon."

* * *

AUGUST IS WAITING for us already as we arrive at the restaurant in the middle of Crystal River. Damon drives us there to meet him.

"He's always punctual," Damon remarks quietly as we pull up and see his brother standing by the front door of the restaurant. "Just like me."

I wait for my contracted master to open the door for me, and then I'm meeting his brother.

August, unlike his criminal sibling, has steel-blue eyes. His hair is a whiskey brown, and wavy. Neat and parted. Even though some of their features are different, there is a striking resemblance to the two men, in the same way as there's one between Damon and Spencer. He's got that Penmayne square jaw and that hint of broad muscular shoulder under his perfectly tailored suit. I bet he's nicely toned, as all the Penmayne brothers seem to be.

He is, undeniably, a very handsome man.

They all sure have won the genetic lottery in that family, haven't they?

"You must be Ava," he says as he greets me.

I smile. "You must be August. *Doctor* August, sorry."

I remember that the man is a famous pediatrician.

Doctor August smiles charmingly. "Don't worry about using titles with me. Just call me August."

"Well, it's lovely to meet you, *just* August."

"You're looking very beautiful tonight," the doctor says. "A picture of *stunning-ness*. Damon does know how to choose a perfect date partner."

I blush. "Oh, you're much more polite than your brother, August. I like you already."

"You're too good for him, Ava," he says. "How about we ditch my brother and you and I get to know each other..."

Next to me, Damon growls. "That's enough of your flirty talk, August. Keep your hands off her. Let's go inside."

As the server greets us at the door and guides us into the empty restaurant, I turn to the doctor.

"You're very different from Damon, even though you two look alike."

"I'm the better-looking brother," August replies, making me laugh. "It's a shame he got the bad looks and the grumpy personality, while I got the brains and the attractive looks."

I can sense Damon listening in to our two-way conversation even as he organizes things with the server. I like making him a little jealous and a little curious.

We're taken to a table set up next to the kitchen at the back of the restaurant. Damon wasn't lying when he said he had booked out the entire place just for us. The Penmaynes really do value their privacy.

"Do you agree with Ava?" August asks Damon when we sit down. "Do you think we are very different?"

"I am nothing like you," my captor replies to his brother.

It's a joke. It takes me a moment to realize that they both share a very dry sense of humor. The two men laugh.

I've never seen Damon like this. *Relaxed.*

The two brothers are clearly comfortable with each other. Their blood runs thick.

"Oh, I think we are pretty similar," August continues.

"You and Spencer were always the smart ones, according to Mother," Damon replies. "The ones with all the promise. I was the one they kept away in case I dared infect your intelligence."

"Don't put yourself down, Damon. You are a hell of a lot smarter than Mother gave you credit for," the doctor remarks.

"It's all in the past," Damon replies.

"To be honest," August says, "I was pretty damn surprised when you told me you had a girl, Damon. I really, really wanted to meet her when you told me about her."

"And what would be so surprising about that?" Damon asks.

"Well, you're not usually the type to... *hang around* when it comes to women in your life," August replies. "Every conquest of yours seems to fall by the wayside pretty damn quickly."

Damon looks at me, and I can't help but let out a chuckle.

"I understand," I say. "Damon and I have both come to an... *arrangement.*"

Now that's spiked the doctor's curiosity. "Oh, really?"

"Yes," Damon grunts. "An arrangement. What she said."

August's curiosity is not extinguished. "What kind of... *arrangement* have you two got going on, then? Anything that I should be privy to? You always loved a good little secret, Damon."

I glance back at Damon. He's staring at August with killer eyes.

"An arrangement you need to know absolutely nothing about," he growls at his brother.

It's clear he wants him to immediately cease this line of questioning.

"Alright, keep your little secrets," the doctor replies with a smirk. "You two are having fun. I see that and I admire that. I must say, though, you sure have picked a very pretty girl to make a so-called *arrangement* with, Damon."

There's another growl from my man. "Don't you start deploying your charming talk again, August. See where that leads you."

I stifle a giggle at Damon's seriousness. He's so very protective of me. I like it.

"Please, no fighting," I joke.

"You know," August says to me, pointing at his brother, "Damon wasn't always the hardened bad boy like he is now? He was once such a shy teenage boy..."

"That's enough," Damon shoots back.

He really doesn't seem to like talking about his past. Even something as cute as when he was a nervous adolescent.

But I'm used to emotionally unavailable men. His past is something that will only be unraveled when he wants it to, I can tell.

The server takes our order in a professional style. When she leaves, it's Damon's turn to aim his guns at his brother.

"Have you got a girl you're hiding from the rest of us, brother?" he asks.

I notice August's cheeks go a very slight shade of pink. Unlike Damon, he clearly can't hide his secrets well.

"No," he replies. "No one."

"August once had a big crush on the daughter of our family maid," Damon tells me. "It was quite something..."

"When we were teenagers," his brother corrects

quickly. "It was a childhood thing. A mere fling. Nothing serious."

"It was quite intense," Damon continues. "Wasn't it? That's what I remember. You were *obsessed* with her for ages if I recall correctly. Didn't you once walk in on her dancing on her own? Didn't you say that it was the most beautiful thing you had ever seen? You liked to call her beautiful if I remember correctly."

August's cheeks somehow shade even more pink. It's sweet.

"Shut up."

"Have you seen her since?" Damon asks. "Ever tried to get back in touch with the girl? You two parted ways, didn't you? Lost each other in the tumult of life and the waves of fate. Would be a shame to lose your one true love just because you can't even be fucked to go out there and look for her."

August rolls his eyes at that.

"Damon can be so controlling," he says to me. "He likes to dominate a conversation."

"Oh, I've noticed," I reply with a smirk.

"But he's loyal," August adds somberly. "Very loyal. He'll go above and beyond for his loved ones. Even if he does tend to rip into them for no reason. He's got a good heart, though."

Damon sits there, next to me, his arms folded. His face is stone as August praises him. I have a feeling these brothers don't compliment each other as seriously as this often.

"But he can get closed off," August continues about his brother with the confidence as if Damon isn't there. "I still don't know much about the time when we disappeared for a few years in New York. Those wilderness years when we didn't even hear a peek from him. No one really knows what went on, not even our other brothers."

"There is nothing to know," Damon replies. "And that's final."

* * *

AFTER THE DELICIOUS MEAL, I have a strong sense that the two brothers want to spend some time talking with each other, and so I excuse myself and head outside to get some fresh air.

It's nice to stretch my legs.

Sitting with the two in there was a very different experience from what I was expecting. I was seeing a whole new side of Damon. A more chilled version of him. I have a feeling that what August was saying was right about him being very closed off - it seems like Damon only lets a select few people through the tough barriers he surrounds himself with, and rightly so. His career demands that of him. But it is good to see him with someone who I can tell he trusts with everything.

I've only ever heard horror stories about the Penmaynes. I never knew how loyal and kind they are to each other. They seem to genuinely care for each other in a way that few other families ever do.

A tight bond strengthened by blood.

It's made me see Damon in a whole new light.

I walk across the road to the main park of Crystal River. It's night now, and everyone is in bed. The streets are empty. The only lights seem to be coming from the restaurant. I spot The Oak across the street on the other side of the park, all closed up for the night.

I take a seat on the playground swings and gently rock,

thinking about Damon and the dress he's made me wear and his carefree laugh.

I could lose myself in the sound of his laugh...

I hear the crunch of grass nearby, and I know someone is close.

My heart beating fast, I turn around.

And there's Luke.

What the fuck now?

He's been waiting for me.

Again.

32

AVA

REALLY, though. *What the fuck does my ex want with me now?*

Luke is clearly drunk. Very, *very* drunk.

I can see it in the way he's staggering on the spot, his knees buckling. I can see it in his half-opened mouth. I can see it in his glazed eyes as they stare, hungrily, at me as I sit on the playground swing in the dark and empty park.

"I want you back, Ava," he says.

Ah. That's what he wants. At least he's straight to the point.

His voice is slurred. It penetrates the night air like a cheap piano that's off-key. A horrible sound.

It's a voice I really don't want to hear right now.

I've seen him drunk like this a few times. It is certainly not a pretty sight, and it usually means that his quick temper is not far away.

That temper I know all too well.

"Luke? What the hell? What are you doing here?"

He takes a step toward me.

"Ava..."

"You're drunk, Luke," I say.

I stand up from the swing in the opposite direction to my ex, but he still limps forward toward me. Even though he is not in complete control of his faculties, the man is literally twice the size of me. And I am *always* aware of that fact. That star high school quarterback figure that I've come to know so well is looking very, very dangerous right now.

"I want you back," he says. "I'm here to get you back. It was wrong of us to break up, Ava."

His voice is really slurring now.

I shake my head, holding my firm ground.

I'm praying that he simply gets tired and walks away back home.

But I'm too optimistic.

Please go away. Please go away.

Luke steps toward me again. And again. It's so quick.

And now he's so close. *Too damn close.*

"I want to kiss you, Ava," he snarls. I can smell the alcohol on his breath.

"Go away," I reply. I start to turn, but I can already see the man's arms rising. He can easily get at me from this close.

Why have I allowed himself to get this fucking close?

"Ava, I want you..."

"Step away from her."

That's not Luke.

That is from a deep, stern voice in the darkness. I recognize that voice immediately.

It's Damon.

And he doesn't look happy.

He's turned up...

Luke turns to the man as well.

Damon is alone. No August beside him.

I have never been so thankful to see the gangster's face.

"I'm not scared of you, Penmayne." Luke's voice is seemingly less slurred now, like he realizes that this has turned into a very different situation for him from the one happening a moment ago. He straightens up, sensing the threat.

Luke towers above me.

He's a big guy.

But so is Damon.

"That's a foolish thing to say," Damon replies coolly. "You should very well be scared of me, boy."

In response, Luke raises his fists.

"I'm willing to have a fight right here and now to see how tough Damon Penmayne really is," he says. "See what he's like without his bodyguards to protect his sorry ass."

I turn back to Damon.

And I see him reaching for his black knife in his belt.

No, no, no.

The knife. That's too much.

I know he could kill Luke. He *would* kill Luke. He's got that knife. He's got the intent.

Damon is, after all, the most dangerous man I've ever met.

It's up to me to stop him. Only me. Luke can't do anything against a man like Damon.

And then, without thinking, I'm running toward Damon, my hands desperately pushing to keep his razor-sharp knife away. To not cause any more pain or trouble.

No killing, no killing.

No violence.

Please.

"Damon... Damon..."

I see the fire burning in the eyes of the man. A burning

desire to rip out the heart of my ex. Aggression. Anger.

Passion.

He's out of control. He would do anything, and Luke would be totally unable to fend for himself.

There would be blood, and it would be spilled over *me*.

And I'm now cradling Damon's face between my hands, whispering to him. Trying my best to keep him away from my ex.

"Focus on me," I whisper. "Ignore Luke."

There's still the anger in those dark eyes...

"Focus on me. Focus on me. Focus on me, Damon."

He growls.

"Don't hurt anyone. Please, Damon. Don't do it. Don't think it."

And then he finally locks eyes with mine, and not with Luke's. He's turning away from committing violence; I can see that.

"I can make him disappear with a mere click of my fingers," he snarls, toward both Luke and me.

"I don't doubt you could," I reply soothingly. "I really don't doubt. But you don't have to. You can come with me back to yours. You can keep your eyes on mine and forget all about Luke. Focus on me."

And Damon does what I ask of him. I see, in real-time, that flame of anger dissolve from behind his eyes as he centers his attention on me.

And now I am taking him by the hand and leading him out of the park as we continue to look at each other, and not at my ex rambling around uselessly behind us.

"This isn't over yet," Luke yells from the distance as we reach Damon's car, but neither of us are interested in the harmless drunk man in the park.

We're staring at each other with such intensity that the whole world is shut off to us.

33

DAMON

I AM SEETHING WITH ANGER.

So much so that I stay completely and utterly silent during the entire drive back to my mansion. The only thing preventing me from doing a sharp U-turn right now and heading back to the park to settle things with that asshole once and for all is Ava sitting so composed beside me as we spin through these dark streets of our hometown. At any other time in my life I would not have hesitated to make that boy vanish as if he'd never existed. Stick my knife in his begging throat. But Ava's got this mysterious, ethereal influence over me that can somehow tame my more... aggressive impulses. She's stopping me from indulging in my worst nature.

When she ran up to me in the park, her hands on my face and her eyes burning into mine, I felt a shift in me that I had never felt before. She was immediately able to make me flip from seeing nothing but red to a strange kind of peaceful stillness in a mere heartbeat with just her calming look.

Focus on me, Damon...

I pull up inside my mansion gates, home at last, and proceed to march into my living room where I finally turn to Ava. She's followed me. Calm and silent. All the way inside. She's impossible. She's like an angel.

I can't even look at something so pure.

Someone who can calm my rage with just a look and some throwaway words.

"I need a drink," I say. The first words I've spoken since the park.

"I'll have one too," my girl says.

I pour two whiskeys and guide Ava to the balcony where we sit under the stars.

I can't get that face out of my mind. Luke's face. Him standing there so close to my girl...

The bastard.

I am still simmering even as I drink my whiskey in silence on my balcony.

And I think Ava notices my anger. She reaches out and takes my hand in hers.

And my heartbeat immediately relaxes.

How the fuck can she do that?

Something about that act... that pure, innocent act, makes something drop inside me.

And I finally *relax*.

Breathe.

In. Out.

In. Out.

In. Out.

"Thank you for tonight," she whispers to me in the starlight. I see in her eyes she is not joking or being defensive, but she is actually serious.

And I lean forward and grip her hand tighter.

"Thank you for being you," I whisper back.

"I'm glad you listened," Ava replies.

I shift in my seat. "I want to tell you something," I say.

Ava doesn't move. "Tell me."

"I was always a leader," I say to her, my voice soft. "Ever since I was a boy, I was the one to take charge of any situation, even in the playground and at school. I have always liked being the one to make decisions and to be the man people look up to, but it is lonely, and it is a lot of responsibility. You have to remove yourself emotionally, otherwise you can't cope with all the consequences of those decisions you have to make. I was meant to join the army. That was always my destiny. It was always what I wanted and what my father wanted from me. To become an officer. To someday become a general. It fitted with who I am as a leader."

"What happened?" Ava asks. She's interested, and that gives me the fuel to carry on. "What happened to you?"

I've not told anyone this, especially not in this kind of detail, but her presence has changed me tonight. I *want* to tell her everything.

The words come tumbling out of me like they never have done before.

"What happened was that I saw something that no boy should ever see," I continue, my voice barely a whisper. "Something no teenage boy should ever have to witness. What happened was that I saw my godfather get assassinated by a gang member. He was my father's best friend and my closest mentor, and I saw him get torn down by bullets as he stood even closer to me as you are sitting now. That one singular moment jolted me out of my life as a member of the billionaire elite and turned everything upside down, and my life hasn't been the same since."

"And what did you do?" Ava asks. "Did you find the guy who did it?"

I might as well continue. She's brought me this far. She's opened me up like this.

"I left my family behind, made my way to New York with nothing but the clothes on my back, and ended up living on the unforgiving streets. I became part of the anonymous crowd, working my way from the bottom up. I was hellbent on revenge, and I was determined to find that gang member who took my godfather from me. I took charge of my godfather's business in New York, rebuilding it stronger and better as one of the most powerful organizations in the city. I took down the men who conspired to kill my godfather, but never found the actual man who pulled the trigger. Everyone kept their mouth shut despite my threats. I tore down that gang and purged it from the inside and made it my own, but there was still no sign of the culprit who killed my godfather. It was a tough few years. I met Jim. I got this scar on my face. It was during this time that I ventured into the alcohol business, needing a legitimate front for my operations. The knife I always carry, the same one I was going to use on your ex tonight, belonged to my godfather. I've kept it by my side all these years to use it on the man responsible for his death."

Ava lets go of my hand.

"That is one crazy story," she whispers. "And one hard life. Thank you for telling me, Damon."

I take in a deep breath. I feel nervous.

Have I really divulged all this? To a fucking girl I barely know?

"I've not told anyone about what happened," I say. "Even my brothers have heard only the bare minimum. I don't let anyone know anything about my past."

"Are you telling me all this because you trust me?" Ava asks.

I glare.

"I find it hard to trust anyone," I whisper. "You have to trust no one in my profession."

"Answer my question, Damon," she replies. "Do you trust me or not?"

God, she looks beautiful in the moonlight.

"Yes," I say. "I trust you. And I don't know why. I don't even know why I said all that just then."

Ava leans back in her chair and continues to stare at me.

"Have you ever got satisfaction from killing?" she asks.

"A big question, Ava. Do you really want to hear my answer?"

"I want you to be honest," she says softly.

"Yes," I reply. "And no."

"I saw something in your eyes tonight in that park," she whispers. "A coldness. You looked at Luke and... I don't know what you had behind your eyes. It was beyond anything I'd ever seen before. Have you killed men with your bare hands and that knife?"

I nod slowly. "I was going to deal with Luke the same way I dealt with the men who conspired to kill my godfather."

"Until I stepped in?" she asks.

"Until you stepped in, yes."

"What would you do if you ever found the man who did it? The man who killed your godfather?"

"He's probably dead by now," I reply. "And not by my hand. That's probably why I haven't found him. Either that or he went into hiding. Found a simple life and kept away from the business for years and years."

"What would you do if you found out he was still alive?" Ava asks.

She's really digging in deep tonight.

And, for some reason, I want to answer every single one of her questions.

"Well, then. If I were to find him, he wouldn't be alive much longer. I am a man of my word, and I've promised myself I would enact my revenge come hell or high water."

"Oh."

"You did something to me tonight in the park," I confess to the girl, my voice trembling. "You... *stopped* me. No one has ever had that power before. I am not a good man, Ava. I've committed countless wrongs, things that I can't honestly say I regret. They were undeniably terrible, and I have become a truly bad man. But you, Ava, you've become the one shining beacon in my life, the single source of light amid this abyss of darkness. Without you, I am utterly adrift."

"You're adrift?"

I look at Ava so that she totally knows my intentions.

"Come closer," I say. "Lean closer."

"Why, Damon?" she asks.

"I have an overwhelming urge to kiss you right now, Ava Matson."

34

AVA

AFTER A LONG AND tender kiss on the balcony under the stars, Damon takes my hand and gently guides me into his bedroom.

I can already tell this is different from all the other times the man has come to take me in order to fuck me. Instead of his normal animalistic domination, he's so tender now.

Soft, even.

His grip on my hand is firm, but there's no rough play or hair-pulling like in the past. He steers me to his master bedroom with a delicate touch, as though he is handling rare, fragile China plates.

He is... dare I say it... *respectable*.

And don't get me wrong, I loved it when he tossed me about like some doll to be fucked the last few times we had sex, but I do cherish witnessing this side of him - a side I know no one else ever gets the chance to see.

It's thrilling to see this man who's so usually assertive and authoritative simply be a *lover*.

Inside his bedroom, he slowly lays me down on his bed, descending with me as we lower onto the soft silk sheets.

I breathe in deep.

He does the same.

We're so connected.

It's like he's listening to me.

His face is barely an inch from mine...

Then he leans in the final inch and kisses me. It's a kiss that's deep and tender, mirroring the way he's held my hand. It lingers in the air between us, unhurried and gentle, yet there's no mistaking his strength. This is a man who's well aware of what he wants right now.

He wants to make love.

And I want that too.

Our kiss continues. And continues. And continues.

And I am lost. I give myself to him.

His hands are all over me, leisurely undressing me even as our lips lock. He knows what he is doing.

My breasts heave as they become free in his delicate hands. He squeezes my tit as I feel his tongue penetrate my tongue.

And soon, his cock is penetrating me.

I close my eyes as he gets deep inside me.

But this is not some quick fuck. This is slow and deliberate.

So tender.

Affectionate, even.

Our kiss breaks as he thrusts inside deep.

"Look at me," the man growls in his deep, sexy voice. "I want to see your beautiful eyes. I want to take in your pretty face."

This is such a different side to him, even if that air of streetwise Damon confidence is still there. He's become more empathetic; more willing to listen to the desires of my body. Attuned to me.

We are so connected. Our bodies rock in the same rhythm.

I open my eyes to his command.

The man is staring at me with danger in his own dark eyes. I bite my lip with an uncontrollable urge as I see him look at me like that.

How could any girl resist such a look of pure wild lust from a man so domineering?

His cock envelops me. Fills me. His hands pin me down. I'm trapped by him, in the most sexy way possible.

And then he's kissing at my neck. Gnawing at me with a ferocious intensity. I sigh again and really let him have his way with me until finally I'm on the cusp of the greatest orgasm of my life.

"I'm going to cum," I moan.

The man growls at my statement and continues to push in deeper.

And deeper.

And deeper.

And I'm panting.

"Cum for me, Ava. I want you to feel everything."

"I can't hold back anymore," I murmur.

Damon glares at me.

"You don't have to. Look at me, Ava, and *finish*."

And I do.

I erupt at the exact same time as this man does one final shudder into me while we stare into each other's eyes like nothing else exists.

My pussy fills with his cum as I totally lose myself in seas of gratification that wash over my body.

And the whole time we continue to look at each other, our connection unbreaking.

"Damon."

"*Ava.*"

35

AVA

I WAKE up to Damon watching me with those dark eyes of his.

"What?" I ask him as I come to, a self-conscious giggle escaping my lips as I notice his stare. I don't know how long he's been looking at me as I lie here, asleep, in his grand bed.

"Nothing," he replies softly. And then... "Just looking at *you*, Ava."

And it's like my heart melts.

But I'm not going to give him the pleasure of knowing that little fact. I've already given *way* too much to this man.

I pull myself up to a sitting position and stretch out my arms with a big yawn. I feel so... *full*. Damon certainly knows how to give my body a good time.

"I want to see Dad today," I announce, now fully awake. "I know it's probably against some clause in the contract, but I want to see him. And this isn't a request, but a statement. I'm going to see him."

I turn to look at Damon.

He's still staring at me, but this time it's with a slight smile.

Something is amusing him.

And then he takes in a sharp breath and speaks.

"I've decided I'm going to drop everything against him."

I blink.

"What? What do you mean?"

"All his debts," he replies slowly and seriously. "Everything. All gone. I've decided that your father owes me nothing."

The fuck...

I am shocked, to say the least.

"Everything?" I ask. "All the debts? You're just going to drop them?"

The man doesn't even hesitate. "Yes."

"Then what about the contract we signed? The whole *mistress* thing?"

"To be honest," Damon replies, "I just wanted a reason to have you in my life. I was caught by something the first time I saw you at my office in New York. I was drawn to you. I needed to have you."

"Drawn to me?"

"I can't put it into words," he mutters, his voice trailing off.

And now I dare utter the thought that's screaming through my head.

"So... this means I'm *free*?" I ask. "No more contract? No more being a mistress?"

Damon nods.

"But one more favor, though," he says. "Will you stay with me for a few more nights?"

"Why?" I ask.

"Well, it's going against everything I've ever thought about myself, but I believe I'm falling for you, Ava."

Holy shit.

I did not expect this to be happening when I woke up this morning.

Is this even true? Is the man falling for me? Is the billionaire gangster who has killed with his bare hands actually going crazy for a former cheerleader with no money?

I think about what he's saying to me. About him wanting me to stay with him. There's a part of me completely terrified to spend even another minute in the company of this dangerous man, but I also can't help to admit there is the other side of me that seems to want him more than my lungs need oxygen.

He laid out his heart to me last night. He bared his soul. He told me things I know he's never told anyone else, and yet he has still done despicable things. Unmentionable parts of his life. My head and my heart are torn between two very different ends of thought.

"Yes, I'll do it," I reply. "But I am worried about a few things."

"Like what?"

"Well, everything you told me last night..."

Damon sighs. "I knew that was a mistake divulging all that to you," he says.

"I'm just concerned about your past and your violence," I explain. "I'm not judging you on your past actions. What you experienced and what you had to do to survive is understandable, but I am not going to be a witness to anything. I do not, under any circumstances, want to see you fight someone. And I definitely don't want you to fight over me like you were going to do last night with Luke."

Damon takes in another sharp breath. "I understand," he says quietly.

I know he's being serious. I've come to get a feeling of

the man since I first moved into this mansion, and I can tell he's not lying. I can tell that he's making a promise.

And if there's one thing I know about Damon Penmayne in the time I've been with him, it's that he never breaks his promises.

And so I lean back over him and kiss him for a long time.

As our lips touch, I feel my heart opening up, and I know it's already too late for me now.

What the hell am I getting myself into?

36

DAMON

Ava ends up not going to her father's. Instead, she stays here. At mine. In my bed.

With me.

Our kisses in bed go from fleeting pecks to longer and longer kisses.

Longer and longer and longer kisses until she is sitting on top of me - her ass balancing on my muscular thighs - smiling at me in that irresistible, sexy way of hers. The same way that I can't help but indulge. We can't help but fall into this.

"You want me?" she asks, a strand of her gorgeous blonde hair dangling temptingly over her soft beautiful eyes as she looks down at me.

"Always," I utter before I reach up and kiss her again.

She melts into me.

And then her hand is finding its way down my hard abs and to my groin. She takes my erect manhood and begins to stroke it as she looks on at me, biting her lip.

I collapse against my bed, convulsing with waves of warmth that emanate from her touch.

Jesus...

"Fuck, Ava. You know how to undo me."

She giggles sexily at that.

"I like being able to please my big, strong man," she whispers.

"Say that again," I command as my cock twitches in her hand.

"My *big*, strong man."

"Good girl," I reply. "Now get on top of me and fuck me until you cum. I want to feel you as you let go."

She sighs with a flutter.

"Gladly, my big, strong man."

I am between her legs as she climbs on top of my hard cock, guiding herself down onto me with a relieved groan from both of us.

This is glorious.

And then she's rocking on me. Rocking in a rhythm that makes her gasp and gasp. I groan as she continues.

Her blonde hair drapes over my face as the girl pleasures herself on my long, thick dick. I don't even have to do anything as she rides me into oblivion.

I don't have to even move.

Ava's using me.

I groan again.

Her breathing deepens.

We both moan in unison.

"So I'm not your mistress anymore?" she asks, breathless.

I shake my head. "No."

"I'm doing this out of my own free will," she says as she leans her head back in ecstasy. "I'm doing this because *I* want to. I'm here to get what I want."

Oh, she definitely is getting what she wants.

Ava doesn't stop rocking until she is tearing at my bedsheets and I am pumping myself deep within her.

And, yes, I can feel her cumming.

And it is the *sexiest* thing I've ever experienced.

* * *

"So, you're falling for me, huh?" Ava asks, tracing her finger down my chest and along the edges of my toned muscles as we lie in bed together.

"You could say that," I say.

"You *just* said that," she replies. "You said it this morning."

"I did? I wouldn't want to inflate your ego."

"Damon. Please answer me."

I let out a chuckle. "Sure. Yes, Ava, I am falling for you."

"Please explain more," she says. "Please tell me everything. Please tell me how you're feeling."

"You want me to open up to you?" I ask, my eyebrow raised.

Ava giggles. "I am sure a big, tough man like you can have a little ounce of emotional maturity. We're here, *alone*. I'm sure you can open up in the privacy of your own mansion to the girl you're falling for."

I take in a long breath.

Fuck it.

"Well, for one thing, you've made me softer," I say. "Fuzzier."

"*Fuzzier?*" she asks, eyebrow raised.

"Ava, it's been a whole lot of new emotions," I reply. "What else do you want me to say? I'm not used to talking about things like this."

She lifts her pretty head up and smiles.

"You don't need to say anything else," she whispers. "How about you shut up now and kiss me."

37

DAMON

AVA WAKES up wrapped in my arms. The morning sunlight streams through the window and onto her face, illuminating her beautiful features. Making me smile.

Over the time I've been with Ava, I've tended to wake up before her, but I am not complaining in the slightest. To see her sleep so peacefully with that pretty face of hers is like a gift every morning. Her warm body snuggles up against mine. I feel the outline of her soft ass against my leg muscles. Her platinum blonde hair slips through my fingers.

I feel totally at peace - a feeling I've not felt for a very long time.

Who is this girl and why is she making me so damn happy?

Why do I laugh along with her? Why does she make me feel so many overwhelming feelings?

Am I having... dare I say... *fun* with her?

I sound like some hopeless romantic and not me. This is fucking crazy. Am I living in an upside-down world?

Ava stirs, and I roll back against the pillow to hide the fact I've been watching her for the past half hour. Her eyes flutter open and she takes a long yawn.

She looks at me.

I look at her.

"Morning," she says.

I smile. "Morning, beautiful."

She smiles at that.

"I want to show you something, Damon."

"What?" I ask.

"It's a secret. But I want to show you it today, if you have time."

"For you," I whisper, "I have all the time in the world."

"Well, we need to drive into Crystal River," Ava replies.

"I'll call my security," I say, but Ava reaches out and takes my hand.

"No," she replies. "Please don't. No security. Not today. Not for this."

"Okay," I say. "Just you and me. Where are you taking me?"

SHE GUIDES me into the center of Crystal River, to the park near the restaurant the other night. I stop the car and turn to her.

"Tell me, where are we going? I'm not a fan of surprises."

Ava laughs. "You've never had someone surprise you?" she asks.

"Every surprise in my life has been something bad," I reply.

"You've never had someone arrange a surprise date for you?"

I shake my head. "I've never been on a date."

"Wait, what? You've never had a date? Surely you're not a virgin, Damon Penmayne?"

"You don't have to... *do* dates when you're someone like me," I reply. "I'm not exactly the *boyfriend type* girls are looking for."

"Ah, so you're the one-night-stand kind of bad boy?" Ava asks with a wink.

"You could put it in words like that," I say.

"Well, how about I take you on your first surprise date, then? I mean, it's not much of a surprise or anything. I just want to take you to somewhere I really love."

"And what's that?" I ask.

Ava points across the road from us. "The Oak coffee shop, where they have the best almond croissants in the world."

"You know," I say, "I've never been there before."

Ava's mouth drops.

"You've never been in The Oak?" she asks, incredulous. "But you grew up here? How could you never even go there at least once? You must be crazy."

I shrug.

"Yeah, I must be crazy, I suppose."

"Okay, well, now you're *definitely* having an almond croissant."

She eagerly takes me inside the coffee shop with all the enthusiasm of an excitable puppy. She practically pushes me through the front door and orders croissants and coffee before we're even inside and purchases them despite my protests.

"I am paying for this," she tells me sternly. "I am paying for you to have the best almond croissant in the world."

"I'm guessing you like these, then?" I ask her as we take our seats in the coffee shop.

"I *love* them," the girl replies enthusiastically.

I take a bite of the pastry. Ava watches me intently.

"You've got such a stern face as you eat that," she remarks.

That makes me laugh. "It's a good croissant. I guess I make stern faces when I'm enjoying something."

"Would you say it's the best almond croissant in the world?" she asks.

"We'll have to see," I reply.

Ava blushes and drinks her coffee.

"I like it when you laugh," she whispers. "You don't do it enough."

"You make me laugh, Ava," I say. "Not many people can claim that."

What the fuck is going on with me? Am I really falling for a girl? Am I actually fucking happy?

We finish the croissants and the coffee. Ava was right: it is pretty damn good here.

"Okay, now that you've taken me somewhere," I say to her, "it's my turn to take you somewhere."

"Oh, where?" she asks.

I smile.

"New York."

38

AVA

DAMON *REALLY* DOES TAKE me to New York. On his private plane. Even though I've already been on this thing before, my breath is still completely taken away when he takes me on board. That opulence inside here... that luxury of a private plane...

It's all too much.

It's like a whole different world. It's just like how these last few weeks have felt like a dream. Living with Damon. Flying on his private plane. Experiencing his opulent life-style. Like it's out of something that Olivia would read - some fantasy novel or something completely made-up. It's like I simply walked from my normal mundane world into Damon's billionaire exciting world.

And I don't think I ever want to leave...

It's just us two and the pilots onboard the jet. Damon really wants me to have a good time, making sure I'm totally relaxed. He seems like he can't take a breath until I'm tended to.

"You okay?" he asks me as we settle in our seats. His usually confident swagger is now full of concern for me. "You've got everything you want?"

He really wants me to be happy. My mood affects him.

This is new.

I smile at him. "I am more than okay, Damon."

"You want a drink?" he asks me. "Anything to eat? I can summon up anything you desire, even on here. Everything is for you, and you alone. Just let me know what you want."

His anxiety is cute. He's clearly never looked after someone like this before.

I wave his worries away. "I am fine, Damon. I have everything I could ever want. Let me soak in this moment. I'm more than happy right now."

And I do soak in this insane, out-of-this-world moment. I stare out of the window at the rolling fields below us for the entire flight, basking in this incredible experience. I'm pretty damn sure looking out of a window this high up will never fail to captivate me. Everything is so breathtaking. Everything is so vast. I lose myself in the clouds and the idea of just how damn big the world truly is. Buildings look like toys. Crystal River looks like a tiny dot.

Everything feels so small.

Me.

Damon.

Everything.

I just sit on the luxury plane next to the crime boss who treats me like a princess, and I shake my head at what the hell I've gotten myself tangled up in.

I still cannot wrap my head around all this.

When we land, Damon has a car already waiting for us. He is very intent on driving us.

By the ease with which he steers us into the city, it's

pretty clear that he *knows* New York intimately. He knows each and every street. Each and every bend.

This is *his* city.

And he wants to show it off to me.

"I'm going to take you to my usual suite at the best hotel in town," he tells me as we zoom through the busy city streets. "But first, I want to take you somewhere that's important to me. Somewhere that I've shown no one else. Are you okay with that?"

I merely nod. I'm overwhelmed by everything.

"Yes, I would like that, Damon. Very much."

"Good."

We duck and dive until we're underneath one of the main bridges of the city. I recognize it from countless films and TV shows, but I can't place the name. Damon pulls the car over and stops, nodding out of the window at the dark alley underneath the bridge.

"What's this?" I ask him, peering down at the grimy spot.

"This is what I want to show you. That's where I spent every night for the first few weeks I was living in this city," Damon replies, his voice soft. "Penniless, hungry, ambitious, and hellbent on revenge. This was where I went after I witnessed my godfather being shot. This is where I disappeared from my privileged life and where I started a new life. This was where I met Jim. This was where everything changed for me."

"You wanted to show me this?" I ask quietly.

"Yes," Damon replies.

"You wanted to show me where you spent the worst time of your life?"

"Yes."

I stroke the man's cheek. I can see the emotion in his eyes. The memories. The pain. The struggle. It's all in there. And there is also the pride he has for crawling out of that bleakest moment of his life.

"A lot has changed since then," I say. "*You've* changed since then."

Damon nods. "True. Now all this city is mine."

"It's your kingdom," I say.

Damon likes that.

"Yes," he replies. "It is my kingdom. And you are my queen."

* * *

DAMON'S SO-CALLED *usual* hotel suite is nothing short of incredible. I stand on the balcony, looking out over this amazing city, the wind blowing through my hair. I can't help but be overwhelmed over how high up we are. And the rooms themselves in this suite are the most lavish rooms I could ever imagine. I've never seen anything as extravagant as this, not even in documentaries or on social media.

It's as opulent as Damon's private jet, and just as much a fairytale. There's a chandelier in the main living space. A separate bedroom that's practically the size of Dad's house back home. A jacuzzi. A dedicated concierge at our beck and call. It feels all so... *indulgent*.

I can't believe I'm here.

I can't believe I'm experiencing this.

I can't believe I'm standing right next to the man of my dreams.

"You like it?" Damon asks me, wrapping his arms around my waist and hugging me from behind as I behold this crazy, impressive view.

"Yeah," I reply quietly.

"Yeah?"

He's taken aback.

"Yeah, I like it just a *little* bit," I say. "A teeny tiny bit."

The man spins me around and takes a moment to longingly kiss me. I find myself melting into his embrace.

There are so many hidden layers to the man. So many I didn't see at first...

"Come to bed," he whispers in my ear once he's done kissing me. "Seeing you naked will be a better view than the one out here."

I shake my head.

"Not just yet," I reply.

"Are you disobeying my direct order, Ava Matson?" he asks.

"Yeah, I am. How about you wait for me in the bedroom," I say to the man. "I have a gift for you."

39

DAMON

As Ava instructs, I wait for her in my hotel suite bedroom while she does whatever she needs to do in the other room.

A gift. For me? From her?

As I lean back on my bed, waiting for her, I imagine what kind of gift she's got planned up her sleeve. She knows I hate surprises. It better be worth it.

Well, I don't have to wait for long.

The door to the bedroom swings open, and there is Ava.

My breath stops, and it's not just because that gorgeous girl is standing there.

It's *what* she's wearing that makes me breathless.

She's dressed in her old cheerleader uniform. Pom poms and all. A sleeveless top. The red and white colors of the Crystal River High's football team. The red skirt. She's even got on the white athletic sneakers and crew-length white socks. She's done the whole lot. She's tied her hair up in a white bow. The fabric of the uniform tightly hugs her deli-cious curves, emphasizing her tits and her ass.

And I am practically salivating.

This is one hell of a gift...

"Come here, girl," I snarl.

"You like what I'm wearing, Mister Penmayne?" Ava asks.

"Fuck yes. I like what you're wearing so much. Come here. Now."

She sticks her tongue out at me rebelliously.

"Make me."

I push myself off my bed and dart toward her. "Oh, I will."

The girl giggles as I scoop her up and fling her over my shoulder. Her tits bounce against my chest as I carry her back toward my bed.

"Oh, you're such a big boy," she whimpers. "Able to carry a cheerleader like me."

"I can do a lot more to you than just simply carry you, Miss Matson."

I toss her onto the hotel bed before I climb on top of her.

"Are you going to fuck me?" she asks. She looks cute with her blonde hair tied back with the little bow.

A little gift wrapped up for me.

"I'm going to admire you in this sexy little uniform you got for me," I reply, my eyes scanning down her curves. "And only *then* I am going to fuck you, my cheerleader."

She giggles.

And I can't help myself. My hands pull her out of her outfit.

I am a creature uncaged, and I want to devour her. Right fucking *now*.

I fuck her fast and hard as my fingers rub her clit. I

cover her mouth as she moans into my hand whilst I bring her to the point of no return.

"My little naughty cheerleader..."

We both come crashing down to earth with an almighty bang. An erupting climax of passion that sends us both grunting in delight as our bodies tangle around each other's.

Fuck me, no other girl has made me feel this way. No other girl has filled me with such craving and lust.

Ava's body, even without her seductive cheerleader uniform, sends me wilder than I could ever imagine.

"I've never finished like that before," I grunt as I lie next to her, completely spent.

The girl, her blonde hair falling around her pretty neck, leans up over me and smiles victoriously.

"I have you wrapped around my finger, don't I?" she remarks. "Just like the bow in my hair."

I snarl at that comment.

But I can't help thinking how possibly true it is...

40

AVA

It seems like Damon owns every piece of New York City, judging from all the places he points out to me that he controls as we drive along in his fancy car.

"Let me guess, you own that building as well," I say to him cheekily as we pass the Empire State Building. Damon glares at me, unamused by my comment. I have to laugh at his seriousness.

It's night as we zoom through the neon streets. It feels like I'm in a movie with all the bright lights and all the famous landmarks of the city flashing past me. Damon is so chilled as he handles the car through the busy New York traffic. He is completely at ease here, even if I am acting like the most awed tourist in the world.

We arrive at a bustling nightclub that's hidden away down a side street like it's a trendy secret. Well, it's not much of a secret with such a long line of people waiting to enter.

"It's gonna take us ages to wait to get inside," I remark to

Damon as we pull up outside, eying the crowd of trendy young New Yorkers standing outside the door.

He hands over the keys to a valet and opens my door chivalrously.

"Yes, it would be a long wait to get inside," he whispers into my ear as he offers a hand to help me out of the vehicle. "It really would be if I didn't *own* the place."

"Oh."

Wow.

Damon simply nods at the security, and we're quickly ushered inside. Everyone here somehow knows who he is. The staff all acknowledge him with a mention of his title – *Mr. Penmayne.* A security man in a dark suit leads us to the VIP section behind closed ropes and we're immediately given an ice bucket with fancy champagne.

"I guess there are some perks in owning a nightclub," I say to Damon as we sit in the lush booth. I can look out over the entire club from here. I can watch everyone dancing. I can feel the music popping.

This is, just simply, crazy.

"I don't usually go out," Damon replies. "I'm usually busy working."

"Well, maybe let your hair down a bit," I say. "For once."

"Only with you."

I blush. "You always seem to know the right things to say, Damon."

He leans close to me and whispers. "I love how you impress me, Ava. I like to flaunt you in front of everyone. I want everyone's eyes on you. I want them to all know that you are mine. *My girl.*"

With those last few words, his hand comes to rest gently on my knee.

Jesus...

His fingers tighten around my thigh, and I find myself melting.

I let out an uncontrollable sigh of pleasure.

Damon watches me as I do so – his dark eyes soaking me up.

I feel like the only girl in the club right now. The only girl the crime boss has ever set eyes on.

He's just so... overwhelming.

A man in a dark suit appears, waiting at the side of our booth for my man. Damon gives him an irritated sideways glance and then tells me that the man's the manager of the club.

The gangster doesn't sound happy to stop what we're doing.

"Please excuse me for a moment," Damon tells me. "I've got to talk business with him."

"You're excused," I reply.

Damon gets up and then spends a few minutes conversing with the suited man, a serious expression on his face. I wonder how stressful a job Damon must have. All these businesses he owns. All these men who are under his employ. All these deals and figures and worries that must occupy his head at all times of the day.

But he still finds time for me...

Damon finally gives the nightclub manager a pat on the back, sending him away into the crowd of dancing bodies, before turning back to me.

He sits down next to me, and his hand finds my thigh again.

"Where were we before I was rudely interrupted?" he asks with a smirk on his face.

But before I can reply, we're approached by a man wearing a backward baseball cap. I instantly recognize him as a world-famous DJ. I've only ever seen him going viral on my social media, playing to record-breaking crowds at music festivals, and now he's here standing in front of us.

"Nice to see you again, Damon," the DJ says, shaking my man's hand. Damon nods at him and then turns to me. He sees how starstruck I am.

"This is Ava," Damon replies, introducing me.

I don't understand what I say next. I nervously fumble over my words as I speak to the famous man. I think I remark how much I love the DJ's music or something. He's very gracious with a girl who can't seem to string a sentence together.

"Well, I have to finish my set," the famous musician says to us, turning back to the nightclub's dancefloor.

And then someone else approaches. Again, I instantly recognize him. This time it's a famous late-night talk show host. I've only ever seen him on my dad's TV.

We all do handshakes and a brief conversation. Again, this celebrity knows Damon by his first name. And again, I fumble over my words as I try to converse to this incredibly famous man.

When the talk show host leaves, I spin around to Damon, spellbound.

I knew he was powerful, but *this* powerful? It feels like he owns half the flipping city. Even celebrities want a piece of him.

"You really *are* the King of New York City, aren't you?" I remark.

Damon leans back into the soft leather of the booth and smiles at me. He likes how impressed I am.

He spreads his legs open like he owns the place.

Well, technically, he does.

"Yes," he replies proudly. "Yes, I am the King of New York City."

41

AVA

I WAKE up to the distant rumbling hum of men talking and a splitting hangover moving like a freight train through my head that makes me want to be sick the instant I open my eyes. It takes me a moment to get my bearings in my new surroundings as I groan and sit up slowly in the bed I find myself in after last night at that cool star-studded nightclub.

Oh. Right. I'm in a hotel. And not just any hotel, but that super fancy one that Damon has brought me to. The chandelier and the view and all that.

And it takes me another moment to recognize the two men I can hear talking.

Damon and Jim.

I pull myself out of bed, my head spinning furiously.

Oh, crap. This hangover is going to kill me.

I would rather just curl up in bed and spend the rest of the morning nursing this terrible self-induced affliction, but the alarmingly raised voices from the two men intrigue me too much for me to ignore. I stagger to the closed door that leads out of the hotel bedroom and place my ear against it in order to decipher what the hell they're going on about, feeling like a sneaky detective.

"You've got to speak to him," Jim is saying on the other side of the door. His voice sounds like it's on the verge of a shout: something I would never imagine someone doing at Damon. I can't picture that man accepting anyone shouting at him and letting them get away with it. "You can't put this off forever."

"Yes, I know," Damon replies in his typical growl.

"He wants to meet," Jim says. "Tonight."

"I'm not going to some meeting with Handsome Jack. I'm with Ava. She takes precedence over any man."

So just who the hell is this Handsome Jack guy?

"Damon, you know you have to do this. You know you have to meet with the guy eventually. It's better that it's a peaceful negotiation now rather than some bloody duel in the future."

Jim is being more persuasive now. It seems like Damon allows this man – and this man *only* – to speak to him like this. I admire their friendship. They've gone to hell and back together, and Damon trusts Jim with his life. He allows him to speak to him as a friend.

I'm sure Damon doesn't have many of those that he can trust.

My head still throbbing with this hangover, I am unaware of my foot pressing down on the nice hotel flooring.

And then there's a squeak of the floorboards as I apply pressure.

Fuck.

I immediately cringe as the sound reverberates through the entire hotel suite.

The two men go silent.

Yep. They heard me.

Why did I allow myself to do that? Now they'll know I'm standing here at the door, listening to them...

And so I try to save myself by opening the door and stepping into the main hotel suite living space with all the confidence in my arsenal. The bright lights momentarily blind my hangover ass as I smile at the two men.

With smudged makeup and my bed hair, I must look like a crazy witch.

"Morning, boys."

Damon is already dressed in one of his nice black suits and looking like he didn't have a drop of alcohol last night, the bastard. They both turn to me, hushing their serious conversation.

"Hello, Ava. How's your hangover?" Jim asks. "I hope we didn't wake you."

I roll my eyes. "Suffering, but I'll survive. What are you two talking about?"

Damon straightens up. "I have a work meeting tonight," he says.

"Nice," I reply. "I'd like to come."

Yes, I know. I'm *bad*.

Damon's eyes narrow. "Really?" he asks. "You want to come?"

I shrug. "I want to see how your business works. I would love to sit in on one of your mysterious work meetings. I'd be totally silent, of course. You won't hear a peep from me. *Nada*."

Damon shakes his head.

"I don't want you to see this. Sorry, Ava. I can't have you coming with me to witness my work."

"Oh, I think I will," I retort. "What type of meeting is it? Where is it? You're not going to leave me here on my own, are you? That would be so *ungentlemanly* of you, Damon."

Damon turns to Jim, who remains stoic. Good for him. He doesn't want to get involved between us.

"It's... at an art gallery opening downtown," Damon explains. "Unusual place for a meeting, I know."

Oh. I can definitely latch onto this.

"An art gallery opening?" I ask. "With the celebrities and everything?"

Damon seems perplexed at my question. "Yes, there'll be celebrities there."

"Fantastic," I reply, beaming. "I'd love to go. I've never been to an art gallery opening or a film premiere, but it's been there on top of my bucket list. I'll come for sure then. What a great idea, Damon."

"No," he replies firmly.

"Please, Damon. I'd love to come."

"This is not your world, Ava."

"I'll have big strong you next to me," I say. "I'm sure I'll be perfectly fine."

Damon looks at Jim. He looks back at me. He looks back at Jim.

And then he sighs.

"You really want to come, Ava?" he asks.

"Yes, Damon. I really want to come."

He sighs again.

"I'm totally against this idea," he says.

"Well, you no longer control me," I reply, not budging. "Our little contract has been ripped up, remember? I want to come, so I'm coming."

"Fuck. Let's do it, then," he says, resigned. "We'll have to find you something nice to wear, though."

"I don't have anything for a nice art gallery opening," I reply. "Nothing fancy enough for one of those."

"What about the dress you were wearing last night?" he asks.

"Damon, a girl simply can't wear the same dress two nights in a row," I retort. I am loving how I'm making him squirm.

Damon sighs yet again.

"Maybe you need to go shopping," he says.

"I'm glad you suggested that," I reply with a wink. "I would never turn down the chance to have a little browse through the famous shops of New York."

"Remember, though," Damon says, "that this is all your idea. Not mine. You can't blame me when everything goes to shit tonight. You got that, Ava?"

"I wouldn't dare, Damon."

"Fine, then."

"Woo."

"I want to spoil you, Ava," Damon growls. "Let's get you a new dress. Let's go and get you spoiled."

I let out a shriek of glee. "This is gonna be fun."

"Go and buy a nice dress," he says. "Go and have a browse. On me."

Oh, I'm loving this.

For the rest of the early afternoon, I take Damon down Fifth Avenue looking for something nice to wear.

And it is a hell of a lot of fun.

"Money is no object," the crime boss tells me. Even though he might be annoyed I am tagging along to his so-called *business meeting* tonight, he's still keen for me to be happy. I like that. He's still happy to let me indulge myself.

As we walk to the next luxury store, I take a glance up

at the man. I can see he's deep in thought. Something is worrying him.

I bet it's tonight's meeting.

At this store, I try on another dress. I look at myself in the mirror.

This feels good.

I step out of the changing room wearing the dress to get Damon's opinion, seeing as he's the one paying the small fortune for it. He rises to meet me. His eyes are on me. He crosses the room and whispers in my ear.

"You look beautiful, Ava."

It's so sincere. So impulsive. I can tell that's what he's actually thinking.

Oh.

And my heart instantly melts.

"Well, in that case," I say, "If you think I look beautiful, then I'll just *have* to get it. Give me your credit card."

42

AVA

THIS IS one hell of a strange world that Damon is pulling me into. *A total trip.* It starts off all innocently enough with the art gallery opening, but then everything quickly spirals into some kind of crazy gangster movie.

Damon is wearing a black suit. It's his typical color, but strange for the glitz and glamor of an art gallery opening.

"Are you going to a funeral?" I ask him as we take the elevator down to the private VIP parking lot of the fancy hotel.

"A meeting with other bosses in my profession is similar to a funeral," Damon replies, his lips tight and pursed. He's clearly very much on edge for this work meeting.

And that puts me on edge. I don't know what it is, but I've learned that if Damon's anxious, I damn well should be too. I used to think the guy is unshakable.

Until tonight.

We're chauffeured downtown to that art gallery in Damon's limo, and let me tell you, the place has got all the razzle and dazzle you'd anticipate for a grand opening in the heart of NYC. Paparazzi, A-listers, politicians - you name it. The big shots you usually only catch on giant billboards, movie posters, or the news, or scrolling through your social feed - they're all here, gracing us mortals with their presence.

And just like every second of this little New York escapade with Damon, I'm utterly floored as our limo trundles up to park outside the red carpet and I see the commotion.

This is certainly a long way away from Crystal River...

We step out of the nice car and onto the VIP carpet leading inside the art gallery. Damon offers his hand to help me out in a gentlemanly manner. I cling to him as we take our first steps up the intimidating red carpet. Paparazzi look up and aim their cameras at Damon and me, but my man casually raises his arm, and the paparazzi respectfully lower their cameras. They know who he is and his reputation. He has power here. He wants his privacy.

I notice Damon's security isn't following us inside. They hover by his limo. A tinge of panic catches in my throat. I don't want to be entering a nest of gangsters without men loyal to Damon by our side.

"What about your bodyguards?" I ask him. "Aren't they coming?"

"It'll be rude for me to bring armed men inside here," Damon replies calmly. "At meetings like this, we all show respect to each other by not causing trouble. We are bound by our code of honor. There will be no guns here. No fights. This is a meeting of the minds, not of steel."

And so we enter the dazzling art gallery without any protection.

My head whips around, taking it all in. It's all so minimalistic in here. All so modern and... well... *arty.*

Stepping into this world is like stepping into a kingdom I've never dreamed of being a part of in my wildest fantasies. Famous faces from magazines, movies, and TV shows surround me, mingling in the elegant ambiance of the fancy-pants art gallery. Impeccably dressed and well-mannered waitstaff move gracefully through the exclusive crowd, offering flutes of bubbly champagne from trays that gleam like polished mirrors. It's a spectacle that leaves me in awe, and I can't help but be utterly taken aback by the sheer grandeur and sophistication on display before my very eyes.

"I'd like to check out the art," I say to Damon, looping my arm around his to stay close. "Or maybe meet some more celebrities..."

"We're not here for the art or the cameras," he says quietly. "We need to go upstairs. That's where the real business is taking place."

Damon nods at a burly-looking security man with a walkie-talkie. The man nods back and gestures for us to follow him. We make our way down the middle of the art gallery, passing by groups of people admiring the art and chit-chatting in voices that reek of old money.

A man stops us and shakes Damon's hand. I instantly recognize him as the Mayor of New York. I've seen him doing press conferences on TV. He's with some old senator who also shakes Damon's hand. They are smiling and practically begging for attention from my man. It's like they are of lower status than Damon and not two of the most powerful political players in the country.

This is insane.

But during all of these whirlwind interactions, Damon's spare hand doesn't leave mine.

The security man eventually wrangles us into a special elevator at the back of the gallery. It's all painted in black and is very imposing. This feels very restricted.

This is definitely not part of the art gallery opening.

The security guy nods at Damon as he presses a button for the top level.

"You're wearing a wire?" he asks my man.

Damon snarls.

"What do you take me for? A rat?"

"Just making sure, sir," the security guy replies, a note of fear etched in his voice.

"You know my reputation," Damon says in a near whisper. "You know how much I hate a rat."

"Yes, sir."

"Good. Don't ever ask me such a fucking stupid question again."

"We are secure now," the man says as we start to ascend. "No one goes this way except on invitation from the boss."

"This boss guy sure does like showing off," I remark. Damon glares at me to remain silent.

I guess this is not the time or place to joke around.

Damon's face is the sternest it's ever been, and that's saying something.

He is worried.

Really fucking worried.

And now I definitely feel frightened.

Maybe it was a mistake coming along tonight.

Maybe there's a reason I should not be in this world.

But it's too late to turn back now. Way too freaking late.

This is definitely a long way away from Crystal River...

The elevator doors open, and I am thrust into the gangster movie of my nightmares.

43

AVA

As we step out of the elevator, way up above the art gallery, a whole squad of beefed-up dudes are stood waiting for Damon and me. They're all rocking black suits, just like Damon. Well, maybe not as dapper as him, but they sure bring the intimidation that makes me gasp.

But, instead of being scared like me, Damon simply holds his head up high and nods at the small gathering like he is their boss. Even in this daunting situation, Damon is an alpha.

Even when he is clearly nervous, Damon is as solid as a rock.

Barely any words are spoken between the males in the room. There is a palpable antagonistic tension in the air - like the men and Damon are lions readying to pounce to determine who is the king of the pack with a clawed fight. I can tell there is a hell of a lot of respect emanating from these men when it comes to Damon, even if it does seem like they want to kill him.

They also seem, dare I say, a little bit *terrified* of him.

"Shall we proceed?" Damon finally asks the room, breaking the tension.

The men all part like Moses' sea to let him and me pass through them. I feel multiple eyes on me as I walk through the crowd, but I remain strong and unblinking – just like I imagine Damon wants me to be. He holds my hand tight, giving me the energy and the will to keep walking proudly beside him. Right now, I feel like Damon's girl, and I want to do right by him. I don't want to be the weak link.

I mean, being stared at doesn't faze me, anyway. I've been stared at before. On the football field. In skimpy cheerleader uniform. The stereotypical blonde bimbo, as salivating men would see me as when I was a teenager. This moment of being stared at – in this room full of gangsters - is nothing compared to those high school experiences.

Men are always men. No matter where they are - on the football field or in a gangster's enclave. They will always try to dominate their power over women.

And women are stronger than they think.

I can be strong for Damon.

Past the beefed-up men, we enter into a long boardroom. It's something that seems like it would fit in a major company's headquarters. In the epicenter of the room sits a long dark table that stretches down the entire length of the space.

There are even more men in suits here. I want to laugh at the sight of them all: it seems like they're playing a game of how many they can fit in one room. Like clowns at a circus fitting in a tiny car. It would be funny if this was not so grim. The lights above the long boardroom table are focused down, giving the lieutenants a dramatic shadow to their serious-looking faces.

Am I meant to feel daunted? Because I freaking do feel daunted.

Everything goes silent when we enter.

Everyone turns to Damon.

There are no other women in here, only me.

Damon's reputation clearly precedes him. His presence is an announcement enough. He can command a room, that's for sure.

I look up at him. Surprisingly, he smirks at the attention.

"Hello," Damon says, greeting the small army.

He's so damn calm. So damn... *cool.* It's impressive.

And kinda sexy.

All the nervousness I saw in him earlier today has completely evaporated.

A man steps forward from the other side of the room. By his own presence, I can sense he's the leader here.

He must be that so-called Handsome Jack.

The man walks with a slow, confident grace toward us, full of implied gravitas. There's certainly some kind of enigmatic allure to him, something I can already tell would make men follow him into battle and girls fall at his feet.

As he gets closer to us, I get a better look at him. He must be in his early thirties, and I'm surprised by that. I honestly would've thought he'd be older, judging from the way Jim and Damon talk about him. Handsome Jack's deep green eyes contain an entire hidden world of mysteries. His brown hair is short and slicked back. He wears a tailored three-piece suit. Around his neck hangs a gold chain. With his style, I can see him effortlessly navigating both the criminal underground and also the high-society world that is gathered at his art gallery opening below our feet.

Yes, this definitely must be Handsome Jack.

I can see the similarities to Damon so well, but I'm sure the two men would balk at being compared like that.

Despite that, they are two wealthy, powerful, confident, and handsome young men at the head of a complex and sprawling organization. It wouldn't be an insult to compare them, even if they would object to that.

Handsome Jack's movement seems to control the other men in here - they all basically bow to him as he passes by them.

I suddenly feel very exposed without Damon's security. Naked.

I really hope this meeting goes well.

"Finally, Damon Penmayne," Handsome Jack says as he stands at the other end of his long table. "You came."

Two alpha men ready to meet.

Damon squeezes my hand. I wonder if it's for support.

Well, I'm here for him no matter what...

"Yes, I did come," Damon replies to the other gangster.

Handsome Jack smiles.

"Please sit," he says. "Both of you. There is a lot to discuss."

44

DAMON

Warily, I take a seat at the long boardroom table and beckon Ava to do so as well with a flick of my hand. Every man in the room is waiting for me as to what happens next, hanging on to every movement I make, sensing for any kind of inclination of what I might be thinking.

They are petrified of what I might do next, even if there are a dozen gangsters in this room and only one of me. My reputation precedes me, clearly. My physicality scares them.

I am used to situations like this, but even then, this feels different.

More dangerous.

And I have every reason to be cautious.

The only man not overtly wary of me in this room is Handsome Jack. He stands on the other end of the table, a smile on his face. This is the closest we've ever been to each other. He, too, is waiting for me to make the first move - the opening gambit in our little power struggle.

I am more than happy to do so.

"This is Ava," I say, gesturing to my girl next to me.

I want to introduce her first. Mark my claim over her. Make the men in this room realize just how important she is to me.

"I was wondering who this beautiful creature might be," Handsome Jack replies smoothly, nodding to Ava. A momentary jolt of both anger and protectiveness passes through me, but I quell it. He is a man I have to tread carefully with, even if he is eyeing up my girl.

"Hello," Ava says.

"My name is Handsome Jack," he tells her. "It's a nickname that's stuck and is not what I think of myself, in case you're wondering."

"I get it," Ava replies.

"The real name is Jacques, but I hate the word," he continues. "It's too... *French*. I blame my Francophile parents for that."

He's got the rich, deep voice of a man totally in control. I can tell he loves to hold a room hostage to his verbal outpourings. I don't like him at all, but I deeply respect him.

I have only seen Handsome Jack in the flesh once before. A few years ago. He is just as he was back then. Nothing's changed in his appearance. He's the son of one of the most powerful mafia families on the Eastern Seaboard – the Contes. His father was shot down by a rival just five years ago in a similar situation as my godfather, and Handsome Jack took over the running of his operations. He is known in our world to be a wily commander. A deeply intelligent strategist. Everything in this business has gone his way thus far. No man has been able to stand between Handsome Jack and his goals. He's wiped out his competition.

But those were other men. Weaker men. Men before Damon Penmayne.

I don't know exactly what he might want with me and what he has called me in for this meeting about, but I can take a few guesses. I can certainly fire off a few shots in the dark as to what Handsome Jack is looking for in this meeting between rivals.

He has been wanting us to meet with a level of urgency that is very alarming.

I've got to be careful with what I say, and so does he. This could very easily turn into a war by just the words we exchange with each other.

I don't want to go into conflict with this man, but I will protect my empire if it comes to that. I am prepared to flip this cold war into a hot one.

"I must say that it's a strange sight seeing a man like Damon Penmayne sitting in the middle of my operations," Handsome Jack says with all the calmness of a man addressing a lifelong close friend.

"I simply came for the art," I reply wryly.

"Ah, an *artist*," he says, practically licking his lips with satisfaction. "Do you like the opening downstairs? All that glitz and glamor? I must admit I hate art, but it is a good front for my business. You can move a lot of money around in the art world without any scrutiny from international authorities. It works wonders."

"Maybe I should open an art gallery across the street," I remark. "Move my own money around. Bring in some culture to this city."

Handsome Jack chuckles at that. "Maybe you should. I enjoy eating up the competition. I will need to head down soon and join my guests. There are a lot of movie stars' hands to shake, as you might expect. A lot of powerful men to schmooze."

"I thought you were above name-dropping," I say.

Handsome Jack sits down at the head of the table facing us, taking his sweet time to lower his ass in his chair.

"I've been wanting to meet up with you for some time, Damon, but you've not answered until now. Why?"

I glance at Ava. She's breathing quickly. Her chest rises and falls. Under the table, I take her hand.

"I've been busy," I say to the man.

Ava is scared, I can tell, and she has every right to be. The man sitting opposite us could well be as dangerous a man as I am. But she wanted to see me conduct business. Well, here she is. She's getting a pretty strong taste of it now.

"Let me cut the bullshit," Handsome Jack says quickly.

"Please do," I reply. "I'm starting to get bored."

The man is unfazed by that comment.

"Let me tell you what I want," he says quietly.

"Go ahead," I say.

"I want New York," he says.

Ah.

"New York is no one's to own," I reply instantly.

Handsome Jack sighs.

"Don't patronize me, Mr. Penmayne. We both know you've slowly turned out the other families to own a majority share of this city. You own casinos, bars, hotels, nightclubs. Everything except this art gallery, apparently. But there's a new power in town. *Me.* I want this city. I want you to give it to me."

"No."

"*Please?*" Handsome Jack asks, his voice dripping in sarcasm.

"You want me to hand it all over to you on a silver platter?" I ask him coolly. "Everything I've built up over the years? All to you because you've asked nicely?"

"I'll pay you handsomely, of course."

"Just like your nickname," I remark.

"I'll even throw in a few of the artworks downstairs," Handsome Jack continues, ignoring my quip. "How about that? Give you some much-needed culture."

"No."

"Would you accept a price way above market offer?" he asks.

I lean back in my seat. "I said no."

"You're really not going to budge?" he asks me.

"No."

"You're only going to say *no* to me, aren't you?"

"Yes."

Handsome Jack is silent for a long time until he finally nods at the other men in the room. Without a word from him, they all shuffle out. It's just him, Ava, and me left now.

I stare at Handsome Jack. He stares back at me.

He waits until everyone is out, and the door is safely shut, before he speaks again.

"I will have to do some horrible things to you if you don't agree to this, Damon," he whispers.

"Don't threaten him."

That was Ava, her voice loud. Her interruption surprises both Handsome Jack and me.

Us two men are silent for a moment – processing Ava's interjection - before Handsome Jack turns to me.

"Control your woman, Damon. She may be pretty, but she's got a nasty mouth."

"What did you say?" I ask him, anger already boiling up in my throat.

"You heard what I said," Handsome Jack replies curtly.

I stand up.

That's it. Meeting over.

"No one disrespects my girl," I say. "Fuck you, and fuck your offer, Jacques."

I take Ava's hand and guide her straight out of the room. *I'm not putting up with that bullshit.*

We pass through the men as we march into the elevator. No one dares to stop us.

Handsome Jack doesn't follow us.

I might have fucked all that up. I might have turned this into a war.

But no one disrespects my girl.

I'd rather this entire city burn to the ground than let anyone insult my woman in front of me.

Both Ava and I are quiet inside as we ride the elevator down the first floor. As the doors open into the main art gallery space, my girl turns to me.

"You didn't have to do that."

"I did," I reply.

"You didn't need to risk everything for my honor," she whispers.

"I do."

"You've just made a dangerous man angry," she remarks.

As if I don't know that.

"I am also a dangerous man," I reply to her. "And he just made *me* very angry."

45

AVA

THAT WHOLE NIGHTMARE with Handsome Jack was last night, but today has been like a dream - a total contrast to whatever went down between those two gangsters in that boardroom.

Have they declared war on each other? Is everything going to go to shit over Handsome Jack insulting me?

But instead of having the time to wrap my head around last night, I've been hanging out with Damon all day. He set up a spa morning at the fancy hotel just for me. I got pampered and massaged and everything a girl might want. I feel so fresh. I feel so... *sexy.*

But I still can't get over what happened at that art gallery, and what it might mean...

Tonight, Damon's taking me out for dinner. At a restaurant he, incidentally, owns.

There is no mention of what happened last night: no visible nerves from Damon - no signs of him stressing out that he might have just launched a turf war in New York City with a very powerful man.

He drives us to Midtown in one of the many sportscars he owns in his fleet. This is a restaurant just like that swanky nightclub the other night, with a long-ass line waiting to get in. But, same as before, we skip the line entirely and get waved in by security as soon as they spot Damon's famous face.

The server gives us the best table in the building, close to the live band playing and the amazing view of the lights of the skyscrapers of New York City.

"This restaurant is usually booked out a year in advance," Damon tells me as we sit across from each other.

I smile and raise my glass of wine to my lips. "And you own it, so you can get any table you like anytime you want. I bet people would kill to get a reservation here."

"It's not about the restaurant that's so special," he replies with a smirk. "It is who I am sitting across from."

That makes me blush.

Just like the rest of today, we don't bring up what went down last night. Handsome Jack's name doesn't come up at all as we sit across from each other in this trendy restaurant. It hits me that we haven't even touched on that topic since we left the art gallery opening.

None of those celebrities and politicians there last night knew what had gone on upstairs above the red carpet.

They didn't know a secret grudge had been all-but-declared between two of the biggest gangsters in the country just above their pretty, over-styled heads.

And now, even as we sit here at the restaurant exactly 24 hours after that horrible meeting, if Damon has been shaken by what went on in that boardroom, he certainly doesn't even hint at it.

Sometimes I look at the man and think that he's a totally different species to the rest of us mere mortals.

But I am really falling for him, despite my better judgment. I can't help myself, but it's happening whether I want it or not. It's just so damn hard not to when he whisks me away to spots like these, gazes into my eyes the way he does, and hangs on to every word I say, no matter how trivial.

The meal is jaw-droppingly good. Lobsters and oysters and caviar and wine. Fit for royalty.

Fit for the king and queen of New York.

It's only when we're finished that I dare utter to Damon what's been plaguing my head.

"So," I whisper as the lights of New York flicker below us, "what's going to happen next?"

"What do you mean?" Damon asks, politely nodding at the server to take away our plates.

"You know... between you and Handsome Jack? What happens now that you two had that big falling out?"

Damon shakes his head. "It wasn't a falling out," he says.

"Well, it seemed like one to me," I reply. "I may not be a gangster and all that, but I have been a teenage girl at high school. Trust me, I know a feud when I see one."

Damon smiles. "Everything is fine," he says. "Don't even give it a second's thought. I have everything under control."

I want to believe him. I want to believe that confident, nonchalant swagger of the man.

But I have a sinking feeling that everything is *not* under control.

But what can I do? I am a nobody next to these kinds of powerful men.

I have no choice but to trust Damon.

* * *

In the elevator back down from the restaurant floor, it's just us alone.

Damon takes a step back so that he's behind me. He kisses my neck. I lean back into him.

Then his lips go to my ear.

"I want to tell you something," he whispers to me.

"What is it?" I ask, closing my eyes and forgetting all about Handsome Jack and that meeting.

"There has been one thought I've had all dinner," he continues.

"Yeah?"

There's a long pause before he speaks.

"It's the most impossible thought in the world, especially to a man like me with my past and my cold heart, but I do believe I'm falling in love with you, Ava."

I turn around. Looking at his face, it's clear he's not joking.

He is deadly serious.

He is falling in love with me.

And I can tell he's waiting for my response with every fiber of his being.

The powerful gangster falling in love with the former cheerleader...

"This may be the most impossible thought with me," I reply, "considering this all started as some kind of blackmail, but I do believe I am also falling in love with you, Damon."

46

DAMON

On the drive back to the hotel, I can't keep my spare hand off her. My fingers gradually work their way up to her inner thigh. Ava offers no resistance at all to my advancement, and instead, she does the sexiest thing she can do.

She *moans*.

And that drives me crazy. Even as I'm driving.

How can a sound from her pretty little mouth send me so damn wild?

"Fuck this," I mutter, immediately pulling the car over and stopping by a park overlooking the Hudson River with the skyscrapers of Manhattan rising up around us.

"What are we doing?" Ava asks me quietly as I halt the car.

"I can't resist you, girl," I snarl. "Don't you dare moan at me like that and expect me, as a hungry man, to do nothing about it. I'm going to fuck you right here and now."

I kiss her. Slow at first, and then with a more urgent speed. Her tongue is in my mouth as I greedily undo her seatbelt. It goes loose, and I wrap my hand around her, squeezing her breast under her dress.

She moans *again*. In my mouth.

And that drives me even more crazy.

Her chest tilts out, encouraging me to continue playing with her supple breasts. My fingers find her tit and I pinch it, eliciting another sexy moan from her.

Fuck. Does she know what she does to me?

Our lips part.

"Someone could see us doing this," Ava remarks in a whisper. "Anyone driving past could glance our way and they would see us doing this in your car..."

"They could," I reply. "And that's what makes it thrilling, don't you think?"

She bites her lip and nods with wide eyes. "Yes."

"You like that we could be discovered doing this?" I ask her.

"Yes."

"You like being so dirty?"

"Yes. I'm *so* wet, Damon. Why don't you do something about it?"

"Get on me," I command darkly. "Let me fuck you. You're such a good girl for me, let me make you cum as good as the good girl you are. Spread open your thighs for me."

I pull the lever by my side, sending my seat back to let me lie down in the car.

Ava, spurred on by my command, hastily and eagerly undoes my belt to let my hard cock spring loose, and then she slides over to sit on me, letting me penetrate her deeply in one smooth motion.

We both let out a moan.

Every time with her feels so damn good. Why would I ever let a girl like this go?

And then she's rocking against me, her hip rolling against my body as she fucks me inside my car.

It's true – anyone could see us like this.

But no one is around to witness my girl fucking me in my car.

I lie back and look up at Ava as she lets herself go free. Her blonde hair cascades down as she sways against me, leading us both into elation.

I need to touch her.

My hand reaches up, my thumb rubbing against her soft plump lips.

She takes my thumb into her willing mouth and begins to suck.

She moans again.

She closes her eyes.

She looks so fucking beautiful.

Her pretty face, sucking on my thumb, makes me enamored with every sexy part of her.

Makes me go over the edge.

She makes me lose control. Every damn time.

And I'm finishing with a groan as Ava sighs in ecstasy.

"Fuck," I whisper as I unload. "*Fuck.*"

Ava opens her eyes and stares at me. My hand drops from her mouth. I'm completely spent.

"You like that?" she asks. "You like what I was able to do to you in your car?"

I nod. "Yep."

"I like to please you," Ava says, breathless but clearly elated. "I like to make my man happy."

I snarl.

"Oh, you most certainly do," I say.

"I do?"

"Yes, Ava. You make me feel so fucking good."

"Show me," she says. "Show me how much I make you happy."

I summon her to lean over and get closer with a flick of my finger.

She does so.

And then I kiss her for a *very* long time.

And now I'm the one who's moaning.

That's proof enough of how happy she makes me.

47

AVA

WE MAKE our way back to Crystal River aboard Damon's private jet, soaring high through the night sky above America. When we finally touch down, it is in the shroud of darkness that blankets our hometown. The air is crisp, and the town feels peaceful and serene under the cover of night. We disembark from the jet. Damon holds my hand. I feel safe.

We hop into Damon's sleek, high-speed car, and the engine roars to life. The piercing beams of the car's headlights breaking the darkness and the occasional glimpse of trees that line our route back into the main drag of Crystal River are the only things I see. Each flash of foliage adds a rhythmic punctuation to the otherwise uninterrupted blackness, a stark contrast to the glitz and glamour of the world we've just left behind.

It's so weird going from that extravagant world to this small town home.

But, as long as I'm with Damon, I am happy.

"I want to take the scenic route," Damon tells me as we speed around a corner.

"What do you mean?" I ask him.

"I want to drive past my brewery," he replies.

I turn to him and place my hand on the back of his neck, stroking him. "I'd like that."

As we turn a few more corners heading in the direction of the brewery, I start to see a bright color above the tops of the trees.

The one thing penetrating the night sky.

Red.

A deep, violent red.

"Is that... a *fire*?" I remark, straining my head forward closer to the car window to better see the alarming color streak across the sky in front of us.

No way. Fire? At the brewery?

My man is already thinking far ahead of me. Damon is deadly calm, even when processing the deadly fact that his most prized possession might be in flames. He presses a button on his steering wheel and is immediately speaking to Jim.

"I think there's a fire at the brewery," he says to his trusted lieutenant.

"A fire?" Jim's gravelly voice is clear through the loud-speakers. He's businesslike, not alarmed in the slightest.

The two men have clearly dealt with panic before. They know how to handle a crisis.

"I can't make it out," Damon continues, "but I think it's where the brewery should be. We're heading to it now. Better send backup, and better make it fast."

"Okay," Jim replies. "I'll send out a security team and alert the emergency services. You're nearly there?"

"Yes."

"Don't do anything reckless, Damon."

"I won't."

"Wait until the security team gets there. I know what you're like. Please don't."

"I won't, Jim."

Damon hangs up with a growl and then starts to shoot toward the brewery, taking us at breakneck speeds around bends in the direction of the fire.

He doesn't say a word as we spin around dangerous country roads.

He is thinking, and I am freaking out.

Fire?

Could it really be? The brewery?

How?

And why?

And then we see it.

Damon's brewery. Or what's left of it.

And it's with a sinking feeling that I realize I was right.

It is a fire.

Most of the beautiful building is in flames. Roaring, uncontrollable flames.

Damon curses under his breath as we speed toward it even faster. He can't help himself.

"Slow down, Damon," I cry out. "We might crash. Pull over."

And he does. Just at the entrance. We can feel the heat emanating from the burning buildings, even from here.

We are both breathing heavily, unable to believe what our eyes are telling us as we come to a stop by the open gates of the complex.

Damon's pride and joy is really, truly on fire.

Fuck. This can't be real. This must be a nightmare.

"Someone's done this," Damon murmurs. They are the first words he's spoken since hanging up on Jim.

"No," I reply. "It must be an accident. Who would do this, Damon?"

He turns to me. I see the fire burning in his eyes. It's as vicious as the real one burning in front of us.

"We both know who might do this, Ava," he whispers.

Handsome Jack...

And then we see him. Both of us do: a man running from the flames not even a hundred yards from us. He hasn't noticed us, but we've certainly spotted him.

He's a dark figure against the roaring inferno, but we can pick him out.

Who is he? What's he up to?

Damon's entire attention is on him.

Whatever this man is doing here in the dead of night, it isn't good. He might be the culprit Damon is looking for.

And at the moment I think that, Damon unclips his seatbelt and is unlocking his door; his eyes totally focused on the shadow of the man leaping away from the flames.

"Stop, Damon," I say, reaching for him. "Wait for Jim and the rest of the team. He said not to do anything reckless..."

"I can't wait that long, Ava," my man replies with anger burning in his voice.

"Please don't," I plead.

"I need to go, Ava."

"I won't forgive you if you hurt someone," I whisper. "Or yourself."

Damon nods toward the fire and the stranger. "He wasn't expecting anyone to be on the scene this fast, and certainly not me. He might escape. I can't let him go. This is my chance to end this."

I look at my man directly. "We're through if you do this. *Please*, Damon."

I truly mean it. I told him I didn't want to witness him

getting in harm's way. I have never been more sure about something in my life. I told him I didn't want to witness violence. I do *not* want to see Damon in the fire beating up this man.

I really do not want to see violence.

Damon stares at me for a long time. I can't imagine what he's thinking behind those cold, dark eyes of his. The fire behind those eyes is still burning brightly as he finally comes to a decision.

He can't do this.

But then he's running away. Out of the car. Toward this man.

Away from me.

Away from my command. Away from my resolution...

We're through if you do this.

I watch him sprint through the flames. I watch him tackle this man to the ground. I watch Damon's fists unload into this man as he lies in the hot dirt. Constant punching.

I witness his violence.

He is on top of the man. He is in full control. He is unleashing his entire physical strength on the intruder.

I see Damon as the criminal he is. I see his brute power. His anger. His dark side.

And I can't look away.

I am in shock.

That is not Damon. Please tell me that's not Damon. That's not the man I know.

But he is the man I believed him to be when I didn't know him - the man that everyone in Crystal River has heard the stories of, the criminal with the cold heart, the man who didn't give a single fuck about anyone else, the man I had come to believe didn't *actually* exist.

But there he is, beating up a man in front of me.

And then there are cars pulling up behind me. Damon's men have arrived.

I open the car door and step out.

I move like I'm in a trance. Jim is here. I see him through the smoke and the bright flames. He comes rushing toward me.

"Are you okay, Ava?" he asks.

"I need a driver," I say in a monotone voice. "I'm going home. Right now. Without Damon."

48

DAMON

I HAVE him tied to a chair - this man who I found at my brewery in the dead of night as it burned. I knew for certain that he was involved in the fire.

And I was not wrong.

I've brought him back here, to my mansion on the outskirts of Crystal River, far away from the law. Down here in my basement, there is no rules of some government we must abide by: only what I command and deem what's right. My kingdom.

The man has blood streaming down one side of his face. Some of it is his. Some of it is mine from when I lunged at him in the fire and smoke to tackle him to the ground.

I don't remember much from that moment when I left Ava in the car to chase after this man. I simply remember my senses going haywire. Burning. Punching. *Anger*.

I leave the man tied in the chair and head upstairs, locking the basement door behind me and nodding to my security to make sure no one goes in or out of that room. I head into my office and immediately pour myself a whiskey.

Fuck this.

I am still so angry. It hasn't faded since I first saw my brewery up in flames on the drive back from the airport.

Over the last hour, I've gotten the name of the man who sent that man downstairs to burn the brewery down. *Success.* It was easy getting the information out of the bleeding man, especially because he knew I was the one who came out of nowhere to take him down as the brewery burned down around us.

He knew exactly who I was the moment he set eyes upon me, and that made extracting information out of him relatively simple. He knew what might happen if he didn't talk. He knew all about Damon Penmayne. I didn't have to resort to any interrogation techniques.

The man who sent him is exactly who I feared it would be.

Handsome Jack.

For fuck's sake.

That was the name the man squealed over and over and over when he could finally glimpse a real look at my face in the dim light of the basement. The act of burning down my brewery late at night was all Handsome Jack's revenge on me turning down his offer to buy out what I own in New York. And that revenge was *fast*, I'd give him that.

But Handsome Jack and his destructive revenge is not what has made me truly angry. *No.*

I've lost Ava.

My girl.

That's what makes me furious.

The first thing I said to Jim when he arrived on the scene of the burning brewery was nothing to do with what was happening around us, but a question about something very different.

"Where is Ava?"

When Jim told me she had been driven back home at her request, I had snapped at him in a way that surprised even Jim. I've never lost control with my second in command like that before, but I was so damn incensed that I had lost her.

She's left me?

I tried calling her, but she never picked up. And I know why. She spelled it out pretty clearly in the car and at the signing of the agreement between us: she would leave me if I committed violence in front of her.

And I had done so. In the clearest of ways.

And now she is gone - just as she said she would be if I dared commit an act of violence in front of her.

The one thing I care about most in the entire world, and I've ruined it all with my desire for revenge.

I storm into the restroom next to my office and furiously wash the bright blood off my knuckles. I glance up at my harried face in the mirror.

Fuck, Damon. You've fucked all this up. First your brewery, and now your girl.

Well, I'm going to fix it all. I will. I'm going to get Ava back.

49

DAMON

I KNOCK on the front door, hoping with every fiber of my being that it is *her* who opens up.

But it's not Ava who greets me, it's her father.

I was not expecting this when I put my fist to the door, and I am momentarily and uncharacteristically taken off guard seeing the man's face in front of me.

Ava's father also seems shaken by seeing me, and I'm not surprised. His debt collector: here in the flesh at the front door to his house. No wonder his expression strongly suggests that he is currently experiencing a violent heart attack just by my mere presence.

We stand here at the front door, staring at each other for a full silent moment before one of us dares speak.

"You look nervous," I remark to the man.

"Damon Penmayne?" Ava's father is obviously very, *very* concerned by my appearance here. It's etched in his voice like permanent ink.

"Don't worry about me turning up like this at your

home," I say. "I am not here for you, sir. I'm sure Ava has told you that I consider your debts to me forgiven?"

"She's not here."

"Who? Ava? Come on, I know she's in there."

"You're not going to see her," Ava's father says.

I look at the man. "I want to see her. I usually get what I want."

The man shakes his head and mutters to the ground. "I don't know what's happened recently with her. I don't know why she's with you, or what she has done with you these past few weeks. I don't know what has happened between you two. But whatever you have done against her, you should know that you should just walk away right now. Walk away from this front door. Go back to your world. Forget about her. She doesn't want to see you."

What the hell?

I want to let loose with this man, but I hold myself back. He is her father, after all.

I take in a deep breath.

No need to lose my temper. That's not going to help anything. Calm yourself, Damon.

"I understand," I say. And I honestly *do* understand - Ava is angry with me, but I need to respect that feeling even if every bone in my body wants to fight to the death for her.

Even if I will do literally *anything* to get her back.

"I think you should leave her alone, Damon," her father says.

I nod. "If that's her wish," I mutter.

Fuck.

It's hard doing this, saying those words. Backing down from a challenge is *very* unnatural for me.

But it must be done if that's what my girl wants.

Ava's father closes the front door on me.

And I am left here on the suburban street. Like a loser. A man tossed aside.

I don't like this.

She really doesn't want to see me. And I really have to respect that decision.

No matter what I've done in my life, no matter how much money I have made or power I have accumulated, all of that simply pales in comparison to this moment and the loss of the love of my life.

I stare at the closed door, not moving.

Nothing has ever hit as hard as this moment.

The world seems empty without Ava in it.

A black hole of nothingness...

50

FIVE WEEKS LATER

AVA

CLUTCHED IN MY HAND, my phone vibrates angrily at me. It makes me jump. I am really no good with surprises.

Tutting at myself, I check what the phone is desperately trying to notify me about. It's a message from my calendar.

DAMON AGREEMENT ENDS TODAY.

OH. Right. *Of course.*

That whole contract thing with Damon was supposed to conclude today, according to the terms we laid out when we signed the thing.

Well, isn't that crazy...

I must've completely forgotten to delete that upcoming notification when everything with him went... *haywire* a few weeks ago. When I decided never to speak to him again.

I overheard Damon and my dad's conversation that night five weeks ago when he rocked up to my family house unannounced. My dad had lied to Damon at the door - I was actually there, at the house. I was standing by the stairs, out of view of the man. I clearly heard Dad telling him that I never wanted to see him again.

It was the truth.

And it also kinda... *wasn't.*

Ever since that night, Damon has kept true to his word – like he always did – and he hasn't even attempted to contact me in any way since then. It has been complete radio silence from him. He clearly respects me enough not to intrude or step on my wishes.

But I have to admit there is a part of me – buried deep inside – that does *kinda* want him to reach out.

I would really love to hear that deep, silky voice of his one more time...

And sometimes, I doubt myself. I question if leaving Damon that night at the brewery fire was the right thing to do. Sometimes, when the world is quiet and I'm left on my own, I spin through a whole range of thoughts about what happened. Was I overreacting by leaving? Was that me defining my boundaries, or just me being selfish?

Do I really want him out of my life forever?

But then I remember seeing Damon lay into that man as the fire raged around them. His fists flying. His anger. The violence on display.

Yeah, it was the right thing to go. I told him I didn't want to witness violence. That was a deal-breaker, and he knew that. And he still broke it.

He can't expect to come crawling back to me, thinking everything will be fine. He crossed that red line, and even I am smart enough to realize that it'll only happen again if I let him back into my life. I've seen enough posts on social media to know that men who break one non-negotiable will only break others.

In the weeks since he rocked up to Dad's place trying to get back with me, I've tried my best to forget about Damon, and all the memories we made together, and focus instead on that last night when it all fell apart. That night at the brewery fire. I focus on how Damon broke his word on that night and committed an act of violence in front of me, despite my protests.

I have really tried my best to forget him.

Since then, I've gone back to college. I've moved back in with Olivia at the dorms, back in my old college bed. Just like the time before Dad told me about his debts and I had my heart broken by Luke.

Like the time before I met Damon Penmayne.

And now I am back in class, studying like a good student for once in my life.

Well, that's where I am meant to be heading to - back to class. I'm crossing the CRU campus when that reminder on my phone goes off in my hands.

Being a good student has come with feeling good about myself, but it also has its downsides. The last few weeks have been *boring*. Like, real *rip-your-hair-out* boring. I was swept up off my feet into a gangster's world in a sudden strange whirlwind and now I've thudded back down to reality with a real crash on my butt.

Sometimes, in the dead of night, when it feels like the whole world is asleep except for me, I allow myself the momentary indulgence to think about Damon. I think about giving him a second chance, and what that might mean. But I know you can't change a man like him: a man with violence embedded in his heart and in his history. My own heart has been broken too many times to dare risk it all again. I don't know if my little heart could take it.

I clutch my phone in my hand and continue my march across campus. I'm about to reach the main door of the lecture hall building when I am stopped dead in my tracks by none other than Luke.

Ha. Talking about broken hearts...

"Jesus," I exclaim, surprised at the sudden appearance of the man I've come to fear in the last few weeks.

Damn, Ava. Why are you so awkward?

My ex grins at me.

"I'm sorry," he says confidently, raising up his palms as if in surrender. He's still smiling as if he's some recent convert to some happy-go-lucky hippy cult.

"You just gave me a shock," I mutter.

I eye him warily. I'm nervous as to what he may do, or even worse, *say*.

And Luke seems to know this. He keeps his hands raised up.

In that new, super smiley way.

"I don't mean to ambush you, Ava," he says cheerily. "I saw you walking and thought I would come over and speak to you."

"What for?" I ask. My voice coming out is more abrasive than I imagined it to be in my head.

"To say sorry," Luke continues. "I'm sorry for the way I acted... *before*. I have not been in a good state recently, but I'm working to change things. I want to start things over again with you."

"You threatened me with spreading rumors," I reply, remaining strong.

Luke shakes his head. "I am sorry for that. I didn't actually go through with it, if you must know."

"It still doesn't change a thing," I say.

"And I don't expect it to," Luke replies. "You're justified in being angry with me. I just wanted to come and say sorry and clear the air between us."

"I've got to go to class," I murmur, trying my best to end this weird conversation. I know Luke. He's a boy full of testosterone and ego; the last thing he might ever be is *sorry*, no matter how big his smile may be. I'm wary enough not to fall for his charms.

"Could we go for a drink?" Luke asks delicately. "Tonight?"

"Why would I even think about something like that, Luke, after the way you've acted?" I question him.

Luke looks at me for a moment. His eyes are soft. He's looking at me in the same way he used to when we first started dating as teenagers. He's looking at me in the same way that made me fall in love with him.

"I feel like I owe you," he says. "I want to apologize, Ava. Really. For everything. In a truthful and serious way."

I sigh.

I've got nothing on tonight, and my life *has* been boring these last few weeks as I've tried to be a good little student. Maybe hearing a real apology from Luke might put some closure on things. Maybe it might help me sleep better at night so that I am no longer thinking about certain men.

Maybe it might actually be an okey time for me to find a conclusion to that part of my life.

Fine. What the hell.

"Sure," I say. "I'm free tonight. One drink, though. And I want it noted I'm doing this just so that you can say sorry properly."

Luke smiles one more time. A genuine smile for once.

And I can't help but feel a short little twinge of something to see him happy that I want to go out with him.

"Perfect," he says. "I'll swing by your dorm room at eight to pick you up."

51

DAMON

I CROUCH by the stone wall.

I am shrouded in the enveloping darkness of the night, exactly as I had meticulously schemed when this daring plan first took shape in my mind.

No one can see me.

I hope.

I really should not be here.

This is dangerous. This is trespassing.

If I were caught here, I'd be dead without a shadow of a doubt.

And I know it. *Oh, I really know it.*

The stone wall is cold against my face, but I am forced to stay here in this uncomfortable position as I wait and wait and wait.

Waiting until the guard – unsuspecting of my presence – slowly walks past the wall on the other side of me.

I patiently squat in cover until he is safely gone before I

leap over the wall and head straight toward the large building.

Directly toward my goal.

I reach the building's wall undetected.

My breath is quick.

My heart rate is fast.

I really should not be here.

It's cold tonight. The stars are dim. It is a perfect night to sneak into a heavily fortified compound on the edges of the city.

No one would ever believe someone could actually *sneak* in here.

But they did not take me into account.

I am a man who, when he puts his mind to an impossible task, executes it with planning and precision.

No one would ever believe someone could infiltrate Handsome Jack's private mansion, but they haven't met *me*.

I'm here, on the outskirts of New York City, to get my revenge on Handsome Jack: the man who burnt my brewery to the ground. I want him to pay for what he did.

Handsome Jack's place is an opulent mansion; it's all perfectly crafted balconies and terraces overlooking fountains and a manicured yard. I would even dare to say it is similar to my own home back in Crystal River.

The architecture is done in an Italian Renaissance style, with towering columns supporting the grand portico entranceway. The rest of the building is a grey stone.

The security here is a heavy presence. As can be expected. Men in black uniforms with automatic rifles. Dozens of them scattered around the place on constant surveillance.

He really doesn't think anyone could break in here, does he?

I cautiously make my way around the wall of his

mansion to one of the locked back doors, shuffling alongside the wall to keep me out of sight of any wandering eyes belonging to a security guard. I've been planning this operation for days, barely eating or sleeping, as I map out this attack on my rival. I've studied maps of this building - everything that Jim and I could find of the layout of this mansion.

But preparation is nothing when you are actually out in the field executing your plan.

Anything can go wrong now, and it can go wrong spectacularly. The odds are against me.

I really should not be here.

I see the door I want further along the wall, just as I planned it would be.

But there is a *slight* problem...

A security guard smoking just outside - an unexpected obstacle that really puts my plan in jeopardy. It looks like he isn't going anywhere, and I realize with a dread that if he simply turns to his right, he will see me clear as day.

Fuck.

I curse myself for getting into such a precarious situation. I was too eager to break in that I didn't take a moment to consider my actions. I moved too damn fast along the wall.

I did not stick to the plan. I should have been slower. I should've never taken a risk.

If this man sees me, I am dead. Without a doubt. I see the rifle ready in his hands, locked and loaded. Handsome Jack's men do not play around, especially with intruders in the man's private space, just like my own men.

So I take the last resort.

I pull out my own gun.

And I shoot the man.

But not with a bullet, but with an old-school tranquilizer dart that I had Jim sort out for me before embarking on this venture. I'm not going to kill these guards when there are other ways to take them out of action. The dart embeds itself into the man's neck and he immediately drops – limp – into a nearby hedge. He'll be back awake in a few hours, unharmed but with a raging headache and a sore pinprick in the side of his neck.

Jim did not want me to do this tonight; he explicitly warned me about taking my revenge on my rival. I told him I was going to do it. I told him I needed to do it. He, like all the other times I've had a crazy idea, simply sighed and immediately went about helping me with the utmost professionalism and skill.

And that's why he's my second in command.

I approach the door to Handsome Jack's mansion. It's locked, as expected. But that proves no impediment to me. I've picked many locks in my life, most a hell of a lot harder than this one.

As the door swings open, I am suddenly reminded of a face.

Ava's face.

The girl whose absence has caused me to act like this - getting obsessive about this revenge. Her absence has caused a void to open up deep in my life, one that can't be filled by doing what I'm doing now. But what else can I do? I've tried to give her the space she clearly wants since she left me, but there has not been a moment since that night at her father's house when I haven't thought about her in some form. The image of her face has been like a constant background in my eyes, and nothing I can do can shake her from my thoughts.

I progress through the mansion. Little is known about the internal floor plan of this place, but I do know where I am heading.

Upstairs.

I pass by lavish rooms. This building has been in the hands of Handsome Jack's wealthy family for generations, and it shows. The foyer is grandiose, with high ceilings decorated with frescos depicting ancient Roman gods and myths. Tapestries don the walls. There is a carved marble fireplace positioned as the centerpiece of the room.

This is the den of my rival.

I am careful. Very careful. I hear people talking, so I keep low and quiet. I avoid lights.

Handsome Jack is very much tied in with his family. This building has clearly been in hands going back generations. It's old, but I can see the man has tried to update it in a modern style and with modern security systems.

But those systems prove no match for me.

I pass by a hallway full of art and sculptures. It's clear Handsome Jack views himself as a cultured man, despite his day business. No wonder he opened an art gallery. No wonder he tries to emplace himself amongst the stars and celebrities and artists of the city when he thinks of himself as more of an art collector than a man who orders deaths for a living.

He values the high life.

And he thinks that no one could break inside his little fortress. Ha.

I make my way upstairs until I'm in front of the door to the room I've been looking for.

Handsome Jack's bedroom.

I sneak in.

He's asleep in the middle of a large bed.

There he is.

I saunter right up to him and place my trusty knife against his throat. The cold black steel against his neck wakes up the man.

His eyes flutter open.

He sees me.

He does not move.

I raise my finger to my lips to shush him. Handsome Jack understands me perfectly well, even in the dark.

He doesn't scream. He doesn't shout. He is, after all, a professional.

He understands that I am here and that I am dangerous, and that – right now - I have his life in my hands.

"I will get straight to the point," I whisper to the prone man. Handsome Jack doesn't reply. He just stares at me. He's acutely aware I currently hold his fate on the edge of my blade. He wants to hear what I have to say. "I know you ordered the brewery fire. But you didn't anticipate I would be there at that time, so I found your man. I'm sure you already know that, and I'm sure you didn't know that I could sneak into your mansion when you're sleeping. I simply want you to know that I can do this, and I can do it again. There's nothing stopping me from doing anything else to you. And I want to let you know that this would normally be the moment when I end your life, but I made a promise to someone important in my life. I'm a changed man now."

Ava wouldn't want me to kill Handsome Jack, even after everything he's done to ruin me. She wouldn't want me to slit his throat.

And, for some insane reason I can barely understand, I am still following her wishes, even if I haven't seen her in weeks.

She's still got a hold over me...

And so I simply nod at Handsome Jack, lower my knife back into its sheath, and I silently walk out of his bedroom, down the stairs, and out the front door.

I sent Handsome Jack a message he can't ignore, and that's all I need to do.

He won't be bothering me anymore.

It's only when I am a few miles away in the dense forest that surrounds Handsome Jack's secluded mansion that I press a beeper on my belt.

It's sending a signal to a helicopter. My helicopter. Telling it to come and get me.

And a short time later, it does; landing in a clearing in the darkness.

I jump in. Unexpectedly, Jim is waiting for me in the other passenger seat.

"I didn't think you'd be here, Jim," I say to him as a kind of greeting. "I didn't kill him, though, if that's what you're here to hear. I'm a changed man."

My second in command turns to me with a solemn expression.

"I'm not here about Handsome Jack. I need to talk to you," he says. "Urgently. I have something important to tell you. Something about Ava."

52

DAMON

"Okay, tell me."

Jim gazes at me from across the helicopter, carefully considering how to share what's on his mind. It must be something deadly serious if he's taking his time to reply.

It's about Ava.

What has happened to her? Is she alright?

"I've been watching Miss Matson," Jim says.

I immediately see red.

"*What?* You've been watching her?"

"I've been following her since you two... ended your agreement," Jim continues. "For security reasons, I hasten to add."

"You've been stalking her without my permission? Without *her* permission?"

I am so angry. Jim has gone behind my back to do this, and only now he's telling me? Weeks on?

It's not right. It's unprofessional of him.

I can't have him undermining my authority, no matter how well-intentioned he might think his actions are.

This is not how I do things.

"Hold on," Jim says, raising his hands as we fly high above rural New York State, anticipating my anger. "I needed to do this because I saw she was also being followed, and not by us."

"Who?" I ask. "Who was following her?"

"That boy she was with. Her ex."

"The motherfucker..."

"I was worried about his intentions and so I ran a thorough background check on him," Jim explains.

"And?"

"Nothing serious or out of the ordinary," he says.

"So why are you bothering me with all this?" I ask, my voice rising. This excuse for following Ava will not be forgotten, but I am more interested - for the moment - in whatever dirt Jim has managed to find on the guy. The last thing I want is for Ava to end up hurt over her ex, especially if he is violent.

Especially if he is stalking her.

She'll need to know. She'll need to protect herself.

"I had a run-through of this Luke Abbott's social media, and... well, you just need to see this. I can't explain it."

And then Jim hands me a print-out.

It's a photo of a man.

And though the years might have aged him somewhat, the memory of that face has been forever seared into my mind since my first – and last – encounter with him.

It's a photo of the man who killed my godfather.

The man I've been hunting for years, and who I could never find. The man who has eluded me for a lifetime.

I see his face in the photo in my hands.

What the hell does he have to do with Ava?

53

AVA

LUKE HAS TAKEN me to a restaurant in town. Very fancy. He *definitely* wouldn't have attempted such a nice date when we were properly together. No way in hell. Back then, it was typically drinks at his place or long make-out sessions in his car in one of the more secluded high school hangout spots on the edge of town. Such a teenage thing. Nothing fancy at all. Nothing like an actual freaking restaurant, with seats and menus and servers and everything.

"This is... *nice*," I say as we settle into our table by the window. Outside is dark; you can barely see the rest of the town. The restaurant is lit by candlelight, giving it a romantic vibe. I know for a certain fact that I am *not* going to sleep with my ex tonight, but – sitting across from him - I do allow myself the briefest of moments to relive our past and all the happy times I've had with him. Times before he changed. Happy, carefree times before he dumped me for the most petty of reasons...

"I wanted to take you somewhere nice," he says with a smile.

And there is the old Luke back - that popular gorgeous teenage boy who'd showed me interest. I can see him sitting in front of me.

It's like a rain cloud has lifted and I can see the sun again.

"What are you thinking of having?" I ask, glancing down at the menu to avoid his intense stare any longer. I don't want to betray any softening of my feelings toward him.

I'm not thinking of him in any way romantic or anything, but I *am* unstiffening. In a cautious way. I'm finding it easier to remember our past and not the last few weeks.

"Let's not think about food just yet," Luke says, gently lowering my menu to get a good look at me. "Let's just be together for a moment."

"What kind of a moment?" I ask.

Luke chuckles. "A moment like we used to have together."

I've promised myself I won't fall for this. And I won't...

"It's been a long time, Luke. A lot has happened since we were together."

"And I still miss you," he replies.

I look at him then, in the eyes.

And I really do see the old Luke. The star quarterback I fell for all those years ago. It feels like an eternity since I've last spoken to that boy.

The rain cloud is truly gone.

"You make it hard for me to miss you, Luke," I whisper.

He shakes his head.

"You've not changed one bit since high school, Ava, you know that?"

"No..."

"Still so stubborn," Luke says.

"I'm not stubborn," I reply.

"See? *Exhibit A.* You're so determined to get your own way, Ava."

"And you're not?" I question him.

"No, you're right," Luke says. "I like to get what I'm owed."

"Are you talking about me?" I ask.

"I just want things to go back to the way things were," he says. "Before... all *this.*"

"All of what, Luke?"

"You know what I'm saying, Ava."

I take in a deep breath.

"You're talking about Damon Penmayne, right?" I ask. "You might as well say his name out loud when you hate him so much. We might as well bring the topic of him out in the open if we're just going to skirt around the edges, yeah?"

Luke goes silent for a moment. I see anger flash behind his eyes. His fist on the table clenches hard enough for it to turn red.

And then he says it. The sentence that breaks us.

"Tell me, Ava, in those weeks with him, did you let Damon fuck you?"

My mouth drops open.

"You... can't... ask *that.*"

I'm absolutely gob-smacked, completely caught off guard by his aggressive tone and the derogatory words spewing from his mouth. The sheer intensity of it all leaves me practically shell-shocked, struggling to process the verbal onslaught.

No, no, no. This is not how I expected tonight to go.

Scrap what I said earlier. This is not nice at all.

"I want to go," I say.

"We haven't even got drinks yet, Ava," Luke mutters.

Why did I let this happen? Why did I agree to this?

"I said I want to go, okay?"

"You want me to drive you home?" he asks.

"No," I reply, my voice quivering. "I can get back by myself."

"Well, how are you gonna get home?" he asks me. "If you're not going to let me drive you. There'll be no taxis around now, you know that."

I inhale another long, deep breath, my chest tightening as I teeter on the brink of tears. The weight of the moment threatens to spill over, and I can sense the emotion welling up, just waiting for the chance to escape.

Please don't make a scene here, Ava. Please don't cry in front of your ex. Not him.

"Okay, just drive me home," I finally splutter. "Don't talk to me, just get me home. I want to go home. I want to go back to the dorm."

We silently walk out of the restaurant, but not together. I'm way ahead of Luke. I don't even bother holding the front door open for him. He follows me, still. I don't look behind, but I can feel his intimidating presence behind me all the way to his car.

It is so dark outside. I feel so very alone.

I reach for the car door handle, but it's still locked. Luke hasn't even pulled out his keys yet.

Instead of unlocking the vehicle, Luke grabs my outstretched wrist.

"You're disgusting for allowing that Penmayne to fuck you," he snarls at me under his breath.

This is what he's been thinking all night. *This* is what he's been wanting to tell me. *This* is the sole reason he invited me out tonight, to smear those words into my face in the dark.

I want to break free from his grip, but he is holding me tight.

Those tears I've been holding back so valiantly start to bubble up to the surface. I'm going to lose my cool any second...

"Please let me go, Luke."

"You really let him fuck you, didn't you?"

"Please... let me go..."

But, deep down, I know he won't let me free.

Oh no.

54

AVA

Iᴛ's at this moment when I am at my most vulnerable with Luke's tight grip around my wrist and I feel at my most frightened, that the most unexpected thing happens.

Damon Penmayne appears.

And he doesn't just appear, he seemingly *emerges* out of the darkness like some kind of vampire. Out of the shadows like some kind of demon…

And straight into our confrontation.

He doesn't say a thing.

Neither Luke nor I have the briefest of moments to even process what is happening before Damon slams into Luke, pushing the former quarterback against his own car with the slightest of ease. The noise of Luke crashing into the car reverberates around the quiet streets of Crystal River. All six-foot-plus of my ex crumbles in front of my eyes as his body is flung around by the man who held me in custody not even six weeks ago.

And then I'm screaming.

"What the hell are you doing, Damon?"

Damon doesn't even look at me.

He doesn't even *acknowledge* me.

He simply walks past me and straight up to Luke lying in a sprawled mess on the ground. I can just make out that my ex is still conscious but groaning in pain as Damon leans over him with a burning snarl.

"Take me to your family home, Luke," the crime boss sneers in a near whisper.

My ex merely lets out another groan. I can't believe how easily Damon knocked down the star quarterback. Damon is so fucking strong.

But what is he doing here, and why does he want to go to Luke's family house?

"Take me to your home, Luke. Right now."

There's another groan from Luke instead of anything approaching articulation.

"Lay off it," I exclaim to Damon. "Can't you see he's hurt? You threw him against the freaking car."

But the man doesn't care, and he doesn't listen to me. Instead, Damon reaches for Luke, grabbing his arm and forcibly pulling him to his feet with no regard for what the former quarterback might be feeling.

"Show me the way to your family home, Luke Abbott."

My ex is struggling to speak from the shock. He only makes out a few words.

"What... why..."

"Leave him alone," I say to Damon, but he still doesn't pay me any attention. "What are you doing? Why are you here? What do you want from Luke?"

Still not even a look my way from the crime boss.

Damon pulls Luke around the car, taking him away from me.

But I follow behind as the two men shuffle into the

darkness. I'm not going to give up on this. Damon must think I'm crazy if I'm just going to let him carry Luke away to do *God-knows-what* to him.

Damon notices I'm close. He turns around. It's the first time he has looked at me.

"Stay here, Ava," he commands. "Don't follow me."

His voice is dark. Controlled. Menacing.

It's a warning as much as a command.

I shake my head at that.

Hell no to that.

"Wherever you're taking him, I'm going," I reply.

Damon says nothing to that.

I continue to follow them as Damon forces Luke around the corner and toward his own parked car.

He must've been following me tonight if he's parked so close. He must have been waiting for us to leave the restaurant. He was waiting to strike. But what does he want to do with my ex?

I'm worried about what Damon is planning to do with my ex. A million scenarios race through my head as we make our way to his car. Is he actually going to kill Luke? I wouldn't put it past him. And why does he want Luke to take him to his family home? What's that all about?

I am so fucking confused.

With his spare hand, Damon opens his passenger car door and forces Luke inside the vehicle. In response, I open the back passenger door and slide inside as well. Luke is groaning and still not making out any recognizable words.

Damon gives me a hard look as I strap myself into the backseat. He clearly doesn't want me here, but he can't do a damn thing about it. I am going to be here, no matter what happens. I am not going to wait behind and leave Luke to Damon's violent hands.

Whatever he's got planned for Luke, I'll be here to witness it.

"Have you been following me?" I ask him when he finally sits in the driver's seat and ignites the engine. "What are you doing here tonight? Were you waiting for Luke and me? I can't believe you would do that to him. I told you *no violence.* I wanted you out of my life, and here you are - breaking your word yet again."

"You should be thanking me for saving you from this boy," Damon mutters under his breath.

"Nope," I reply. "Not in a million years. I'm capable of handling myself."

"Right."

"I wanted you to leave me alone. Forever," I say to the man's reflection in the rearview mirror. "So why are you back here for me?"

"I am not here for you, Ava," Damon says coolly. "I'm here for Luke's father."

And that makes me silent.

Luke's father?

What the hell?

55

DAMON

EUGENE ABBOTT HASN'T CHANGED in all the years since I last saw him on the worst day of my life.

He's still the same man whose face is permanently etched on my memory.

I burst through the door of Luke's family home, located not far from the restaurant where he's taken Ava on that pathetic so-called *date*. It was a short drive with the boy strapped in next to me and Ava sitting in the back seat. She's completely confused over what I'm doing – and I don't blame her for wanting to know what the hell's happening – but I have a lot more problems to deal with right now than to stop and explain myself to her. She thinks I'm going to beat up her shitty ex-boyfriend for some perceived slight or something, but I have no care for Luke Abbott when it's his father I'm truly after.

I hold the brat's shirt collar tightly as I make my dramatic announcement into the house, scanning around for the man I've come here for: the brat's very own father.

I don't have to search for long.

Eugene Abbott is sitting on the couch, watching some football game on TV, when I come crashing in. His head swivels toward me, a look of pure surprise on his face.

That same face I saw all those years ago.

Yeah, he still looks exactly the same as I remember...

I've been darkly curious as to whether the man would even recall my face from the last time we saw each other, but the instant recognition in his eyes when he sees me confirms it pretty damn quickly.

I snarl at the sight of the man.

"Eugene Abbott. *Finally.*"

Despite the fury and the action of the previous few minutes, I am not out of breath. I am full of testosterone and adrenaline. *Years* of it, waiting for this very moment.

The man simply stares at me dumbly.

I bet he wasn't expecting this turn of events on this lazy night. I bet he wasn't expecting to see an avenging angel smash through his front door with his name on his lips.

He has no idea what's in store for him now.

"Damon... what the..."

Ava has followed me inside. Her voice pierces my back as she surveys my ferocious entry. I must look a strange sight with a drooling Luke Abbott in my hand and my lips sneering at some unsuspecting middle-aged man sitting in front of me.

"This man, Ava," I say quietly, gesturing at the frozen Eugene a mere step away from me as I tightly hold on to his son, "is the man I've told you about. He is the man I've spent years of my life looking for. Eugene Abbott is the man who shot and killed my godfather right in front of my eyes on the streets of Chicago."

Ava darts to my side, dumbstruck. We're both now

totally ignoring her pathetic ex as I cling to his collar by my other side.

"Wait... *what?*" she asks. "He's really the one who did that? The one you've never found? Are you sure that's him?"

Eugene is still frozen in his chair. His eyes swivel between Ava and me. He's not saying a word. He knows it's too late for him. I'm in control, just as I was in control at Handsome Jack's mansion.

I nod at Ava and then turn my attention back to the man. "I saw his face that day, clear as it is right now. I will never forget that face, and here he is. I can't believe he was here all this time, living in Crystal *fucking* River, of all places. All that time searching for a man who turned out to be the father of your ex..."

"This is crazy, Damon," Ava says. She sees the burning in my eyes. She knows what's coming. "Stop for a moment. Consider this for a second. *Think.* Don't do anything rash..."

"I have done enough thinking," I say, pulling out my trusty knife with my spare hand. "I have had my godfather's knife with me all these years, waiting *exactly* for this moment. This knife has had one purpose, and that's to exact its revenge on this man."

Finally.

Eugene is still totally shackled in shock to his chair. He seems utterly resigned to his fate. There's nowhere for him to go, nowhere for him to escape.

I am certain – without a shadow of a doubt – that this is my man. He's got the same light shade of blonde hair. The same curled lips. The same eyes.

It's him, for sure.

One hundred fucking percent.

And now it can finally happen.

My godfather's revenge. What I've been thinking about for so very long...

I raise the knife high – the black blade which has my godfather's name engraved on it - ready to plunge down into Eugene Abbott.

Nothing can stop me now.

And then Ava steps in front of me and in the way of my revenge.

56

AVA

I HAVE no choice - I have to stand in front of Damon and his target.

I have to stand in front of his falling knife.

I can't believe what Damon has said... Luke's dad is the man who killed Damon's godfather? Did he really shoot him all those years ago?

It can't be...

I know this man sitting there in front of the TV watching football. I've spent so much of my life in this house when I dated Luke. I have sat at his dinner table. I've spoken with him so many times. He's written me Christmas cards. I once spent Thanksgiving here in this very room with this man carving the turkey.

Eugene doesn't seem like the type to commit a gang murder to me.

But I see that look of certainty in Damon's eyes. He has the look of a man who knows he is in the right.

And I don't doubt him for a heartbeat. Damon really

believes Luke's dad is that man who destroyed his life and that of his godfather's all those years ago. I know Damon well enough to know he is totally hellbent on killing the man I've known for so very long right here and right now.

And that's why I have to stand in front of him.

I bet even Luke didn't know about any of this; he didn't know who his dad was, or what he might've once done to the crime boss.

"Don't do this, Damon," I say as I put myself between the man and Eugene.

"Ava, get out of the way," the gangster says to me, determined to follow through with the motion of his knife.

"Please don't do this," I whisper in defiance.

I gaze directly into Damon's eyes, and in that moment, it feels as if the entire world has dissolved around us. It's as though we're the only two souls present, locked in an overpowering connection.

For the two of us, Luke is no longer here. Eugene is no longer here.

This is a struggle only Damon and I can figure out. *Together*.

"Ava, this man killed the man I loved," Damon says. He is almost begging. He wants me to move out of the way with every fiber of his being. He can't do anything until I move.

I shake my head at the insanity of it all. I just want him to see sense. I know Damon isn't truly like this.

I *hope* Damon isn't truly like this.

"If you are right, then Eugene has done a lot of bad things, and I know that you made a vow to fulfill your revenge, but there are other ways for him to pay," I explain, my voice shaking. "There are other ways that don't contain spilled blood. Damon, this should not be an eye for an eye."

"Ava. You don't understand. This man did the worst thing in the world..."

Damon's voice is soft. Childlike. I can see that moment behind those dark eyes of his: that time a teenage Damon witnessed his godfather shot down in a hail of bullets.

He attempts to interrupt me, but my resolve is stronger than his effort. I haven't said everything I need to say, and neither Damon nor his burning intensity can silence me now.

"I know you've never received any true satisfaction from hurting others, Damon," I reply sternly. "I've really gotten to know you over the last few weeks, and I know that this is not you. No matter what you might say."

"I have to do this," Damon replies. "I have to avenge my godfather."

"I understand, Damon. But this isn't the way to do it. This isn't *you*."

"Ava..."

"*Damon.*"

A hint of uncertainty briefly crosses his gaze, an unusual moment of doubt for Damon.

But I know him. I know his true character.

Sometimes he needs a reminder as to who he really is.

"I have to do this..."

His voice is weaker now than it was before. He's less convinced than he was a moment ago.

I lift up my hands and tenderly cradle his face.

"Focus on me. Focus on me. Focus on *me*, Damon."

It's like that time at the park with Luke after we met August. I am trying to calm the man down, but I can still see the anger in his eyes.

But you know what?

The anger is starting to fade...

"I've waited for this moment, Ava, for so long," he whispers, his voice faltering. "So fucking long."

"You may have done bad things, Damon," I say, "but you are a good man."

"But what about Joshua Hall?" he asks. "What about my godfather?"

"You have a choice," I murmur. "You always have a choice. You can end this all right now."

And then he drops his knife. It clatters to the floor between our feet and slides away, but we both ignore it.

I realize that he's done all this because of me, because I've been able to truly *see* him, just as I did in the park with Luke.

I can see his true character.

"I'm proud of you for doing that," I whisper to my man. "I love you, Damon."

The man lets out a long breath. Like relief from deep within him. It's like he's letting out all the tension built up in his body, letting out all those years of hurt and pain and focus on revenge to simply be himself again.

And he just *looks* at me.

We're together, in complete connection.

But then I hear movement behind me, and our focus is immediately shattered.

I glance down at the source of the sound.

It's Eugene. He's reaching for the knife. He's looking at me as he does so.

It is too late to move.

The man is fast, faster than I'm anticipating. He shoots up, knife in hand.

And he's aiming straight for me.

57

DAMON

I SPOT the knife in Eugene's hand a mere moment after Ava does, but it is too late for me to snatch the weapon back. It's too late for me to yank the blade out of the hands of Luke's father. Too late for me to stop the man from plunging the knife right toward Ava's beating heart.

But there *is* enough time for me to push my girl aside. There is enough time for me to take a slight step forward. Enough of a step so that it is I, and not Ava, who now stands in the way of the thrusting knife.

It all happens so quickly. I'm acting on pure instinct.

Anything for Ava...

Anything for my girl.

And then there's a searing pain in my stomach. My legs buckle underneath me as I lose all the energy in my body. It seeps out of me. *Gushing.*

I can register what's happened, but I can't process it.

I have been stabbed before. I've had knives and guns

aimed at me plenty of times to know what it feels like to be hurt.

But I have had nothing like this.

I've had nothing like this pain.

It's too late for me to even save myself.

This feels serious.

I look down and stare at the handle of my godfather's knife lodged deep in me as I fall to the ground.

Fuck. This feels fatal...

58

AVA

I'M JUST STANDING and watching on as Damon falls to the ground. His fall looks so... *unnatural*. It is so unlike him. He's usually all swagger, in charge of everything, but now he's just falling.

Falling.

Falling.

And I'm watching.

And then my attention switches...

To Eugene.

The knife. Oh, fuck. The knife.

He *aimed* it at me. The blade was meant for me, but Damon pushed me aside and put himself in its sights. He got stabbed.

Eugene wanted to kill *me*.

And he still can.

I watch as Eugene quickly reaches again for the knife. This time it's lodged deep in Damon's side as he lies on the ground. The man doesn't need to reach far to retrieve it, though.

I can't run. I'm way too close to the man to escape. I am trapped.

He's got me exactly where he needs me.

Oh.

But then, to my complete surprise, someone lunges out of nowhere and tackles Eugene. The man flies away out of my sight as he is attacked.

Luke.

He has his own dad pinned against the ground in a perfect football tackle, just like one of the ones he used to do in front of adoring high school crowds. He holds his own dad's hands down. He has come out of nowhere to tackle his own father.

"Luke!"

Eugene's voice is breathless. He can't believe his own son has turned against him.

But Luke ignores him.

He turns to me.

"Make... sure... Damon... is... okay..."

I look at my ex as his words slowly sink in.

Damon...

And the next few moments are a fast blur.

Luke sits on top of his dad as I spin around.

I'm in tears.

And I'm on the ground and I am cradling Damon in my arms.

I notice his eyes are shut. There is blood. Redness. A whole load of it.

He is not okay.

My phone is out. I'm calling emergency.

Is he still alive? This man who leaped in front of a knife for me?

I wait for the ambulance, Damon's motionless head in my lap. His body leaning against me.

I'm crying floods of tears now.

Luke stares at me, his dad pinned below him.

I'm gripping Damon Penmayne's body.

And I wait.

And I wait.

And I wait...

59

AVA

I STAND OUTSIDE the main doors of Damon Penmayne's mansion and take in a deep, long breath.

When I was last staying here, holed up in that guestroom upstairs, this building was damn intimidating. But today's visit is even more stressful – way more so than those weeks I spent as Damon's *guest* - and now this place feels like a nightmare in the flesh.

Today, this mansion comes across even more like a fortress than I remember. It's as if it's been an eternity since I last strolled through those tall, imposing gates, even though it has only been a couple of weeks.

Man, and haven't these past couple of weeks been absolutely insane...

I knock tentatively on the front door. I mean, I really don't have to. It is pretty damn obvious the security for this mansion would've seen me coming within a mile of this place and would've been hella ready for my sorry ass, but I feel like I have to do something to announce my arrival and to just keep my freaking hands occupied. Being here, on a day like today, is making me so terrifyingly nervous.

I'm practically shaking.

The door opens.

It's Jim standing on the other side.

It's been a few weeks since I last saw him. All the way back then on the worst day of my life. I remember Jim's face at Luke's family house amongst the sea of security and paramedics and police and Damon's men and blood. He was the one who made me finally let go of Damon's unresponsive hand after what seemed like an eternity of holding him as we sat in the back of the ambulance being driven to the hospital.

He stayed with me the entire time we waited to hear news about Damon's critical condition. Him silent. Me pacing. Those bright hospital corridors and endless stale tasteless coffees gave us migraines as we waited and waited and waited.

Jim looks different now as he opens the door the Damon's mansion. He's a hell of a lot more gaunt. More cheekbones, less fat. Sunken eyes in his face. He clearly hasn't eaten or slept much in weeks.

In that case, I guess I must look in a pretty similar state. I can't blame him for looking like a husk of his former self.

I've not eaten or slept much either.

"Ava."

Jim's voice comes out as a soft sigh. Almost a relief. I think he was dreading who he might be opening the door to. More journalists sniffing around? More bad news?

"It's good to see you, Jim," I reply sadly.

"Come inside," he says, taking a step back to allow me room. "You must be tired."

"You have *no* idea, Jim, just how tired I am."

The man smiles wryly. "Oh, I think I have some idea."

"Upstairs?" I ask, nodding up.

Jim merely nods back in response.

And I find myself slowly taking the stairs up and up into the depths of Damon's mansion.

This was where I was for all that time I was under that strange contract – all that time waiting for whatever that gangster was going to do to me under the terms of our agreement. *Anything he wanted*, that's what I signed up for. How I was scared of him back then, but also secretly thrilled at the prospect of being his captive.

All under this roof.

And all not very long ago at all, even though it seems like years after what's gone down recently.

All of the shit that's happened…

Luke's house.

Eugene.

The *knife* and the *stabbing* and the *blood* and the *tears*.

There have been times in the past few weeks I thought I would never step foot in this mansion ever again, until today.

Damon's top-class lawyers are making sure that Eugene is going to get locked up for a very long time. There is *more* than enough evidence that those well-paid lawyers can play around with in order to fuck up the former assassin and send him away. They've assured me that they do not intend to involve Luke in their prosecution. He won't be implicated in the sins of his father. Like I suspected, he didn't know anything about his dad's past, nor about his role in the gang shooting of Damon's godfather. Luke is guilty of being a shitty ex, but not of murder. I'm happy that he's not going to get wrapped up in this crazy court case. He saved me by tackling his dad, and that's got to count for something.

This is the justice that Eugene deserves: holed up in some horrible place for the rest of his life. That's much more justice than a swift knife in the ribs. He's going to rot for the shit he pulled.

And, surprisingly, yesterday I received a handwritten letter from Luke apologizing for the way he acted toward me and for the actions of his dad. It was honest and heartfelt and detailed. It seems like even assholes can sometimes have moments of self-reflection.

But I don't want him to blame himself for the actions of his dad - there has already been enough generational pain here, and I don't want to cause more. Too many people have been tied up in the actions of a few bad men.

I make my way to the top of the stairs and past my old bedroom - that room I spent so much time in – and continue to Damon's master bedroom. I glance inside his dark, wooden office, expecting to see him pacing around in that serious way he does, but of course he isn't there.

I should know he wouldn't be around here.

I wish he was.

That tall, gorgeous, dark man I had grown to care for... I wish he was wandering around that room or sitting behind his desk hashing out some deal in his criminal enterprise.

Anything to see him like that again.

I remember what it was like the first time I walked in here. The awe I felt. The overwhelming nature of the crime boss and the titillating fact that he wanted me to be his mistress. All those nights longing for him in the guest bedroom. All those nights we shared the same bed. Sitting under the stars together.

Damon opening up his true deepest feelings to me...

In those few weeks of being the crime boss' captive mistress, I felt like an entire lifetime had passed - a wonderful, erotic, deepening lifetime full of passion and love and partnership.

And then it ended as abruptly as it had begun.

And now I'm here in this quiet mansion with no Damon in his office and no love between these walls.

And I am feeling a sense of dread.

I'm wanting the world to swallow me whole.

There's only one more place in this sad building to go...

The door to his master bedroom is shut. For a heartbeat, I'm worried it's locked, but all it takes is for me to turn to handle and I'm inside the room.

60

AVA

THE MOMENT I walk into Damon's master bedroom, I am hit with a glaring wall of monitors - all data and images and things that just blind me with their... *unnaturalness.* There are tons of the devices, way too many to keep count of at first glance. Bright blue screens. And the wires are everywhere. It is so damn overwhelming at first.

And then I see him.

Lying in his bed, hooked up to all these medical machines.

My poor Damon...

The room is dark. Jim is evidently not letting much sunlight into the space while his boss is stuck in here. I resist my caring, womanly urge to rush over and rip open the curtains to let the fresh air in.

I bet Damon – the *dark, cool* man he likes to be – doesn't want to be bathed in sunlight while recovering in bed.

"Damon?"

My tiny voice echoes feebly across the room like a mouse's squeak.

The man in the bed stirs at the sound. I see his head start to rise from the pillow.

He's moving...

"Ava?"

His voice is soft, but still there. It's still – somehow - that same deep resonating baritone that haunts my dreams.

It's still the Damon I remember. Hidden by pain and restricted by wounds and quietened by struggle, but it is still *him*.

"You're awake?" I ask. "Can I come in properly?"

The man moves again in his bed. His dark eyes shine at me through the blackness.

"This isn't a dream?" he asks. "It's really you, Ava? You've come to see me?"

"Of course I have come to see you," I reply. "And, yes, last time I checked, I wasn't a dream. You can pinch me to make sure, though. Jesus, you're like Dracula in this room."

And then he really moves. In one movement, Damon launches himself – *erupts* - from the bed, letting out a grunt as he rises to his feet.

It's all so... *improbable*. Surreal. He ought to be bedridden. The man received a knife into his stomach, and it's not even been weeks since he was on life-support in hospital.

He certainly should *not* be standing, but here he is doing so.

Defying all odds.

And simply because I'm here.

"I hate all this crap," Damon barks, gesturing at the machines and cables surrounding him. And as if to prove his point, the man suddenly starts ripping out all the cords attached to his body. The saline drip. The heart rate monitor. *Everything*. It all violently goes as he strips himself free from their hold in front of me.

To be honest, I'm not surprised. I wouldn't take Damon to be a man who's held down by things such as medical devices. I bet he'd rather die on his feet than spend a lifetime in bed.

And he's ripping them out because of *me*.

"What are you doing?" I ask him. "You can't do that!"

Damon laughs. "I'm not going to spend another fucking minute stuck in that fucking bed feeling bad for myself, especially not when you're in the same room as me. I want to see you properly, Ava. I want to stand above you and take you in as a man."

That makes me laugh, despite my concern for him. "Of course, *you* wouldn't allow something as minor as a near-fatal knife wound to stop you from getting up close and personal with me."

"Nothing would," Damon says quietly, leaning forward so that our faces are nearly touching. "Nothing could separate me from you, Ava."

"Really?"

"Yes."

"You're sweet," I reply. "But maybe you should go back to bed. I don't think it's super wise to be up on your feet right now, no matter how much you want to be with me."

The man shakes his head. "I've been doing a lot of thinking, Ava, trapped here in this bed. Thinking that I want to share with you. *Urgently*."

I raise an eyebrow. "You have? What about?"

"You and me," Damon replies.

"And what about *you and me*?" I ask him.

"About what an asshole I've been," he whispers. "And all the shit things I did that I should really stop and apologize for."

"Damon…"

I try to object - I try to tell him that now is not the time – but Damon cuts me off. He doesn't want to hear it. He wants to say what he's going to say, and my protests won't halt him.

"Let me tell you what's been stuck in my head while I've been stuck in this bed," he says.

"Okay, Damon," I say. "Go ahead. Tell me what's been stuck in your head."

"Ava, I broke my promise to you back at my brewery fire," he says softly and very seriously. "I crossed that line, and it was my mistake. It was my fault. Totally my fault. I take all the responsibility for what I did, and there is no excuse for my actions. I fully understand why you would want nothing to do with me after all that, and especially after I gave my word that I wouldn't commit violence in front of you. I wouldn't want to have anything to do with me if I were you. I understand why you would want to turn your back on me."

"Your nature to revert to violence nearly got us both killed," I whisper. "Eugene with that knife…"

Damon sighs. "I know. I was wrong. So *very* wrong. I was blinded by my hate, by my need to exact revenge. And, by my actions, I put you in harm's way. And I don't think I can ever forgive myself for doing that. It was wrong, I admit that."

"Even you can admit that?" I ask.

"Yes, Ava. Even me."

I stare deep into his eyes. I can see the remorse there: the thinking he's truly been doing as he's laid here in this bed. This man is genuine.

"You understand what you did?" I ask him somberly.

Damon nods slowly. "Yes, I do."

"You told me you wouldn't commit any violence," I mutter.

"And I did," he replies, "and I am truly sorry for breaking my word."

I continue to stare deep into his eyes and the sincere apology that lies behind it.

He's really telling the truth. He really is sorry.

"Maybe everyone deserves a second chance," I whisper.

"And do you think I deserve a second chance?" Damon asks tentatively.

His apprehension is uncharacteristic of him, but sweet.

And shows how much his apology means…

I shrug. "Maybe you do deserve a second chance," I reply.

The man takes in a long, deep breath. It's as if – with my approval and acceptance - he can finally breathe again.

And then he smiles. "I never got to finish that little conversation we were having when we were rudely interrupted by Luke's father," he says with a hell of a load of cheekiness.

"What little conversation?" I ask.

"The conversation when you told me you love me," Damon replies.

I let out a nervous giggle. "Oh."

"While I was lying there waiting for the ambulance and looking up at you as my eyes started to close, I remember one thought," Damon whispers. "I remember thinking that now, with you, I have got a life to live for. For once. And that's how I know I love you with every ounce of my body. I have never been so sure of something before in my life. And that was what I was going to say before I got myself stabbed and was so rudely interrupted. And now I finally get to say that to you, Ava."

His words wash over me like warm water, and I am caught in his beautiful stare.

This feels right.

Everyone does deserve a second chance, especially when they say something like this.

He is a guarded man speaking from his heart. This is a rare thing. It's a *truthful* thing.

"You did take a knife in the stomach for me," I reply. "And it was true what I said back there at the Abbott house. I love you, Damon."

"Even after everything I've done?" Damon asks. "Even if I am a bad man?"

"You are a good man to me," I reply.

Damon takes a step back as if my words have pushed him physically. He seems… relieved. Relaxed.

At peace.

We both look at each other for a lingering moment before he speaks again. It is a moment full of love.

"Come, follow me," Damon says, offering his hand. "I've got something for you."

61

DAMON

I ᴛᴀᴋᴇ her into my office. It has been a while since I've been in here - before that... *incident* at Luke's place.

To be brutally blunt, walking is a bit of a struggle for me, even the walk from my bedroom to the office is getting me out of breath, but I do my utmost to conceal my pain from Ava. She is right in saying that I'm not going to let a little thing like a knife wound stop me.

And I'm not going to be stopped when Ava is here.

Like hell I'm not.

I had felt like a prisoner for these last few weeks - all of my agency stripped from me as I lay in that fucking bed having nothing to do but think of my apology to my girl. Doing fuck-all in bed was all so unfamiliar to me. I hated every moment of relying on other people's care, of being nothing more than a number. Nothing more than a blood test. Nothing more than a fucking *patient*.

The weight of it all was slowly crushing me.

Until today. *Until Ava.*

Hearing her voice echo across my bedroom just then really did feel like a dream. It sounds so strange, but just her voice – her *presence* – gave me the energy I needed to finally get out of the bed-bound haze I was in. I *needed* to apologize to her.

And now I am *me* again, all thanks to my girl.

I lead her by the hand to my desk in my office.

I've got something to show her.

She's looking at me with expectant mixed-color eyes.

"I've got a new arrangement for you, Ava," I say to her as we come to a stop next to my chair.

Her eyes narrow at my statement.

"What do you mean?" she asks.

"A new arrangement to repay your debt to me," I reply.

Ava crosses her arms. She's pissed. "I don't owe you anything, Damon."

I smile. "I'm just joking," I tease.

"Oh. *Very* funny. Hilarious."

"But I'm not joking about having a new arrangement between us," I say.

"What arrangement?" Ava asks, suspicious again. "What are you talking about, Damon?"

I take in a breath.

"I want you to be my one and only mistress," I say with utter serious earnestness. "A new arrangement. A new contract. For forever."

Ava's mouth drops.

"What?"

And then I get down on my knee. I take out a ring that's been hiding in a drawer in my desk.

A ring I have been saving for a very long time.

A ring only for a girl like Ava Matson.

"I've never been so sure of anything in my life before," I explain. "I've been an idiot and nearly drove you away, but I know what I want. And that's *you*, Ava. Marry me, and make me a very happy man."

62

DAMON

AND SHE SAYS YES.

And it is the biggest relief of my life. I don't usually get down on my knee in front of anyone, but for Ava, I want to show her how vulnerable I can be. How much I can promise her. What I will do for her. The life I will provide for her.

Because she is my world.

She is my everything.

Strange words for a criminal to say, but here we are. A girl like Ava can do that to even the most hardened of gangsters, and I am proof enough.

She's got me – hook, line, and fucking sinker.

This time, *I* am her captive. My heart's her captive. And I don't ever want to be free.

My heart beats fast as she nods and cries and tells me yes. It's strange to feel it like this... my entire body like this. Nerves are not my thing, but getting down in front of Ava Matson and proposing is definitely the most frightening experience of my life. Asking your love to spend eternity with you is *terrifying*.

I would rather get another knife in my stomach than go through that again.

"*Yes*, Damon."

I get back on my feet. I take her beautiful face in my hands. I tilt her body back, supporting her.

"I love you," I whisper.

"I love you too," she whispers back.

And then I kiss her.

Slowly.

Longingly.

Deeply.

My future wife closes her eyes and lets herself go in my embrace.

We love each other.

And now that love will be forever.

"Let's go to my bedroom," I sigh by her neck, my lips caressing her skin. "Let's consummate this new arrangement."

My fiancée nods. "Yes, let's."

"And this time I don't need you to sit on my knee to prove anything."

Ava laughs. "No, I do not."

This time she guides me to my bedroom, holding my hand and keeping her eyes on me the entire walk across from my office.

My heart is still going so fast. I'm worried about what effect it might have on my recovering body.

My God, the way she looks at me...

It's enough to send any reasonable man crazy.

I just feel an overwhelming sense of love for this girl.

If only the past me could see this. Me in love. He would be so shocked.

But it's the truth. I am in love with the girl I once thought of as someone I could just fuck and keep as my captive. I am willingly giving every part of me over to her. She's completely got me in her hands like putty, especially when she guides me through my mansion with her eyes focused wholly on mine.

It's enough to make my knees buckle.

She's the woman I'm going to spend the rest of my life with.

It is, simply put, the best decision I have ever made.

And her saying yes is the best thing to have ever happened to me.

Ava takes me into my bedroom and jumps onto the bed, facing me on all fours.

"I hope you're well enough for me," she says with an alluring twinkle in her mixed-color eyes.

"Don't you dare even doubt me," I snarl back, before I strip myself down.

"I am."

Her eyes dart down to my ready erection.

"I am certainly well enough to fuck you, Ava," I say. "My fiancée."

"Come here and show me, then," Ava teases. "My *future* husband."

I snarl again before I pounce on her.

And I prove to her that I am certainly well enough to fuck her.

I prove it to her three times in a row.

63

AVA

I LET my finger trace down the middle of Damon's muscular chest. He is *glistening* in sweat, but I really don't mind. Everything about him is sexy to me. Every atom of this gorgeous man.

And he's alive. And he's getting better. And he gets to be mine forever.

I have no doubt in my mind over what his feelings for me truly are anymore. Those days of moping around in this mansion wondering what he thought about me are long, long, long gone.

He proposed to me. Holy shit, the gangster just proposed... to me.

It was totally unexpected. I really didn't think that would be happening *at all* when I arrived here today. It was truly the very, very last thing on my mind when I took in a nervous breath outside his mansion.

But it is the most welcome surprise in the world.

"You know," Damon whispers as my finger continues to

trace down his toned body. "I once told you that every day I wake up and I am always looking to be the best in what I do, and how that conviction is what's got me to where I am."

"Yeah, I remember," I reply.

"And you told me that maybe life is about more than being the best," he says. "You said that maybe life is about relationships and connections and doing the best for your family. Giving your all to the people you love. That maybe there's something *greater* than perfection."

"Yeah?"

"And I told you that it was trash," Damon continues. "But now... getting to know you... getting to love you... I think I'm starting to get around to what you were saying. I think I understand, and I think I agree with you."

"You do?" I ask him, looking up into his eyes.

He nods slowly.

And I feel my love for him surge up from deep within me.

As my finger reaches the edge of his groin, Damon lets out a low chuckle.

"You're ready for round two, my fiancée?" he asks.

The way he says that...

My fiancée...

The way he would say it makes me realize I would do anything for this man. In his embrace, I feel so secure.

"Yes, I am," I reply.

"So am I, Beauty."

Beauty. That nickname he has for me. It takes me back to that first time in his office, when I felt so nervous and so apprehensive about this crime boss who was about to make me his.

Well, how times have changed, hey?

I'm no longer his captive.

I'm his girl.

And I'm soon going to be his wife.

The criminal's wife.

It's a naughty thought to have, but I do like the sound of that.

* * *

I TAKE a seat on the park bench, grasping the hot chocolate to-go cup in between my fingers, feeling the warmth soak through my hands.

I look up at the park. At the playground. At the sun streaming down. I look up and let the sunlight bathe my face. After all the craziness of the last few months, being here in the park is so calm.

I close my eyes.

Peace.

And Dad sits down next to me, a coffee cup in between his own fingers.

"It's a beautiful day," he remarks, taking a long sip of his caffeine. I open my eyes to look at him.

"Yes, it so is."

We've just been to The Oak. We've already devoured our almond croissants before we even reached the park bench.

"Do you remember us doing this when you were just a little girl, Ava?" Dad asks me with a beaming smile. "Coming here to the park to drink hot drinks?"

He looks so happy. This is the first time I've seen him like this in a hell of a long time.

Years.

"I'm a little bit bigger now, Dad, than the last time we did this," I say.

He chuckles at that.

"Yeah, you are," he replies. "You've grown into your

own woman now, and I am so, so proud of you. I am so proud to be your father. I'm so proud to witness you transform into the strong woman you are today."

That brings a tear to my eye.

I feel like I've finally got my dad back after all this time: the dad I remember from that time in the meadow when we saw that butterfly with the same mixed colors as my eyes.

And I see in his eyes that he is thinking the same thing.

All the badness is over. No more debts. No more secrets. No more broken hearts.

Damon and me and my father.

Everyone is fine.

It's all finally over.

"I love you, Dad."

"I love you, Ava."

I lean over and rest my head on my father's shoulder and watch the peaceful park.

And I remember that wish I had made in that meadow all those years ago, and I realize it's come true.

Be happy with Daddy forever.

EPILOGUE

AVA

THANK God that Olivia is here. Someone to hang on to in this crazy place.

"Hey!"

She greets me with the biggest smile.

Yeah, thank God a million times she's here.

"Hey, Olivia."

We wrap ourselves in a big hug.

"Where's Spencer?" I ask her, looking around for her man.

"He's already inside," Olivia replies with a roll of her eyes. "He wants to talk to everyone. He loves a good talk like the English Literature professor he is."

"Ha. Sure."

"You ready for this?" she asks me, nodding at the front door. "Ready for all the commotion?"

I shake my head. "Nope. I am not ready. Not in a million, billion years."

"Ava is simply pretending," Damon says from behind me. He's parked the car and has bounded up to us girls in his trademark black suit. "She can't turn down a party."

I turn to him. "Shut up, Damon."

My fiancé grins, his dark, rugged, handsome face lighting up. "Never."

I roll my eyes at him and Olivia giggles.

"Come on," Damon says. "We can't keep the family waiting, girls. Let's get inside."

"No, we can't keep them waiting," I remark. "Not the Penmaynes, of all people."

The Penmayne family mansion is a hell of a lot bigger than Damon's place. This building – this *complex* – has clearly been built in mind to best intimidate anyone who is not part of the Penmayne dynasty. High walls. Security. An impressive façade that screams wealth beyond your wildest imaginings. We're just outside Crystal River.

A member of the Penmayne security opens the front door for us as we approach. Damon has told me that the mansion is designed in a Colonial Revival style, whatever that means. Architecture is not my strongest subject. There is a quiet simplicity to the grounds of this place, though. It's as if the Penmayne family *knows* they are rich and don't have to display it in some gaudy, tacky style like new millionaires do. It's like they are above the rest of society.

A different breed.

It's scary to think how much I don't belong in this world, but then I think of Olivia and Spencer and the love they so clearly share: two different worlds that have come together in true love.

And it's the same between Damon and me.

I look up at the white columns that support the portico of the mansion and the dark red brick that supports the place. I can't help thinking that this was where Damon grew up. This is his childhood home.

I imagine telling the younger me that one day I would be walking the grounds of the famous Penmayne mansion. Younger me definitely wouldn't have believed older me.

She'd have thought I am insane.

Through the main door, Damon leads us into the main living room and past the impressive foyer with the impossibly large staircase that sweeps up into the higher levels. It looks bigger on the inside than it does on the outside.

I see Spencer first. The cool, suave professor gives me a nod before he comes over and takes Olivia's hand lovingly. He's got that Penmayne cocky confidence about him – the kind that instantly commands a room.

I feel Damon's presence behind me. He, too, takes my hand. His reassuring touch makes me feel grounded, despite all my nerves about being here in the den of the Penmaynes.

"How are you, Spencer?" I ask the professor.

"All good," he replies. "Better to see Olivia here. She's a beacon in the darkness."

"Stop being cute," she says to him, her cheeks blushing.

"You ready to chat to Father?" Spencer asks Damon, nodding behind him at the imposing, older suited man standing by a bookcase. I don't need to be told that man is Waylen Penmayne, the patriarch and the billionaire media mogul.

"Of course," Damon replies. "Ava, come with me."

And he takes me to his father. My nerves are really playing up now.

Here goes.

"Father."

Damon greets his dad in a serious tone. The same way he greeted Handsome Jack in that art gallery meeting.

His father gives him a slight smile before turning to me.

"You must be Ava," he says. I can see where the Penmayne boys have got their deep voices and handsome looks from: the man is a silver fox. He must've been one hell of a playboy charmer back in his prime. Rich and intelligent and incredibly good looking. A real heartbreaker. I wonder what Damon's mother must've done to nail down such an eligible bachelor. She must be an amazing woman, and he must be a *very* lucky man.

"I am," I reply to the patriarch. "Did Damon tell you about me?"

The man laughs then. A deep belly chuckle. "No. Absolutely not. Damon doesn't disclose a single thing about his life to us. I have other ways to find out who my boys have proposed to."

"Right. For a second there I forgot you are a billionaire with the power to kill anyone in the world just by picking up your phone," I say. "Of course you have *other ways* to find out about your sons."

Now Waylen *really* laughs. "I like her," he says to Damon. "I really like her. Keep her around, son."

I guess I've got his seal of approval then.

"I hope you're not trying to scare off Damon's girl," says a voice from behind me. I turn my neck to see it's August Penmayne.

"I'm not *that* scary," Waylen replies to his other son. He winks at me before heading off to talk to Spencer.

He's a man who glides through a room. A powerful man who charms you one second and then is gone the next.

"Hey," I say to August, spinning to face him properly. It's nice I can have a chat with him.

He smiles and shakes my hand politely. "Nice to see you again, Ava. You're looking resplendent."

That Penmayne charisma...

"It's nice to see you, too."

"Last time I saw you it seemed like things didn't end very well," August says. "You disappeared suddenly from that restaurant, and Damon went running after you. He kind of told me what happened next, but not enough to understand fully. There was some kind of altercation, is that so? Something about ex-boyfriend troubles?"

I shoot a glance at Damon. "Yeah, it's a long story," I reply. "But Damon helped."

"I came to her rescue," Damon says. "She really needed me."

"He likes to exaggerate his involvement," I say with a laugh. "But yes. It's a long story, all that's happened recently."

"I'd love to hear it," August replies in that smooth Penmayne way I've come to familiarize with all the brothers. "In detail, please."

"So Damon didn't give you the full run-down of what's happened?" I ask. "The knife wound? Everything that's happened?"

Damon growls. August shakes his head.

"We've heard nothing," he says. "Knife wound? The only thing we know is that he's been out of contact for *weeks*."

"I hope Damon can talk to you about it," I say.

"I certainly hope he will," Damon's brother replies.

"Waylen was just saying that Damon hasn't said a word about me," I say. "So, Damon doesn't tell you guys a thing, then? Nothing?"

"Nope. Never. His lips have been firmly shut since being a teenager," August says, speaking like his brother isn't standing in front of him. "The man likes to pretend to be an enigma. We would love to hear him say his own story, though. For once. We hate having to hear it through Father's spies..."

"That's enough, August," Damon says.

August raises his hands in mock surrender. "Sure. Sure."

And then a woman appears. She approaches us with a graceful and dignified swoop across the floor like she's floating on air. Without even needing an introduction, I can already tell that she's the matriarch of the Penmayne family.

My heart skips a beat.

Here we really fucking go...

And, as if to confirm my suspicions, both Damon and August turn to the woman reverently.

And, inside, I am freaking out.

"Mother," Damon utters to the approaching woman, almost bowing.

Ha. Never seen him do that before.

The two brothers give their mum an air kiss on both cheeks.

It's all so very... *European.*

So very refined.

It's kind of terrifying for a small-town American cheerleader like me with none of that cultural finesse. I don't know how to act. I feel so very uncivilized.

"Hello, boys," Mother Penmayne purrs. Like her husband, her voice is dripping with wealth.

She is a woman who takes her time with everything she does. She is a woman who expects the world to bend around her and her will.

And it clearly does.

It's kinda inspiring.

Go, girl.

"And who is this?" she asks, turning her slow attention to my little sorry ass.

"You've met Ava before, right?" Damon asks his mother. And both Mother Penmayne and I shake our heads.

"Damon's been such a bad son," Mother Penmayne whispers conspiratorially to me, even though her sons can clearly hear her. "Not introducing me to his lady friends."

Damon sighs.

"My apologies for not introducing you two sooner. Mother, this is Ava," he says, gesturing at me. Then he gestures at his mother. "Ava, this is Alda Penmayne."

Ah. Alda. Such a unique name for a unique woman. I wouldn't expect anything less from such an intimidating lady.

"Lovely to meet you," I say to her, unsure whether I should shake her hand or give her an air kiss on the cheeks or to just get down and bow to her like some Pharoah queen.

"Very nice to meet the woman that Damon has chosen for himself," she says before turning to August. "And what about you, son? Any women here that you need to introduce me to? Any other women that my sons are hiding from me?"

August's cheeks go a bright shade of pink.

"No one, Mother."

"Shame," she says. "I guess you're so wrapped up in your work, aren't you?"

"I guess you could say that," the doctor replies.

"I think I should find you a woman," Alda says coolly. "You need a woman, August. I could set you up with some respectable ladies. I'm acquainted with one or two."

Damon sighs again. "Please, Mother. No talking about your matchmaking prowess in front of Ava."

Alda gives me a knowing wink, just like Waylen Penmayne, before she drifts away with a simple farewell.

"Adios."

August turns to Damon when their mum is safely out of earshot.

"*Mother*," he exhales as if it's some form of explanation.

"You were always her favorite, August," Damon remarks. "Let her find you a nice, reputable woman from her pool of upper-crust contacts. She would love that."

The doctor groans at that joke. "Never. I'm not letting her anywhere near my love life."

"Better find that childhood maid crush of yours soon," Damon says. "Otherwise, Mother will truly have her claws in you. She'll have every good match on the Eastern Seaboard lined up."

"Ha. I can only dream," August replies. "The last thing I need is for Mother to act as my own personal dating app."

"You certainly don't want that," Damon confirms.

"Well, I need to go, you two," August proclaims. "I need to mingle with the rest of the family and try my utmost to avoid talk of who I might be currently sleeping with. Always lovely to see you, Ava. Take care of my brother for me."

I smile. "Will do."

And with that, August heads over to talk to Olivia, leaving Damon and me alone.

"So, you haven't said a word to your family?" I ask my fiancé, deadly serious. "Nothing about what's happened to you in the last few weeks? Being stabbed? You didn't think of letting them know you were so close to death?"

Damon is silent for a moment. "I've not told them anything since I witnessed my godfather dying."

"What? Really?"

"Yes."

"Why not?" I ask.

"It's just not... *me* to open up like that."

"But you heard August just then," I reply sincerely.

"They would *love* to hear you talk. I'm sure telling them about your godfather and your years in New York would help them. Hell, at the very least I'm sure it would help *you*."

Again, Damon falls silent. I can tell he's pondering my words.

"You really think I should open up to them?" he asks me softly.

"I think you should do what you want to do," I reply. "I think you should do whatever helps you. But me? I personally think opening up will help you heal some wounds that you have buried deep."

And, for the third time, Damon goes quiet.

"Maybe I shall. Thanks to you, Ava."

I watch as my fiancé raises his voice to get his family's attention.

"*Everyone.*"

And they all turn to him.

"I've got something to say," he announces to the room. "Something that I've kept hidden from you all for far too long..."

He's really doing it, isn't he?

Because of me.

He's going to tell them everything.

I watch as my fiancé begins to talk about what really has happened to him all these years. I watch his family listen to him for the first proper time, really understanding his story. He talks about Joshua Hall, and the shootings, and the hard years spent in New York City, and Eugene Abbott, and the knife wound that nearly killed him.

And *me*.

He talks about me in such a loving and caring way.

He tells them about how I have healed him. How I have

given him a second life. How I have pulled him out of the darkest hole and into the light.

How I am to be his wife forever.

I watch on proudly as my fiancé finally opens up to his family about everything that has happened to him since that day he saw his godfather murdered.

And I realize how truly in love I am with this man.

Want to read August's story?

Go to rebeccacastle.com to find the links for The Doctor's Destiny

ABOUT THE AUTHOR

Rebecca has had the storytelling bug since... forever!

What Rebecca likes most is writing steamy hot filthy romances with sweet happy endings sprinkled with some delicious bad boys.

Born and raised in an Aussie coastal town, she loves travelling around the world - meeting new people and discovering their stories.

Aside from adventuring she also enjoys a good rainy day in with a good book or at a hot beach catching the sun.

She's a world-class napping professional. You'll most likely find her asleep snuggled up on a sofa somewhere cozy.

For other titles and information please visit
rebeccacastle.com

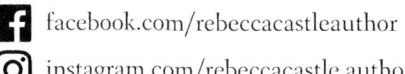

facebook.com/rebeccacastleauthor

instagram.com/rebeccacastle.author

Printed in Great Britain
by Amazon